BLOOD MAGIC

BLOOD MAGIC

MATTHEW COOK

JUNO

Blood Magic
Copyright © 2008 by Matthew R. Cook

Cover art copyright © 2008 by Timothy Lantz
www.stygiandarkness.com

Cover design copyright © 2008 by Stephen H. Segal

Interior design copyright © 2008 by Paula Guran

ISBN-10: 0809572001
ISBN-13: 978-0809572007

Juno Books
Rockville, MD
www.juno-books.com
info@juno-books.com

For my grandfather, Roy Durling,
who saw what others could not.

On the ragged edge of the world I'll roam,
And the home of the wolf shall be my home,
And a bunch of bones on the boundless snows
The end of my trail . . . who knows, who knows!
                                        ~Robert Service

Acknowledgements

I used to read other authors' acknowledgements and wonder why they'd thank so many people. Now that I've completed this, my first novel, I know. Maybe some writers can shoulder the work of an entire novel all on their own, but I'm not one of them.

Heartfelt thanks go to Jennifer McCollam, my self-described "Constant Reader" and all-around wonderful reviewer. Almost every single chapter went to her first, usually while in appallingly rough form, and her plot and character suggestions, keen eye for grammatical deviance and constant encouragement kept me afloat more times than I can count. Equal thanks go to my editor, Paula Guran, who decided to take a chance on a first-time author and his mostly-completed manuscript. Many, many thanks, Paula, for all your advice and guidance.

I would also like to thank all the members of the Columbus, Ohio Writeshop group, particularly (but not limited to): Cory Daughton, Gary Wedlund, Katrina Kidder, Dan Lissman, Lucy Snyder, Tom Barlow, Holly Bell and especially Jerry Robinette. Every aspiring writer should be as lucky in their friends as I am. Thanks for being so tough on me in all those Sunday critiques—I'm a much better writer as a result.

Last, I'd like to thank my wife, Kara (who suggested one possible idea for the ending which gave me nightmares but also was better than my original idea, so I used it) and my kids, Grayson and Raven, who put up with many early mornings while I was working in coffee houses, as well as countless distracted nights while I sat and pondered tough plot complications. I love you guys.

Dublin, Ohio
July 2007

CHAPTER ONE

For three days we run, and the Mor follow. Three days of burning sun, and dust, and constant, grinding pain—limbs growing heavier and heavier, slowing us down, making men stumble. More and more, those who fall do not rise, and we must leave them behind.

Three nights of hurried cold camps; never risking a fire, afraid to sleep lest the enemy come upon us unaware. Three nights of scouting along our back trail, doing what I can to obfuscate the marks of our passage; a hopeless task for more than two dozen men, all heavily booted, all no longer caring to tread lightly, but I cannot help but to try.

Three days and nights since the doomed battle of Gamth's Pass, where five thousand men faced off against a force a tenth their number, and were annihilated just the same. Five thousand men cut down by the Mor's unearthly strength; stone-like limbs scything, claws ripping through manflesh and horseflesh both with appalling ease, while arrows and blades bounced like gentle spring rain from their shield-like carapaces.

I was at the rear when the final charge met the Mor's irregular battle lines, breaking like waves against a rocky shore. I fired arrow after arrow down into the foe, knowing that only one in a hundred shafts might find some vulnerable place. My sweetlings, with their horned limbs and thorny hides, might have had better luck in the fray but I had been forbidden by the priests from calling them.

Pious fools. What good were their prayers against such a foe? What use their magics against beings of such strength? From my vantage point, I saw our line crumble, the Mor cutting it apart like monstrous ants dissecting and devouring a flailing earthworm.

Then there was nothing but screams and chaos as men abandoned their formations, scattering like leaves in a gale, screaming, shouting, begging for mercy. I ran down into the swirling mêlée, searching for Jazen Tor, dodging the swipes and jabs of the Mor. I found him soon after, still fighting amongst the remains of his company, and we fled.

THE FOURTH DAY DAWNS. I do not pause for rest, but continue to scout the perimeter while the men snatch a few precious minutes of sleep. None grumble any more about relying on a woman; such prideful concerns have long since been forgotten. We are all refugees now, all prey.

My body yearns for rest, and sustenance; the hard uneven ground the men are sprawled upon looks as enticing as a featherbed. I push aside my weakness and run back along our trail, before my traitorous body can succumb to temptation. I am dismayed to find the Mor are less than three miles behind. They are gaining, moving at their implacable pace while we—burdened by our need for sleep, for food and drink—slow. If the Mor have such weaknesses, they have never displayed them.

Before I return, I kill a deer with my bow and use its still-warm body to summon one of my dark children. I place it along our trail, commanding it to kill anything that it sees. I dislike using animals, for the resulting creation is slow and stupid and weak, a pale shadow of what my sweetlings are usually capable of, but it should slow the Mor for a few precious minutes.

I return to find the sentries asleep on their feet. I clatter a bit as I roll my few meager possessions, giving them time to come awake. The sound is insufficient to rouse most of them and, finally, I must resort to shaking and shouting.

Soon, all are on their feet and we set out. The men are too exhausted to even groan, shuffling forward like zombies. Jazen Tor, whom I allowed to share my blankets a million years ago, before Gamth's Pass, smiles and offers me a bit of biscuit.

"Eat up," he says, his voice a whispery croak, so different from his usual melodious baritone. "No need to ration. At this pace, we'll be at Fort Azure by mid-day."

I take the morsel with a nod of thanks and place it in my pouch. I am never hungry after birthing one of my precious ones, as if the act of creation fills some bodily need in me.

I lean forward and whisper, "We must increase the pace. The Mor are gaining. At this rate they will be on us before we reach the fort."

Tor looks over his shoulder at Captain Hollern. He knows, as do I, that our commander will not listen to any tactical advice I have to offer. Hollern is a follower of the Lightbringer, and barely tolerates my presence.

"I'll spread the word," Tor says with a weary sigh. "One final run, then we will be behind thick walls, eh?"

I smile in what I hope is a reassuring way and he moves back. He whispers in a man's ear and I see the glazed look of exhaustion in his eyes shift to cornered fear. Tor grips his shoulder for a moment, seeming to will strength into the man, then moves to speak to another. Soon, the column begins to accelerate, just a bit, but maybe enough.

Hollern is oblivious to the change and soon is at the rear of the group. He picks up his pace without seeming to notice, the vacant look in his eyes never flickering. I wish he would just lie down like so many others have already done, putting his command in Jazen Tor's more capable hands.

We come across the Fort Azure road and our pace increases further still. Homesteads are scattered along the road. All are abandoned, all burnt. The Mor, I know, always put our settlements to the torch after raiding, as if they cannot bear the very sight of any human structure. Most are abandoned, but some are surrounded by the shattered bodies of their former inhabitants; men, women, children, limbs scattered and scavenger-chewed, heads missing. We do not stop to bury the fallen.

Mid-morning, we come to a stream and the men stop to refill their canteens. I whisper to Tor to not wait for me and slip away. I run back along our trail, gritting my teeth at the pain in my feet and legs. I will soon be behind thick walls, guarded by archers and pikemen, I tell myself. I can rest then.

I pass by one of the homesteads and check the bodies. None are usable. Without heads or limbs, the fallen are too damaged to call forth one of my sweetlings. The house has been burned to the foundation and its stones scattered. The ashen smell lies thick in my nose.

A horn blast splits the quiet air. Jazen's horn. There is only one reason he would betray his position. I run back, panting, chest like a furnace, wondering if I am already too late.

I slow as I approach the spot where I left the men. The sound of battle reaches my ears, the slithering ring of blades striking rock-like skin, the hoarse grunts and shouts of men mixed with the eerie piping of the Mor. I leave the road, slipping like a ghost into the bushes. I reach the edge of the clearing, drawing forth an arrow and nocking it to the string.

Men lie scattered about the clearing in spreading pools of blood. The survivors, with Hollern and Jazen Tor among them, stand in a tight knot, back-to-back-to-back, sixteen men against three Mor.

The Mor tower over the soldiers, eight feet of stone-gray armor and leathery flesh, their massive, clawed upper arms rising and falling like threshing tools. Weapons are clutched in the smaller, lower limbs: stone hammers and knives. The blades glow a sullen orange, hot as lava, a result of one of the work of one of their shamans.

I draw my arrow back to my cheek, searching for a vulnerable joint, then see there are bodies not five feet from my position. They are horribly torn, the edges of their wounds blackened and smoking, but the Mor have not yet torn them asunder. I smile bloodlessly and take the arrow from the string.

As I open my inner eye, my sister crows in triumph inside my head. I tell her to be still. She spares me a mocking laugh, but falls silent, gods be praised.

I see the spirits of the fallen men, standing near their former vessels. The specters are dazed, wandering about, some crying, others peering at their former flesh with hopeless expressions.

Silently, I call out to the souls of the soldiers. They turn and listen, their ghostly faces pale and translucent in the wan sunlight. I whisper a song of blood and revenge, thrilling as one by one they drift back toward the fleshly remains.

The first Mor does not even have time to scream out a warning as my sweetling leaps upon its armored back. Then a second of my children, and a third, tear themselves free from their still-warm cocoons, shambling forth to take their revenge.

They charge forward, their skinless, rope-muscled limbs lashing, bone blades and horns hissing through the air. As one, they clamber up the Mor's hulking body. They are surprisingly nimble for such ruined-looking things; ugly in a way that only a mother can love. I know that such alacrity will fade in time, as their tissues dry and tighten, but right now they are a whirlwind of muscle and sinew driven by the spirits of the recently dead and my own insatiable desires.

A Mor screams as the talons of one of my children saws across a seam in its armored belly. Its intestines, or what passes for them, tumble out in a vibrant blue spill, smoking in the chill morning air. The Mor warrior falls to one knee, my children still hacking and tearing.

"Kirin, no!" Hollern screams, seeing what I have summoned. "Oh, gods, no!"

The remaining Mor, caught between my dark children and the remnants of the company, make a break for the trees. Jazen Tor leaps at one, his sword stabbing at his opponent's lightly armored back. His blade transfixes a stout leg, busting through the Mor's knee from behind.

It stumbles and Tor is pulled forward, falling face down, his hand still clasping his blade. The Mor turns, seeing what has hurt it. In its smaller, inner hand is a stone knife. The air ripples with laval heat.

"Jazen! No!" I scream, seeing what is about to happen. I give the silent command for my sweetlings to attack, to save him, but I know I am already too late.

The Mor's blade saws across Tor's face in a shower of blood. The crimson flood boils into steam as it pours across the knife. Jazen's scream fills the world. The knife stabs down, burying itself to the hilt in his breast, just as my sweetlings pile onto the enemy.

The Mor's eyes, cloudy, jade-like, almost glowing behind the armored slit of its face armor, lock with mine as my children begin slaughtering it. I cannot tell if it is smiling behind the overlapping bone plates. Soon, my children find a weak spot in its armor and it is over.

"I ordered you to never . . . to never . . ." Hollern pants. "Oh, gods! What have you *done?*"

"Shut up or you'll be next," I say, kneeling beside Jazen, uncaring that my words or my desire to see Hollern's blood are treason. I grab the stone knife's hilt and pull it from my lover's body, all too aware that it is too late. Even through the leather of my gloves, the hilt scalds my palms. I toss it into the stream, and the water boils evilly as it sinks with a hissing splash.

"Shhhh . . ." I whisper to Jazen, stroking his crisped hair. "It will all be over soon. You will rise again, and we will be together. Together."

"D-d . . . don't . . . please . . ." he says, the words a bubbling hiss through the split, oozing wasteland of his face. His one remaining eye rolls and looks into my own. "Kirin . . . I'm afraid . . ."

I bend and kiss him, drawing his breath into my body. It tastes of brimstone and charred meat and his own treasured sweetness. The fiery blade has cooked him from within. I know he is in terrible pain, but cannot bring myself to do what is necessary to end his suffering. Inside, my sister spits and reviles me for a weakling, screaming that I am weak, am weak, am weak, that I will die beside him, in blood and fire.

I hold him, cradled in my lap, until his breath finally stops.

CHAPTER TWO

Kirin was not the name I was born with; it belonged to my twin sister. Back in the happy days when we were girls, Kirin was forever the dreamer, the one who had everything planned. Those were the days when nothing was more important to her than I, her twin, her other half. Before Marcus and the ruinous events that would lead to her death and our rebirth.

Kirin always knew what she wanted. At least, it seemed that way. Find the perfect men, sons of a wealthy family, then settle down in cottages on the same road, or even, if the gods were kind, neighboring town houses in the distant City; cherished wives of sophisticated, urban husbands.

She dreamed of a life filled with children and wealth, shared with dutiful, doting companions, purchased with our fair faces and slender bodies. Kirin was always the one who was so painfully aware of her gods-given beauty and what it could win for us, and who took such pains to display those gifts to their best advantage.

Growing up, she filled the air with nonstop chatter and demands. "Comb those cockleburs from your hair," she would tell me. Or "Stand up straight. Slouching makes you look common. Ladies have dignity and good posture." Or, her favorite, and mother's: "Can't you at least *try* to make yourself pretty?"

Kirin always dictated to me, the quiet one, the studious one, how we would live our lives. Even now she would do so, if she could. That she loathes the state of my life is no secret, for she takes every opportunity to remind me of how I am ruining myself.

Now that I am a woman grown, I can ignore her constant barbs. Most of the time. When I cannot, on those days when I am overly weary, which is seldom, or sick, which is almost never, I simply remind myself of her terrible fate, and pity stays my bitter reply.

There are days, sometimes entire weeks, when I do not curse the perverse knowledge that has allowed me to survive for so long; the same knowledge which keeps my sister bound to me. But when she whispers to me, whispers to me in the long still hours of the dark, on those days I would give every last golden rukh I have ever had or will have for a chance to go back and unlearn what I know. To join my sister in her simple, shallow plans. To be that compliant, frustrated girl again.

Mother did her best to raise us as proper young women. She spent hours with the two of us, laying out her family's tarnished silver and the yellowed porcelain that she said was too fine for any current company we might entertain. Endless lessons followed on how to lay a proper, elegant table, Mother frowning when I misplaced a fork or accidentally banged the side of my soup bowl with my spoon, or on how to start and maintain entertaining, empty conversation, steering clear of any subject that might cause offense or discord.

While we labored, she filled our ears with tales of her own girlhood. In her day, Mother had been a celebrated beauty, living a privileged life at court. Her days were filled with endless, drowsy lawn parties, where high-bred ladies met and mingled; her nights with extravagant banquets and costume balls, where the true powers of the empire plotted behind their masks of revelry.

That was during the time of Emperor Albrecht, before his assassination and the subsequent rule of Contessa, his faithless wife, who was later called by many unpleasant

names, the kindliest of which was "The Mad." Before
Contessa sent away all those loyal to the former Emperor;
the better, or so mother always said, to clear the way for
her lover Berthold, captain of the Emperor's former guard.
All before my family fell on hard times, their wealth and
position stripped away upon my grandfather's fall from
grace and banishment from court.

Kirin devoured such knowledge, seeing it as practice for
the day when she would inevitably marry back into the life
that had been stripped from our mother, becoming a Grand
Lady of the Empire.

Following Grandfather's exile, Mother and her two
sisters were sent away to live with their aunt, while my
uncles, older than they and both officers in the Empire's
army, left for far-away lands at the head of their companies,
there to pass from my mother's stories forever. Mother later
married her landlord's son, Rupert, the man who would be
my father. It was the best match she could make, she often
told us, under such rude circumstances.

My sister's bottomless appetite for Mother's tales was
not one I shared. For my part, I was never happier than when
I was able to slip away and wander my father's modest
holdings, exploring every stream and copse, often alone, but
sometimes accompanied by the children of his field hands
or tenants. I played come-along-sweet, or take-the-castle,
or sometimes even the-ogre-and-the-maiden with them,
laughing and running and acting out in a most unbecoming
manner.

I suppose in many ways it was an idyllic childhood,
despite my boredom and disinterest in my sister's prattle.
We seldom fought, for Kirin had inherited not only Mother's
leaf-green eyes and pale skin, physical traits we, naturally,
shared, but also her skill for inspiring guilt with a simple
glance or weary sigh. No, it was easier to allow myself to

be drawn along in her wake, and to let her chart the course for the adult life that still seemed so very far away. Alas, childhood, like all things, must eventually pass.

Marcus Allaire, the youngest son of Richard the Huntsman, was the sort of boy that all the girls told stories about. Clean-limbed and blessed with a strong chin, flowing nut-brown hair and eyes the color of a cloudless summertime sky, it seemed destined that girls would swoon at his feet. And swoon they did, amongst the buzz of gossip and chatter that always followed in the wake of his enormous black charger. He often rode through town after a successful hunt, mounted in the saddle proudly, his massive bow aslant across his back and his latest kill draped across his saddlebags, a look of insufferable smugness twisting his full lips.

I admit that I despised him. He never went to the school that Mother demanded we attend and Father worked so hard to afford; Marcus often said such learning was beneath a man of action like himself. I remember many an afternoon, walking home from a long day of instruction, when he and his cronies would descend on us, hooting and cat-calling, their ponies splattering us with mud as Kirin and I clung to one another.

Such teasing, of course, ended as soon as our breasts began to swell, replaced with a different but equally unwelcome sort of attention. Almost before I knew it, Kirin's flush of rage shifted, becoming an altogether different kind of blush when Marcus's eyes would roam over her body.

I had always assumed my sister's all-consuming ambition and endless fascination for Mother's tales of courtly life in the City would armor her against pretty, callous fools like Marcus. Assumed her dalliance with him, which began in the spring of our fifteenth year, was a passing thing, another trophy in her long chain of broken hearts. At first I even admired her for her boldness, for the Allaire family was

not one to be trifled with, particularly the cruel, if lovely,
Marcus.

So I willfully ignored the signs as their involvement deep-
ened, becoming more open. Their displays of affection grew,
from furtive kisses stolen behind Miller Osram's granary to
public strolling and hand-holding of a most alarming nature.

Later, she began to slip from the house in the dead of
night, creeping out our window after she thought me safely
asleep. When she returned, her eyes were bright, like a
fever victim's, and straw was tangled in her hair. When I
demanded that she tell me what had happened, she laughed
at me and called me a little girl and a fool.

I tried to warn her, but she, of course, had heard all the
same stories about Marcus as I. How he had been caught,
unashamed, even proud, with the Widow Marsten at the
scandalous age of fourteen. How he had professed his
endless love for Anna Coltsfoot, a girl who later ran away
from home with him for three days and nights before her
father and brothers went and brought her back from whatever
hideaway she had allowed herself to be taken to.

All the girls knew about how Anna had been quite
suddenly and without explanation sent far away to live with
relatives a month later, just as we also knew that Marcus
had boasted about his conquest of her in the tavern upon
his return. We all knew the reason for her banishment, even
though we would never openly admit it, for such talk was
unseemly for young ladies such as we.

Why would Kirin continue to pursue this rough, callow
young man, a person of limited prospects and questionable
family, knowing full well his roguish reputation? True, the
Allaires made a decent living, as their furs were of the best
quality, but they were, when all was said and done, country
folk, uneducated and coarse, certainly not what Mother had
trained Kirin to pursue.

The more I tried to convince her of the danger of her actions, the firmer she became in her defense of him. It was as if a madness had come upon her, one that drove deeper and deeper the more that I tried to show her the error of her ways.

Mother, of course, eventually found out about Kirin. How could she not, with every tongue wagging about it? Their quarrels filled the air for many nights, drifting down from upstairs while I sat with Father, trying to read from one of my storybooks while he quietly drank glass after glass of bitter wine.

He did not interfere; he never did, for Mother had made it quite clear that his assistance was neither helpful nor welcome. Still, I shall never forget the way he would turn his bloodshot eyes up, searching the top of the stairs whenever the yelling became particularly loud, like a hound patiently awaiting its master's summons.

I still do not know if Mother finally realized Kirin was more than her match for stubbornness, or if she had some other, deeper scheme in mind, but eventually the quarrelling, like a wild fire that has finally exhausted its fuel, stopped. Even after Mother had given up, however, I still tried to make my sister see the folly of her decision.

But Kirin had won, a fact she was all too aware of. She no longer argued; she simply reminded me that Mother had grown silent on the issue, and suggested I do the same. When it was obvious she would brook no further discussion of the matter, I gave up, an act that I fear she must have seen as permission for what happened next.

Marcus's boyhood friend was Urik, Miller Osram's son. Both my sister and her loutish new beau made it clear that if I were to take up with Urik, all parties would be quite satisfied with such a development.

Urik was not unpleasant to look upon, even though he did share his father's barrel-chest and ruddy complexion.

His hair was sandy blond and receding, a fact he tried to conceal by allowing it to grow long, wearing the corn silk curls about his shoulders.

Worst of all, Kirin often spoke of his prospects and his family's modest wealth, trying to tempt me with visions of the life of ease that she had somehow managed to mislay in her pursuit of Marcus.

By late summer, my sister's courtship had flowered into a full-fledged betrothal. Kirin set the date: our sixteenth birthday, the day we would officially become women.

Urik followed suit days later, stammering out his proposal with one knee sunk in the mud behind his father's mill. He looked so confused, kneeling there in the dirt, his face even redder than usual, either from embarrassment or excitement. I bade him wait three days for my answer, and went to see my sister.

She knew. Of course she knew. She and Marcus had it all planned, just as she always did. Certainly it would not do for Kirin to wed while her sister did not. All of my attempts to remind my sister of her grandiose schemes and plans, as well as Marcus's childhood cruelty, were fruitless.

When it was clear my resistance was enduring, she stopped speaking to me for a time; I usually capitulated to her demands without much of a fight. The next day she came to me, an unexpected ally at her side. Mother.

Kirin prattled endlessly about the size of Miller Osram's warehouses and how his flours were prized by the finest bakers in the far-off City, a fact that Mother found endlessly fascinating. That Mother no longer turned her shrew's eye on Kirin's continued courtship by Marcus was not lost on me.

When Kirin's arguments were all played out, it was Mother's turn. Where my sister's flawed logic and empty promises failed, Mother's tears and sobbing entreaties triumphed. I did not, nor do I now, understand why Mother gave up on her dreams for our family's return to the good life in the City, but Kirin had certainly said something to her during their heated arguments, discovered some chink in the armor of Mother's resolve, for all she could speak of was how we should look to make the best match that we could under the circumstances.

When I reminded her that she had made a similar bargain years before, she slapped me. The blow, so unexpected, for Mother had never raised anything but her voice to me, brought stinging tears to my eyes. We ended up in each other's arms, sobbing, Mother's tears wetting my shoulder while Kirin sat, smiling, untouched by the storm she had called down.

Eventually, I bowed to their wishes and accepted Urik's ring, telling myself over and over that he was indeed the better half of the pair. He was occasionally thoughtful and generally mild, a man who often brought me untidy bouquets of pansies and boxes of sweets imported from the far-off City.

That he usually ended up eating the majority of the candy himself did not trouble me, for was I not always told the thought is more important than the deed? I will grow to love him in time, I told myself every night, over and over, until the words became a jumble of meaningless sounds.

As summer slid towards autumn and my wedding, I resigned myself to my fate. My only consolation was that I would no longer have to deal with Marcus once the deed was done. I would be a proper woman, a wife and later a mother, burdened with the myriad chores of keeping my husband's house and rearing his children, far too busy with life's details to be troubled with Marcus or even, should I choose it, Kirin.

In that, of course, I was wrong.

Our wedding was a complex affair, what with two brides and two grooms and the attending families of all, but we managed. Kirin looked so happy in her sky-blue wedding silks, standing before the priest. I managed to say my vows without stumble or stammer, which was all I had asked for from the fickle gods.

The Allaires brought their entire clan, all six brothers and their wives and their feral children. As the evening wore on and Father's wine flowed, brawls broke out, every one a knot of chaos with an Allaire brother at its heart, laughing as they punched and kicked. Mother was horrified and retired early, before the worst of the night's embarrassments. If Kirin noticed, she gave no sign; her attention was only for her new husband.

I watched Marcus as well. I knew what kind of man he was, what kind of man he must be, coming from such a feared and wild family. My mistake was thinking that my poor, sweet, dimwitted Urik was any better.

Had I known on that day I was following Kirin down a road leading only to blood and pain and death, I would have fled, gods forgive me, abandoning her to the fate she so stubbornly insisted for herself. But, of course, we never know what fate the gods have in store for us, do we?

CHAPTER THREE

Smoke rises beyond the trees in a black column. Fort Azure lies at the end of this road. Fort Azure, with its promise of high walls and hot food, and sleep, gods-blessed sleep.

The men have noticed. Some groan at the sight. Others merely stare, their eyes as hard and flat as creek stones.

"What is that?" Hollern asks, his voice almost trembling. "What is that smoke?"

"It is the fort," I say, not even trying to hide the disgust in my voice.

"Are they under attack?" Hollern asks. I walk away without answering. Soon enough, we will know.

I draw and nock an arrow, mentally commanding my sweetlings to fall in behind me. I pick the path carefully; my children are not known for their woodcraft, and do not understand what it means to walk lightly. In this they are much like the soldiers.

The men do not like my children, and stare at them with weary looks of disgust and fear. But, other than Hollern, they do not complain. When we have reached a place of safety, their feelings will doubtless change, but for now the soldiers are driven by desperation to tolerate their presence. They have seen what the sweetlings are capable of in battle, and so long as that strength serves to protect them, I know they will not turn on me.

A few minutes later, I see the glimmer of sunlight ahead. The border of the woods, at last. The breeze shifts, and the first smell of burning reaches me, wood smoke and something else, something like meat skewers roasting over a faire-day fire. I command Hollern and my sweetlings to stay put, then stalk to the tree line.

The Fort stands close to the trees' edge, no more than a bow shot from the forest's verge. Keeping the space between clear must have been a full-time endeavor. Beyond lie the lower slopes and rolling foothills leading up to the mountains to the North.

Fort Azure's piled-stone walls are still standing, but the gates which barred the entrance are lying on the trampled grass before them, their thick timbers splintered and charred. Some enormous force has torn them from their hinges. The timbers are covered by pairs of deep gouges.

The Mor have already been here.

Something is burning inside the square walls, the source of the dense black cloud and the smell. The croaking and squabbling of crows is audible all the way from the woods.

I hear Hollern thrashing through the underbrush after me. I can just imagine his chest swelling with indignation, ready to bluster about not taking orders from a lowly scout. I whirl anyway, as if someone like him could ever come upon me unaware, drawing the bow all the way to my cheek and centering the murderous barb square between his eyes. Ten feet away, Hollern freezes, his eyes wide. I hold the shaft for a long moment, then slowly relax.

"I thought I told you to stay back," I whisper, turning away to stare at the burning fort.

"I refuse to stand there in the presence of those . . . those . . ."

"Be wary of what you say," I grate. "They saved your worthless hide, remember. Next time, they just might not."

"Are you threatening . . ." he sputters, his wide, peasant face, a farmer's face, all doughy, large-pored skin and freckles, flushing beet-red.

"They might be inside still," I say, nodding towards the fort. "We should go around. Head overland to Fort Jasper."

"That's three days' march," he protests.

"True. But the Mor have been here, and recently. They might not have reached Jasper."

"The men need rest and supplies. We can patch the gate and retake the fort."

I spare him a long look, waiting for him to back down. The defiant jut of his jaw tells me the outcome of this farce. He shall not be turned aside from this path.

Damn. *Damn*. This is my fault. I can see he has chosen this because I do not wish it. Men are always so painfully aware of any perceived slight to their authority. I should have humbly suggested, and let him think that it was his idea. But, I have always had little patience for fools.

I shrug and sit, commanding my sweetlings to move up. A moment later, I hear them, pushing through the underbrush. Hollern gulps and steps back, his hand on his blade, as my children step forth.

The dark child I have summoned from the remains of a swarthy-faced soldier stops to pick one of the delicate mossflowers growing on the bark of a nearby oak. He stares at the tiny, shell-green blossom for a moment with one weeping, opal eye, before thrusting the flower into his fanged mouth. He chews for a moment, then seems to forget what he is about. The mangled flower droops from the corner of his lipless mouth.

Hollern shudders and sketches the sign of Loran Light-bringer in my direction, then storms off. A few minutes later, the men emerge cautiously from the trees. Hollern is at the rear. I can hear him commanding the men to move forward.

Two men are assigned to go inside the shattered gates, and, just for a moment, I dare to hope that the men will mutiny. But the habit of obedience is strong, and after sharing a long look, the pair slip inside, shields upraised, swords naked in their fists.

They return almost immediately. One rushes to the wall and the meager remains of his last meal come up in a liquid rush. The other sits, only answering Hollern's bleating commands for a report after being kicked. Hollern turns, shooting a withering look back in my direction, before going inside.

As much as I despise their commander, the men need help. This place is not safe. Jazen, dearest Jazen, would have known what to do; he would have jollied, or argued, or convinced his lead-headed commanding officer to do the right thing. But Jazen can no longer speak a language that Hollern can understand.

I look over at the child I have called from his flesh, and a sadness I have carefully trained myself to ignore ripples through me like nausea. I can still see Jazen's lovely features on one half of the sweetling's face, staring out at me with slack-eyed blankness. The other half is pure nightmare, the legacy of the Mor's blade, a yawning, blackened canyon framing the stumps of shattered teeth, skin peeled back to expose the ripple and slide of leather-hard tendons.

A face only a mother could love.

Sighing, I sling my bow and command my children to take up positions at the corners of the walls, beneath the watchtowers. When they lie down, they look disturbingly like skinned bodies. I turn for the gates.

INSIDE, DEAD MEN ARE SCATTERED, as numerous as shells on a beach. All bear the gaping, jagged-edged wounds of the Mor. Many have been dismembered. Others have been cut in half. None have heads; this is indeed the Mor's handiwork, as if the shattered gate left any doubt.

A murder of crows fills the air above us, a cawing, vertiginous cloud of flapping darkness. The bold creatures return moments after being shooed away, gory beaks dipping, landing to pluck another succulent, grisly morsel from the fallen.

The smoke comes from a pyre of horses. For some reason, the Mor have stacked and set ablaze the dozen-odd horses stabled here, mounts for message couriers and long-range scouts, while leaving the bodies of the men to rot.

"You four men, fall out for burial detail," Hollern commands, pointing to his chosen. "The rest, help me with this wagon. Ah, Kirin, I see you've come to your senses and have decided to join us."

"This is folly," I blurt. "You cannot secure this location. If the Mor return . . ."

"Then we have your bow. And the advantage of elevation." He and the men wrestle the wagon to the opening in the wall, where they are to overturn it. They begin rocking it. Finally it turns on its side, half-blocking the gate.

Hollern has gone mad. It is the only explanation. Assigning four men with three shovels between them the task of burying almost three-score bodies; trying to improvise a gate—which will not open if we should want to retreat—out of an overturned wagon and some hastily-piled crates.

I am readying my gear, intending to put as much distance as possible between myself and this place of death before darkness falls, when one of the men catches my eye. He stares at me like a starving man might eye a slice of roast, a desperate, almost feral gleam in his eye. He knows, as do I, that if I go, he will die here. I long to tell him that even if I remain, the outcome will almost certainly be the same. There is nothing I can do for them.

Yet, hours later, I am still at the fort, stationed at the northwest watchtower. The men toil outside the wall, below me, digging shallow graves. They have completed half a dozen, and now afternoon is lengthening into dusk.

Hollern has constructed a great mound of debris in front of the gate, and now turns to commanding the men to police the bodies of the fallen. Once he is satisfied that his orders are being followed, he retires inside of the fort's keep. It, too, is damaged, its door hanging askew on a single bent hinge.

When it grows too dark for the men outside to work, we spend a tense half hour shifting the debris blocking the gate in order to allow them to come inside. I help with the work, trying, and failing, to imagine this heap of rubbish slowing, let alone stopping, a charging Mor.

The men build a proper fire from the remains of the pyre, sharing around whatever horse meat is still edible. Half man the walls while the remainder eat, or try to rest.

I take my meal, the cold remains of dried meat and biscuit from the bottom of my pack, up to the guard tower. I am careful to keep the fire at my back, lest it ruin my night vision.

The forest is a line of impenetrable blackness beneath the milky river of stars above. Anything could be hidden there. Anything. I know that I will never be able to rest in such a state.

As soon as my replacement takes his post, I slip over the wall. I dash across the open space between the walls and the forest, my eyes roaming, searching for any movement, any reflection of the moonlight. I wish my sweetlings could come with me; I would feel better for some company, but they are needed back at the fort. Besides, I will move faster, and far more silently, if I travel alone.

I patrol the woods for hours, ranging far afield before heading back, always alert for signs of the Mor. In the still hours of the darkest part of the night, I find an oak and climb into its branches, fashioning a tenuous perch for myself in a convenient bough. It is not the most comfortable bed, but its concealment gives me comfort.

Dawn is a breathless promise hanging in the still air when I hear them. Heavy footsteps, breaking through the undergrowth. They are not trying to be quiet. They do not care for subtlety.

I still have time. Time to run to the fort. Time to tell the men to run. Time to warn them.

And they might—just might—listen to me. If Hollern sleeps deeply, I may have time to convince enough of the men of the coming danger before it is too late for them to flee.

But in my tree, I am safe. They will not think to look for me here. They cannot track me.

In the black, a crack sounds as something heavier than a Woodstrider steps on brittle wood. The sound, sharp and explosive, makes me jump.

Then I am scrambling down, the bark scratching at my hands, my clothes. My cloak snags on a broken branch and almost throttles me before I can free it.

I sprint across the open ground, arms upraised, calling out, "Scout returning! Scout returning! To arms! To arms! The enemy approaches!" desperately hoping one of the half-awake guards will not loose an arrow at me.

I claw at the mound of debris, slipping between the wagon and the crates, while all around the men rouse themselves with sleepy groans and cries.

They surround me, their grimed, stubbled faces pale in the fading moonlight, mouths open with questions. How many? How far off? Are they coming? Are they coming? Are they coming?

"There is still time to flee," I hiss, hoping that they will hear me. "We must go. Now. Before they arrive. We must—"

"Silence!" Hollern is here. Is coming through the broken keep door, uniform rumpled and hair wild, naked steel in his fist.

"We must flee. They are in the woods. They are coming this way," I say, facing the commander but speaking to the men. Hollern, I know, will not be swayed. But the men might.

"To arms, all men to the battlements. We'll drive them back, in Loran's name," he says, a wild gleam in his bloodshot eyes.

"No! The gate will not hold!"

I see doubt bloom in some of the men's eyes, a poison flower that is their only true salvation. The seed takes hold in the fertile soil of the men's fear. Inside, my sister crows in triumph, and for once I am glad of it.

"You men!" Hollern shouts. He has seen it too. "You men; be true. This is Fort Azure. We can defend this place. We have walls, and gates."

"The men stationed here had those as well," I say, not bothering to mention that Hollern's gate is mere rubbish. The men know. "They had five times our number, as well as a stout, intact gate, and even with all that, they were no match for the Mor."

I see the men look to one another. Some nod. As one, they move to the improvised barricade, begin tearing it down.

"When you get outside, run for the trees," I say, helping them pull aside boxes and furniture. "Scatter. Do not stop to fight; you cannot hope to win. The Mor are powerful, but are not quick. They are no match for your fleetness.

"And do not stop, no matter what. Try to find water; they do not like it. Head for the road, and then keep going."

"This is mutiny! I'll see you all hanged, starting with you, you treacherous bitch!" Hollern rages.

"Cut out 'is tongue. That'll shut 'is yap right quick," one of the men suggests. That stops his words. Hollern moves aside, glaring daggers at me, cowed for the moment.

"Movement in the trees!" a sentry shouts. The words turn my blood to ice. "Movement!" a second calls out.

As one, we look up from our labor, the pile only chest high now, and see them.

The Mor flow from the concealing forest. Three. Six. A dozen, and still more. Their hulking shoulders gleam like burnished stone in the growing dawnlight. Their inhuman faces, like armored masks, stare at us, eyes glowing with laval heat, full of hate.

They emerge from the trees, a ragged yet impassable line of armored death. Behind us are the foothills of the mountains, rising up and up, the ground turning to stone. Far above, snow glitters with the promise of eternal, peaceful cold.

It is too late. They have come.

CHAPTER FOUR

We moved into Kirin's dream cottages soon after the wedding. The gardens we cultivated near our shared wall were my sister's treasure. She loved flowers, Kirin did, and spent every morning planting daisies and snapdragons and morning's glory. Bunches of sun-yellow marigolds vied with climbing rose, their alternately pungent and sweet scents vying for attention.

Ever the practical one, I focused on more mundane, useful crops. Tansy and thyme and mint. Chamomile for teas and hyssop to help with the winter's coughs. All this and more I grew, the plants in ordered, neat rows, surrounded by the desperate riot of Kirin's flowers. I did not know it then, but I would lay those same blooms, with mud-caked hands, on her defiled grave a scant year later.

Pregnancy came fast for Kirin, and I watched with envy as her reed-like body swelled with its preparations for motherhood. Knowing what I know now, about the body's changes in response to the growth of a child and the resulting blood and pain that is the gateway into life, I marvel I still retain such sentimentality about the process. Certainly, the girl I was felt an undeniable stab of jealousy every time I saw her, hands cradling the swell of her belly, her face serene and knowing, thoughts turned inwards.

Urik and I tried and tried to match her but no child quickened in my belly. At first, Urik said nothing, but as the months passed and Kirin's time drew closer, he began to first question, than accuse me, demanding to know if I or my father had known I was barren. I defended Father, of course, once going so far as to suggest that perhaps the fault was Urik's, not mine. The look he gave me was so full of fear and black hate that my blood ran cold. He told me I was to never repeat such hateful lies.

As Kirin's pregnancy advanced, Marcus's journeys away from home grew longer and longer. He became distant and cold. Rumors began to spread that he had a mistress in a nearby town, and I often saw my sister's eyes ringed with the unmistakable red of weeping when we met near the garden wall.

The day Kirin's baby finally arrived, red-faced and screaming on a raw, gray winter's day, was one of the most terrifying and thrilling experiences of my young life. The child was breech, and only the quick thinking of the midwife spared the life of mother and child both, but the delivery necessitated that she be cut most deeply. Never before had I seen such blood, blood enough to drown in, it seemed. That Kirin survived at all was a miracle, and the hard labor forced her to her bed for weeks afterwards. She named the babe Vanessa, after our storied grandmother.

Marcus, of course, was absent for the event, out on one of his "hunting trips." When he finally returned, three days later, he could barely walk, swaying drunkenly across the muddied yard. His bellows waked the babe, and she screamed in her father's face in terror, causing Marcus to shout even louder. He rode out that very night, headed for the tavern and "some peace and quiet," and did not return until the next morning.

After the birth, Marcus did seem to try to mend his ways. His trips grew shorter, and he spent the better part of the winter at home. Things were always difficult when he was around, however; men such as Marcus do not have much love for inactivity, and the six long months of winter crept by with painful slowness.

Finally, spring arrived and with it the return of Marcus's waywardness. Even as his absences grew longer and longer, Kirin would hear nothing ill of him. It was as if her love for him had stolen away not only her ambition but also her very reason. My entreaties for her to run away, for her own good as well as that of her newborn child, were met with stubborn silence.

One day in the late spring, close to Vanessa's mid-cycle birthday, he returned, reeling with drink and smelling like a whorehouse, bellowing for her to come and fix his supper. She refused and confronted him, her shouts of accusation drifting over the wall. Soon, they fell abruptly, ominously silent. When I saw her next, her face bore the hand-shaped bruise of his displeasure. She wore the mark for days.

I pleaded with Urik to talk to his friend, but he would not; either out of friendship or fear I know not. Worst, the poison that had infected Marcus was contagious, and began to taint his simple spirit. The next months were a torture, filled with the white heat of arguments and the helpless, creeping doom of waiting for my husband and his loutish friend to return from the tavern or from one of their increasingly frequent trips.

My first life ended on the day my husband hit me. Urik, for his part, apologized profusely and tearfully, swearing over and over it was a momentary lapse, brought on in the heat of anger. That it would never happen again. But the deed was done. The long summer drew out like a blade, endless days of stifling heat and dreary days of waiting for my husband to return.

When he did finally arrive, more often than not, we fought. About the chores he promised to attend to but never seemed to finish. About the way his endless drinking was bloating his already soft body. About the accounts that needed paying. Soon enough, despite his promises, I was to feel the pain of my husband's hand again.

Divorce is not unheard of among my people, for the gods want all men and women to be happy and fruitful. Yet, a lifetime of instruction in what is and is not seemly and proper for a woman of my breeding had left me unwilling to endure the humiliation. The whispers and openly curious stares that followed me whenever I went into town began to disgust, then enrage me. I spent more and more time alone.

With Kirin lost in her world of denial, and Mother's refusal to become involved in anything distasteful and embarrassing, my only confidante was Edena, the old wise woman that lived up in the hills. Kirin and I sometimes traded the herbs I cultivated and gathered to her in exchange for the potions that soothed our monthly troubles and the healing poultices which Kirin's infant always seemed to need. There were many stories about Edena, tales that spoke of her dancing, nude, in the moonlight on summer's eve, or of strange men who were seen to live for a week, or a month, on her property, disappearing afterwards without a trace.

Yet she was always kind to me, her aged face open and inviting, ice blue eyes sparkling with merriment above rose-tinged cheeks. She seemed to me much more of a grandmotherly figure than my own storied ancestor, always bustling about her workshop, crushing herbs or boiling potions, her gray hair wreathed in fragrant steam.

More than once, however, I spied a dusty book or scroll winking out at me from beneath a shawl or folded blanket. I reminded myself that young ladies do not help themselves to others' things, even such a small and harmless thing as stealing a simple glance, all the while burning with curiosity.

I still do not know if it was her plan to entrap me with her knowledge. A lonely young woman, desperate for affection and starved for the chance to learn; she must have known what sort of student I would prove to be, always eager to read anything that passed through my hands. The whole town knew, why not she?

Eventually, I let curiosity overwhelm my manners. After reading the first page, I knew I wanted to know more. I went to her, the book open in my hands.

"My wisdom isn't for the idle or curious," she snarled, her usually smiling lips twisting with an expression of cruelty, waving away my promises and assurances that I would do anything she asked if she would only teach me more. "Nor is it for those lacking in courage, for I know of such things that would rattle the very fibers of a timid woman's heart and mind. Go back to your garden, little bird. Go back to the life that your sister has chosen for you."

I bent my head, letting my hair fall over my bruised eye, the painful legacy of last night's fight. It was true; I did lack the courage to stand up to my sister and to what my husband had become. But sitting there, head bent beneath Edena's stony glare, so different from her usual welcoming smile, I decided that I wanted to have that courage. To learn the things she kept hidden away like dragon's gold.

When I raised my head she must have seen it, for she met my challenging stare, holding my eyes with hers for what felt like a fortnight before dropping her gaze and nodding.

I still remember that first book as if I had just looked upon it yesterday—such a marvel. An atlas of the human body, illustrated in surreal detail, the body's layers drawn on translucent vellum, which peeled away to expose the hidden secrets beneath. The colors were so vivid, more lurid and enticing than any mummer's show. It was an ancient thing, made through artistry the likes of which I'd never seen before, more precious than gold. Once that door was opened, I had no choice but to pass through.

Every day that Urik was away, I would hurry to finish my daily chores, then trudge the well-worn path to Edena's cottage. Then my studies would begin: long hours bent over my small desk, memorizing chants and herbal mixtures and the names of a thousand bodily parts from all manner of beasts and birds. When she deemed I was ready, we proceeded to a study of a different animal.

Eagerly, I studied the intricacies of the human body and how it reacts to death, transforming from a hunk of dead meat to the birthplace of miraculous new life. How nature wastes not the smallest particle after we leave our mortal shells behind.

As I began to master the physical mysteries, she spoke more and more of the nature of our souls. It was she who first showed me how the human spirit often lingers near the place where it is ripped from its earthly shell.

What she taught me filled me with a dark glee, which I hid away, like a precious stone I feared would be stolen. Even then I understood that our forbidden knowledge was power.

Once, we traveled in the dark of the night to the place were three highwaymen had been hanged and left as a warning beside the road. I'll never forget the sickly-sweet smell that wafted forth as we cut them down, repulsive, yet oddly compelling. The way that her oils and unguents opened my secret eye, granting me a glimpse of the robbers' shades, still lingering near their decaying bodies.

At my mistress's whispered command, those souls drifted back into their former bodies. They awoke from their endless slumber, her devoted, if not very nimble or swift-witted, servants. My education dispelled my fear of them.

My excursions did not go unnoticed. Kirin began to question me about my doings when I was away from home. She smirked when I assured her I was simply helping the old woman with her chores and keeping her company through the long nights. I am sure she assumed I had taken a lover, and I did nothing to disabuse her of that notion.

One night, Marcus and Urik returned from a days-long hunting trip, reeking of beer and women. I watched from a far-away place outside of myself as my husband, once so tender and shy, used me. The stench of another woman lay thick on his skin. He giggled as he put his filthy hands on me, grinning as if he thought the smell might arouse me. I knew the time to depart had come. I slipped away when his snores filled the cottage; the herbal mixture I had put in his wine would assure his slumber for at least a day.

I scratched at Kirin's window, my pack already slung over my shoulder. I was certain she would follow. Were we not sisters? Twins? I would dazzle her with my new-found skills and knowledge and we would take our places at my mistress's side, beholden to no man. When she did not reply, I crept to the door and quietly unlatched it.

The familiar, dread smell struck me first, a mixture of copper and the heavy, organic smell of death. Blood spattered the walls. From beneath the kitchen table, an ivory hand could be seen in the dim firelight.

Her breast bore the crimson stains of her lifeblood. The weapon, a carving knife of rare Ulean steel that my own father had given her as a bride gift, lay on the floor. She looked surprised, as if death had played a sudden and not terribly funny joke on her. A wine-besotted snore reached me from the back bedroom.

I stood and watched him for what seemed like hours as my mind struggled to accept what he had done. Marcus lay there, his once-beautiful face swollen with drink, mouth open in a slack-jawed snore. Her blood was crusted on his hands, staining the pillowcases and sheet and the wine bottle he still clutched.

I knew what must be done, but whatever remaining wisps of the girl I had once been screamed at me that it was wrong, wrong, *wrong*. I closed my eyes and made my decision, stilling the last feeble protests. When next they opened, they were dull, lifeless windows; portals looking in on an empty room. The girl was gone. I was ready.

My clothes gave a whisper-soft rustle as I dropped my skirts and tunic to the floor, then slipped into my sister's bed. The moonlight slanting through the window made my skin luminous, glowing. I reached out and brushed the sweat-damp hair from Marcus's brow with a steady hand, then leaned forward to brush his lips with mine. I felt him stiffen at my touch, and moved so that he slipped inside of me.

Before the forbidden power reached out to snare his lifeblood, he muttered my sister's name—the name I would soon take as my own—telling me in a drunken mumble how sorry he was for killing me. Begging my forgiveness. It was not until my hands were on his flesh and my eyes shifted from white to black in the extremity of my transformation that he knew what shared his bed. I whispered that all was forgiven, allowing him the luxury of a last, unbroken look.

He tried to scream then, his mouth stretched in a soundless howl of agony, but my power held fast to the very roots of his breath, and the capacity was denied him at my whim. As he struggled and thrashed, his body desperately clinging to life, I rode him, my body lifting with his last desperate thrusts. My thighs and breasts and hands were slick with the blood that boiled from his eyes, his nose, anyplace and every place. The thick taste of copper was bright in my mouth as I threw back my head and moaned in mingled ecstasy and loathing.

Blood magic. Such power; such pain. All gleaned from a single, accidentally discovered book, found deep within one of Edena's chests. I never even considered that perhaps she was hiding it from me. Or from herself.

Of course I read it, knowing as each page was turned that one day I would make use of such a thing. Edena discovered the book several days after I had taken it, buried beneath my tablet and the papers strewn across my desk. By then it was too late; I had memorized it.

She railed at me, her fury reducing me to tears, screaming I was not ready for such things, that I might never be ready. I had assured her I would listen to her warnings and never use the knowledge she forbade me.

Now that same knowledge sang a song of lust and power, of sorrow and revenge, in my veins, drowning out my fears as my sister's murderer grew weaker and finally fell still beneath me. I watched in fascination as the black blood sparking on my breasts was absorbed. As dry clay drinks water, the blood sank slowly into my skin until no trace remained.

The babe slept through it all, and for that alone I give thanks to the gods. Afterwards, I stood over Vanessa's crib, watching the gentle rise and fall of her chest, fascinated with the way her dark lashes rested against her cheek. She, too, bore the marks of her father's rage, four finger-shaped bruises on her arm.

I returned to my home, and stood over Urik. He sprawled on the bed, his mouth stretched in a wet snore. The herbs I had given him would assure that he felt no pain. Kirin's knife, sticky-slippery, rested in my hand. The memory of Marcus' blood on my body sang inside of me, more seductive than any lover's promises.

In the end, I left the bloodied knife in the bed beside him. Let him sleep beside a new mistress tonight, I thought.

I do not know why I spared him. Perhaps, given what happened later, I should have ended his life there, but a part of me still is glad I did not take that road.

I returned to Kirin's and gathered up the babe, shushing her sleepy cries. It took most of the night to walk to my parents' house. Dawn's first indigo traces were in the eastern sky when I laid her basket on my mother's step. I fled then, before Vanessa could wake and rouse the household.

I did not shed tears for Kirin. I knew that death was merely a transition from one land to the next. No, my tears were for myself, for I knew my life was over, just as surely as if Marcus had plunged the knife into my own breast. Like my mistress's servants, I was dead, yet still I walked.

I left immediately, bringing nothing but the clothes on my back and the meager contents of my traveling pack. My own Ulean knife, the twin of the one Father had given Kirin on our wedding day, rested inside.

The old woman rejoiced to see me when she glimpsed my gear, but her good humor fled when she looked into my blackened eyes, orbs of purest jet within which my green irises shone like hot jewels. When I told her what I had done, the faintest spark of fear shone deep in her rheumy old eyes, but she did not turn me away.

The next morning I threw myself into my studies, delving deeply into her small library of scrolls and musty books. Within the first week I discovered the *rede* that I required to make my soul complete.

When the townsfolk came, led by the Allaire patriarch and searching for Marcus's murderer, the old woman hid me in the secret space beneath her barn. I lay in the dusty heat beneath the floorboards. The cold, unbreathing bodies of our servants were packed close around me, their twitches and rustlings oddly comforting. The Allaires left soon after with many a warding gesture and mumbled curse, unmanned by her unblinking good humor and the sight of the countless talismans hanging from the cottage eaves, trinkets of twisted hair and bone which she often sold to the lovesick and ignorant.

Three weeks later, in the enveloping darkness of the new moon, I slipped back into town. I lingered for an hour in the garden that once brought my sister so much joy, harvesting a bouquet of marigolds and roses from the chaotic riot into which it had lapsed. I gathered my tools and walked to the cemetery.

As required, I uncovered her body with my own hands. The earth was still soft and easy to turn with my shovel. I pried the nails loose one by one. Her coffin lid yielded with a shriek.

In the grave's stifling darkness, my hands traced the familiar features of my twin, her eyes sunken in death, skin like paper, cool and dry. They had buried her in the same silks in which she had wed, and I fingered them for a long while, imagining what color they must be now after almost a month in the ground. The smell of her transformation was thick in my nose, and the thousand tiny sounds of the new life her body was giving birth to was loud in the pit. I drew forth my knife.

I ate with relish, three mouthfuls as required, watching with my secret eye as my sister's lingering shade was drawn to me by the power of the ritual. The meat was soft, and tasted sweeter than the finest venison.

Then my sister's voice was in my mind, whispering to me the strange, alien wisdom of the vale beyond death as her thoughts mingled with mine, at once familiar and strange. I took her name as my own on that night. Kirin: one name for two souls.

The morning sun rose on her grave, carefully restored to its former condition, the only trace of my work the bouquet of flowers propped against the head stone. I would never see my parents or my home again.

CHAPTER FIVE

Jazen Tor dies in my arms for the second time.

I look up, tears burning in my blackened green eyes. A second return from beyond the Vale is impossible, as I know all too well. He is lost to me forever.

The squat, surprisingly heavy body begins to shrivel, becoming in moments as light and brittle as a wasp's nest rustling in the wind. His face — one half the beloved features that once filled so many passionate nights, the other the ravaged, blackened wasteland that the Mor's knife created — sinks inward, crumbling. Before I can bend to plant a last kiss on Tor's ravaged face, all that's left in my lap is a pile of coarse ash. It slips from between my grasping fingers.

All around, the sounds of the dead and dying echo from the stone walls of Fort Azure. I look up to where the men are making their last stand, packed close behind the remaining shreds of cover offered by the hastily re-piled rubbish. Beyond the barricade, the Mor are choked, packed shoulder to hulking shoulder, disdaining to even attempt to try breaching, or scaling, the walls.

Our last remaining archers, both of them, flank the remains of the gate, loosing their shafts whenever a target presents itself. Their quivers are almost empty, as is mine. Every few moments, their efforts are rewarded with an unearthly bellow of pain, as one of the darts finds a sensitive spot, but such small triumphs are heartbreakingly few.

Jazen was the last of my sweetlings. The others have all fallen, torn limb from limb by the fury of the Mor. Before they finally succumbed, I saw them drag down half-a-dozen of our attackers, throttling them, stabbing at them from behind with their blade-like limbs.

Then the Mor finally noticed that what they had taken for dead bodies were very much alive, and had turned, pausing at their assault, to deal with the new threat. It gave the men a few precious moments to rebuild the barricade, at least, for all the good it will do.

"To arms! To arms! Glory be to Loran Lightbringer!" The cry snaps me back to the conflict about me.

Hollern, surprisingly, stands at the van, his sword hacking at the forest of chitinous limbs that tear at our last bulwark. Desperation, it seems, has finally given the man spine enough to fight. Too bad it did not give him the brains to flee when we had the time. Now we are trapped, the only exit the blocked gate.

I watch as he screams obscenities at the Mor, taunting them, entreating them to try harder to reach his blood, and the men react, redoubling their efforts. For one glorious moment it looks as if it might actually work; the Mor flow back from the opening, leaving behind severed limbs, the stumps streaming the foul black ichor that serves as their blood.

The respite is brief. A moment later, a rumbling cry fills the air. The wounded part, stepping aside to make room for a new assault. A fresh cadre of Mor crashes into the barricade like a wave. The cart groans as two of its wheels snap and buckle. Wood flies as the enemies' powerful upper limbs rip and tear.

One of the men screams as a smaller limb pistons forward, a blocky sledge clutched in the four-fingered, twin-thumbed hand. Time slows, giving me a chance to see the brass bangles twirling merrily from thongs wrapped around the Mor's wrist. One looks like a tiny six-limbed lizard. Its eyes are delicate chips of glittering obsidian.

Then the sledge crunches home and the man reels back, his mouth howling, his cheek a pulped crimson ruin. His eye flops, horribly, against his cheek. Then he is gone, lost in the chaos.

I stand, the last wisps of Jazen's desiccated flesh swirling away, my sister's voice keening in a savage cry. My bow is in my hands. I must will my hand to be still; rage makes it tremble.

The arrow flies true, striking a Mor in its laval eye, sinking deep, only a bare inch of shaft and the black feathers showing. Then it reels back, its bellow lost in the cacophony. Another takes its place.

When there are no more arrows, I drop the useless bow and draw my short sword. I find myself next to Hollern, the grinning madman. He has found glory in the moment, once more calling forth the power of Loran Lightbringer. The remaining men pack close to us, shields upraised, a dense knot of desperate flesh and steel.

My battle scream rends the air as I thrust forward, taking a Mor in the seam between crotch and leg. It pulls back, dragging me along as I clutch the slippery handle. The Mor lifts its huge claw, ready to strike me dead.

Hollern's sweeping cut cracks against the horn-like skin, deflecting the blow. The claws bury themselves in the churned, bloody earth. The pause is momentary, but it is sufficient for two soldiers to hack at the exposed joints with their knives. The Mor goes down, piping, and we shift aside, lest it eviscerate one of us with its death throes.

"We must flee! Make for the trees!" I scream. "The trees!"

"For the glory of Loran!" Hollern shouts, standing his ground. I bark out a sob; he will not flee. Battle madness has come to our commander; I have seen this before. He will die where he stands, along with all of the rest of us.

The blow comes from my left, faster than I can follow, a crushing backhand that lifts me into the air like a kicked child's toy. For a moment I am weightless, tumbling through the air. Then, like a stricken bird, I crash back to earth, landing in a painful sprawl. I fetch up against the unyielding stones of the wall, a dozen strides from the fighting.

The impact drives the breath from my lungs and sets the world spinning. Sounds deaden, as if I have plunged my head underwater.

I look up and see a Mor drive its knife completely *through* Hollern's chest, the fiery blade crisping the thick leather of his breastplate. His tabard smokes and chars, as tiny flames blossom like wildflowers. His scream erupts in a cloud of bloody steam as he crumples forward.

The men, as one, give a wailing groan as their commander falls. A dozen bodies litter the courtyard. Soon all of the rest will follow. I will follow.

After the rigors of combat, I lack the strength to summon so many of my children all at once. But what choice have I?

I open my inner eye and see the spirits of the fallen. Hollern's shade stares down at his body in mute shock. When I call to him, he looks at me with an eternal, undying contempt, but he cannot—or will not—resist the call. He slips back towards his smoking body, followed by the others.

When I open my eyes, I see the stirrings of my sweetlings as they rip themselves from their fleshy prisons. The Mor hesitate for a moment, perhaps unsure of what is happening, perhaps already knowing. The last remaining men do not question their good fortune, and instead make a break for the gates.

Then my children are awake at last, rising to their twisted feet, trailing shreds and scraps of their birth cocoons as they shamble forward to take revenge on their killers. Horned limb meets chitinous claw in a slithering rasp.

The world dims as the summoning I have accomplished takes its toll. The air turns cold, so cold. I cannot seem to draw a breath. The world tilts as I fall to the stones, my body leaden, impossible to control.

"For Jazen," I mutter. "Avenge your brother, my sweet ones."

The battle is furious, but never really in doubt—the Mor are too many and my children too recently awakened, still clumsy in their newly-granted life. Still, they take a toll on their inhuman attackers, fighting until they are literally ripped limb from limb; still hacking, still tearing, until the very moment they succumb to their second deaths. My black eyes weep as, one by one, my children's lights are extinguished.

When the call comes, at first I do not recognize it. A voice, a woman's voice raised in exultation, cuts across the courtyard's din. The words she sings are in a language unknown to me, yet are somehow familiar. If only I could think, but the world has grown too dark and too cold.

The Mor pause in their butchery and turn towards the gate. I move, agonizing inches, until I can see.

Outside the gates I spy a figure, clad in shining, pale silks, gesturing. Her hands are wreathed in coronas of pale lightning, crackling in the growing dawnlight. Next to her, I see a robed figure, the hooked crosier of Shanira held forth in a warding gesture. He too, is surrounded by a nimbus of light, pale yellow and misty, twirling like fog.

The Mor, caught between this new threat and my remaining sweetlings, hesitate. I feel the hair on my arms prickle as it stands erect.

The woman finishes her invocation with a scream and the skies themselves answer her call. The rumble of thunder washes over the fort like an avalanche a moment before the world erupts in light.

A thunderbolt reaches down like the finger of a god, striking the Mor. The thunder is a physical thing, a noise beyond noise, sucking the breath from my lungs. I scream, the sound lost in the titanic rumble, inaudible even to my ears.

Screaming still, I fall into a bottomless black well.

CHAPTER SIX

I almost ended my life several times in the weeks following my departure. My sister, unexpectedly, railed at me day and night, until I was ready to do almost anything to silence her. I did not understand. Did I not bring her back to me from the icy lands of death? Wasn't she grateful for what I had done?

Her journey beyond life had changed my sweet sister. I hesitate to call what she had become madness, but oft times her behavior approached that extreme. She would sing the same few lines of song, over and over and over, sometimes during the dark hours before dawn, making sleep impossible. Or she would weep, or laugh, for hour upon hour.

When she was calm, quiet, sometimes she would whisper to me about her travels beyond the vale. We would talk of the spirits she had met, explorers of the dark shore beyond the fields that we know. Of the beauty of the Higher Powers, which sometimes reached down from whatever afterlife they ruled to offer a place to some chosen one.

She told me of darker things as well, things that my mistress had never spoken of. Of the predators that roamed the border between this life and the next, inhumanly fast and savage, more tenacious, more inescapable, than death itself. Things that fed on the last lingering energies of the soul.

Her periods of calm, however, never lasted long, and soon enough she would set off on another round of weeping, or shouting, or raving, filling my head with her clamor until the idea of purchasing a few blessed hours of quiet at the price of my own life began to seem appealing.

I was not accustomed, then, to the hardships of the road, of living outside amongst the elements. Those first few days, struggling with the simple necessities of fire and shelter, nearly broke me. When I woke, huddled miserably beneath whatever rude shelter I had built, dripping with rain and shivering from cold, I felt older than the eldest crone in our town, a miserable, decrepit thing.

Thankfully, water and game were plentiful, available even to one as ignorant as myself. The lands through which I traveled were gentle, for the most part, with many chuckling, clear streams. If I were to look at that land with my new eyes, with the wisdom I have purchased, I would think them a cornucopia, with food only an arm's-length away, but I was inexperienced, then, in the ways of the wood. The thought of killing and dressing an animal was terrifying to me, so I ate berries and mushrooms. Some made me very, very sick. I grew thinner, until my clothes hung off my back like a scarecrow's.

If I had set out in wintertime, or if the land had experienced one of the droughts that occurred every few years, I would have perished. Even still, those first few weeks were among the hardest I have ever experienced.

A month after I set out, I made a discovery. A cave. Shallow. Drafty. But smooth-floored and deep enough to shelter me from all but the heaviest rain. A pool of clear water, fed by run-off trickling down the cliff walls, sat just outside the entrance.

I had spent days learning to use Marcus's flint and steel, and soon I had a fire crackling in a riverstone ring, next to the pallet of pine needles and moss that was my bed. I was comfortable for the first time in recent memory. I began to roam outwards, exploring and cataloging the places where useful herbs and roots grew.

My new home was far enough from the civilized lands that I seldom saw other people. The foothills and valleys north of my old home were rumored to be the haunt of any number of savage and inhuman beasts, but I saw no evidence of them. Still, I stayed alert, lest something come upon me unawares.

I discovered several homesteads within a few hours' walk of my new home, places where hopeful families had built rude, thatch-roofed houses and cleared a small patch of land. Crops grew there, just enough to support them, supplemented by the meat that the menfolk could hunt. I never approached them. I feared that news of my crime might have reached them; feared how they would react to my disturbing, black-eyed gaze.

One day I came upon a homestead that was abandoned, the house's front door hanging open to the wind. Signs of violence were all around: picked-clean bones, human and animal; the thatched roof half-fallen into the walls; broken tools. Any tracks had been erased by months and years of weather. I searched with my secret eye, but the spirits of the dead had long since departed.

I was tempted to stay, to repair the roof and sleep once again in a proper house, but the circumstances of the previous tenants' departure made me wary. What if whatever killed them returned? In the end, I decided to move some of the house's choicer goods—a chair and small table, a rusted but still solid cook pot, some wooden utensils and musty-smelling blankets—up to my cave. As I made the long walk back, I carefully erased my tracks behind me.

Weeks passed. Weeks of solitude, just my sister and me, alone and hunted. She had grown quiet as my strength ebbed away, but now that I was settled and comfortable, beginning to gain back the weight I had lost in those first desperate weeks, her voice grew louder and louder. Once more she shrilled and raged at me, calling me names most foul before lapsing into crying fits that could last for hours or even days.

I tried to reason with her. I tried cajoling her, or sometimes even singing to her, as I had sometimes done with her child when she was colicky, but nothing worked. When I looked at myself in a nearby pool's still water, I saw my eyes had become glittering, wet-black stones surrounded by bruised flesh, the legacy of so many sleepless nights.

One day I could take no more. As I sat, rocking in the plundered chair I had brought to my cave, trying to will away the chanting that filled my head, a thought occurred to me: *If I die, there are none to bind me here. It will be like sleep; like endless, silent sleep.*

Like a sleepwalker, I rose and languidly strolled to the water's edge. I looked down into my reflection, met my own black-and-green stare, willing my sister to see me.

My fingers wandered to the hilt of the Ulean steel knife, the wedding present that father had given me. My hand drew it out as if possessed of a will of its own. I held the blade to my face, the sharp point pressed to the hot skin beneath my eye. The blade's reflection sparkled, the chill glitter of violence casting jewels of light across the surface of the water.

"Look at this, sweet sister. Do you recognize it?" I whispered.

The voice, the maddening voice, went still. Then my mind was filled with a raging, a screaming louder than any tempest, soundless and deafening. I clenched the handle until my muscles knotted, lest the cacophony cause me to drop it.

I pressed, feeling the point pierce the tender skin beneath my eye. Blood ran down like tears.

Before me was the flat rock where I scrubbed my clothes, a table-sized plane of smooth, implacable stone. I whispered, "I shall fall, and the blade will be driven deep. Hopefully deep enough to reach you, sister. To cut you and silence you, even though it cost me my own life."

The screaming stopped, sharp as a rope snapping. I held my breath and counted my heartbeats. A dozen. Two. Silence. Such blessed silence.

Then, a whisper, barely heard through the ragged pant of my breath.

What do you want?

I let out my breath, but kept the knife where it was, a threat and promise.

"Peace," I whispered. "What I did, I did for love. For love. I can no more live without you than I could if my heart were cut from my chest. Losing you would drive me mad. I'm sorry, I'm so sorry for what I did. But it was a necessity. I need you. I love you. But I must have peace, or one of us must forever die."

My sister remained silent, as I prayed that my words were reaching her, that some part of her remained that was capable of hearing me. After a time, I heard her reply, so quiet that it might have been the sound of blood rushing through my ears.

I love you, but I can never forgive.

She spoke no more, and I could tell that, for now, I had mastered her.

Trembling, half-expecting her to begin her raving anew, I stretched out on my pallet and surrendered to sleep's grasping hands. They pulled me deep, deep into the black waters, deeper than even dreams could go.

I WOKE TO THE TUGGING OF ROUGH HANDS and coarse, braying laughter. Men had come into my cave, my shelter, my rude sanctuary while I slept more deeply than sounds could reach. Faintly, far behind my eyes, I heard the sound of laughter, papery like the rustle of shed snake skin.

Bandits. Highwaymen. Led to my shelter, no doubt, by the smoke from my dying fire. I was always so careful to bank it, lest it give me away, but after confronting my sister I had been so tired . . .

I opened my eyes a narrow crack.

"'Ello, poppet. Have a nice rest, did we?" one of them said, his face a stretched, humorlessly smiling mask.

There were four of them, dressed in tattered homespuns and rude, mended boots. Some of their garments were ill-fitting, as if taken from someone much larger or smaller than they. All were stained with the marks of a hard life lived outside, in uncouth shelter. Their hair was shiny with grease, wild as birds' nests. Their unshaven faces were dark with dirt.

"See 'ere wut we done caught, boys," said the man who had spoken. He was no less begrimed or ragged than the others, but a single hoop of ruddy gold winked in one dusty lobe, so I labeled him as their leader. I tried to rise, but a second man, the one who had wakened me with his pawing hands, knotted his fist in the collar of my shirt, hauling me to my feet like a child.

"Wha's she doing way out here by her lonesome?" the third asked. He was young, barely a man at all, his lip fuzzed with the first scanty promise of a beard. He looked scared, glancing around the cave as if he expected to be ambushed. I looked at him and he flinched away from my gaze. "Lor'! Lookee that," he breathed. "Lookit 'er eyes. Is she sick?"

The fourth man, older, balding, sketched the warding symbol of Loran in the air. "She's possessed," the unexpectedly pious one said, drawing his knife. "Put 'er down and back off, Mick. I'll see to 'er." He moved towards me, averting his gaze from mine, as if he feared I could infect him with a look.

"Fuck that, Tendy," the leader growled. "You wanna do off wit' 'er after, you can, but we's gonna have us a taste of 'er first."

Tendy, his knife ready, looked as if he meant for a moment to argue, and I coiled. If the men were to squabble or, even better, to fight, I might slip away in the confusion. But he dropped his eyes a moment later and moved back, swearing softly.

"Best you leave her 'lone," he muttered. "I'll not be dirtying m'self with her."

"More for us then," the leader said, his swarthy face splitting in a brown-toothed grin. "I've been meaning t'make young Karl into a man for quite a spell, I have. Tonight's yer lucky night, boy!"

Behind me, Mick twisted harder, and my shirt twisted tight around my neck. I gasped, batting at his rough hands, ineffective as a kitten in the jaws of a hound. The young man, Karl, smiled a sickly smile, nodding, but he backed away, turning his attention back to rooting though my simple cookware.

"Please," I whispered through my tight throat, looking into the leader's eyes, pleading now, not defiant. "Please." I could say no more.

"You want me hold 'er down, Barrett?" Mick said. "I likes it when they struggle a bit. Makes th' blood run hot, it does."

"The day I needs your help to rape a whore is the day I'll give over, you pocksy bastard," Barrett, the leader, laughed. They seemed happy, jovial, their banter ringing like a mummer's rehearsed words. They had done this before. They would, doubtless, do it again. If I were lucky, and put up enough of a struggle to harm one of them, then they might kill me swiftly, in a rage, after they had taken their pleasure. If I were unlucky . . . I did not know how many times they would violate me.

Makes th' blood run hot, it does, Mick had said. Then I knew what I must do.

"Please," I repeated, so breathless the words made no sound. My eyes pleaded. To my surprise, Barrett's smile faded, and confusion came into his piggy eyes. He shook his head, like a horse troubled by the buzzing of a fly.

"Let 'er down for a shake," he said, scowling. "I wanna hear wha' she has t'say."

My captor grunted softly and hesitated. The blood rushed through my ears, muffling sound. A terrible swelling seemed to fill my face, and my vision began to dim, flashing at the edges with bright sparks. Then I was down and coughing, the awful pressure receding. I drew in the sweetest breath I had ever taken, thick with the smell of my cold campfire and the reeking tang of unwashed bodies.

Barrett's split boot toes came into my vision, and I looked up. I willed the coughing to stop as I met his eyes.

"I'll do anything you want," I panted, low and quiet, so only he could hear. "*Anything*. But . . . just you first. Over there." I pointed over to a looming boulder, screened with undergrowth.

"Don' listen to her!" Tendy, the pious one, said, repeating his warding gesture. "She's got something inside of her, behind her eyes, she does!"

"Wouldn't you rather have me willing? Eager?" I whispered, never looking away, holding Barrett's dog-brown eyes with mine. "Just you. And then, if you want, the others. I'll not struggle. Much."

And I smiled, all the while hating . . . loathing . . . myself for the words. My sister, hidden inside, in her secret place, chuckled as if at a dirty joke.

"Pack this shit up right quick," Barrett said. "We'll be over there for a spell if you need me. I'll be back in a shake, then you can have a turn. Work it out amongst yerselves who's t'go next."

He grabbed my arm, tearing it out of Mick's loose grasp, then propelled me towards the shelter of the boulder. I stumbled, hands outthrust, trying to keep my feet beneath me, and he followed, his knife clutched in his fist.

No sooner had we reached the shelter of the leeside than he pushed me roughly down, panting, eyes rolling with lust, or fear. His stubby fingers fumbled at the laces of his breeches, trying to open them one-handed.

"Here," I whispered, gagging down the screams I wanted to utter, trying to ignore my sister's rising cackle, "let me do that." I reached up, pushed his hand away, and opened the fastening.

He moaned as my hands slid across his skin, the hair of his lower belly as coarse and bristly as a boar's. I looked over, saw that he still held the knife in a loose-fingered grasp.

My hands on his skin were all that I needed. I hesitated, appalled at what I meant to do. Then I remembered—

I likes it when they struggle a bit. Makes th' blood run hot, it does.

The day I needs your help to rape a whore is the day I'll give over, you pocksy bastard.

My false smile dropped away as I reached inside with the phantom fingers of my power, twining them in the hot, wet tangle of his belly. Then, with a thought, I *squeezed*.

Barrettt's moans whistled to a stop as my power pulled the very blood away from his heart. I had been a good student and had memorized all of the wonderful diagrams in my mistress's books. I knew that, without the bellows beneath the lungs, Barrettt could not scream for help.

So I *squeezed*, my phantom fingers reaching up, up, wrapping around the small, muscled sac and collapsing it. Barrett's eyes went wide as his mouth flopped open like that of a landed fish.

His body spasmed, every muscle going rigid as the blood magic began to draw forth his life. I took away my hand, leaving behind the scarlet imprint of my palm and fingers, a weeping sigil that turned into a gushing, hot rush. I cupped my hands beneath the flow, my head dizzy at its hot spill. The blood filled them, and I brought them to my lips.

They were empty by the time I put them to my mouth, his blood absorbed by my flesh in moments. I laughed then, a throaty sound the likes of which I had never made before, strange and sensuous and alien to my own ears.

My would-be rapist stood, his pale face sheened with greasy sweat, his lips and fingers already going blue. Veins stood out in his suddenly translucent flesh like tattoos, his lips skinned back from his pale gums. The freshet of blood slowed, slowed, then finally stopped. He fell then, bonelessly, his sightless eyes staring from blackened sockets.

The second man, Mick, he who so liked a nice struggle to warm his victim's blood, died a moment later. Barrett's life still rushed through my veins, filling me with his bull-like strength. It was child's play to reach out, grab his head in my hands, and twist. The body was still falling, his startled face looking backwards over his shoulder, when I turned to Tendy.

He was ready, a crossbow trained at me. Behind him, the boy, Karl, crouched beside the fire. He looked up at the sound of the body falling, and his eyes went big as saucers.

I dove forward, the unnatural strength making me fast, terribly fast, but not fast enough.

I heard the flat snap of the string as I leaped forward, and I felt a distant, unimportant impact in my leg. Then my hands were on Tendy, my power reaching out, silently crooning a song of blood and pain only I could hear. His vitality rushed into me, and I laughed once again, throwing back my head as the red, salty rain misted my face and breasts.

I dropped the body, light as a child's now, dry and desiccated, and turned to Karl. I smiled, reveling in the sticky slide of my shirt across my breasts. He began to cry, but did not run. I stepped forward.

"Please," he whispered, "please, I didn't . . . I wouldn't . . . I didn't *want to!*" The smell of piss filled the air.

My sister howled at his words, screaming at the injustice of them. I reached forth to stroke the young face, for once in agreement with her.

"But, you would have," I said, pronouncing our judgment. The blood sang in my veins, pushing away the soft call of mercy. Then, gently, I bent, my lips fastening on the hot skin of his neck.

CHAPTER SEVEN

I wake to the sound of song.

I lay, eyes closed, the sweet melody rolling over me; it has been so long since I had the luxury of being close to anything beautiful. My body is heavy and languid, my head cushioned against a soft, warm pillow which vibrates softly in time to the music.

Sighing, I pry open my gummed lids, then wince as the early morning light stabs deep, calling forth pain that I had mercifully forgotten. I look up, and see that I am stretched on the dusty ground, head cradled in a woman's lap. She strokes my hair, her voice as soothing as cool mist, gentle as a mother with her babe. Seeing I am awake, she smiles down at me.

"What . . . ?" I breathe and she stops singing, shaking her head gently.

"Don't try to speak. You're fine now, thanks to Brother Ato and the grace of Shanira. Just take a moment and come back to yourself; it was a very near thing."

Her voice is as lovely and delicate as she is, all airy consonants and bell-like vowels. I find myself, for just a moment, lost in her sapphire eyes. Her hair is chestnut, highlighted with ruddy bronze where the sun kisses it, twisted in a complex double-bun and secured with jeweled sticks.

Looking at her, I feel small and shabby, a discarded broken thing. My neck is coated with a residue of sweat and grime and I wonder, a part of me marveling at the absurdity of it, whether or not I am soiling her white silken leggings.

Vain! my sister's voice shrills in my head, the sound echoing in my ears like the flutter of raven's wings. *Vain and wicked sister! See what you might have been had you not thrown all my plans away!*

I try to roll to my feet and the ache in my head transforms into a spike of crystalline agony. I writhe in the dust, tears of pain leaking from my eyes. The singer's hand is cool against my fevered brow, stroking as she murmurs wordless sounds of comfort.

"Leave her be. She will recover in time," a man's voice calls out, haughty and imperious.

Blinking away the tears, I look over, into the unsmiling face of a priest of Shanira. An indigo open-hand tattoo rides between his lowered brows, elegant in its stark simplicity, lacking the baroque ornamentation that is a hallmark of his order. He is still a Brother, then, still tasked with wandering the lands, healing all injury and sickness that comes into his sight. Priests of Shanira are never supposed to break that vow, no matter what, but I know that they can.

He meets my gaze, and flinches at the sight of my eyes, his lip curling into a snarl. I find his reaction comforting, familiar, the sight of his prejudice recalling simpler, more orderly times. I slump back, reveling in the feel of warm flesh and clean silk.

"You healed me?" I croak, eyes closed. I hear his grunt of affirmation. "Then I thank you."

"I do not require your thanks for doing the Lady's work," he says, biting off the words. "'All shall be made whole in Her sight, and in so doing, shall be made clean.' There is no higher calling."

"The priests of Ur would disagree," I say, naming the red-handed God of War. Inside, my sister chortles, even as she scolds me for my rudeness. I hear the priest's indrawn breath, imagine his scowl deepening, before he stomps away.

"That was a very poor way to treat the man who quite possibly saved your life," the woman says gently. "Brother Ato takes his vows very seriously."

"All of them do," I sigh. "So very seriously."

I open my eyes, gingerly, fearing the return of the pain. The morning sunlight, golden and newly minted, is still dazzling, but the terrible agony in my head is receding.

Above me, the singer's face is a pale, lovely moon, and once more I find myself caught in her jewel-blue eyes. This close, I can see that the road has left its mark on her face, in the corners of those wide eyes and beside her compassionate mouth; she cannot have seen more than eighteen summers, twenty at the most, but already creases mar her porcelain skin, tracing down across freckled cheeks. Looking at her, I feel old. Old and so very ill-used.

"Better now?" she asks, and I nod. She helps me to my feet.

All around lie the bodies of the Mor, shattered, blackened things, leaking dark fluid from cracked, split armor. The smell of their burning is pungent and thick, a reek unlike anything I have ever experienced, more like burning reeds and charred fish and the stench of a smithy than anything else. The power that rent their lives and their inhuman flesh has also taken its toll on the walls of the fort, and a pile of freshly-fallen rubble fills a quarter of the central court, from which protrude more blackened, armored limbs.

"You . . . you did this?" I ask, gesturing to the fallen creatures.

She nods, the smile trickling away like melting snow. The lines surrounding her eyes deepen.

"I have received training in the Arts Elemental from the Western Academy," she says, stammering a bit. "I only meant to stop them from harming you further, but I must have summoned too much . . ."

"You did the right thing," I say, holding up an unsteady hand. The smell and the smoke fill my head. The ground seems to tilt, ever so slowly. "They would have killed us all, without mercy. I have seen their handiwork. You did well."

She beams at the compliment, as if my opinion mattered in some way, then, seeing my discomfort, takes my arm and leads me towards the shattered barricade. As I walk, I look for my sweetlings. Nothing remains of them, not even ashes. The wind has scattered the last traces. My sister's lament twists through my mind like a barbed hook, joining my own silent call of grief.

"My name is Lia Cho," my rescuer says, helping me past the overturned cart. The air clears outside the walls and I feel my strength returning. "My companion is Brother Daedalius Ato."

"Kirin," I reply, my eyes sweeping the trees. I see Brother Ato, eyes restless at the border of the forest. I appreciate his vigilance.

"Kirin," Lia repeats, turning my name into something sweet, like honey on her tongue. "It suits you." My sister howls soundlessly and I shush her. I do not want this priest to suspect her presence in me, lest he think me possessed.

"Kirin," she continues, "when we came, when I called down the storm, I saw you, in the smoke, fighting. There were . . . *others* with you."

"Yes," I say, meeting her gaze. For the first time, she frowns looking into them. Perhaps she knows what my black eyes mean, perhaps not. Ato knows, I am sure of it, and I see no benefit in lying. I cannot fight the two of them if they decide that my sins have earned the penalty of death, nor would I. I am too weary to fight.

"They were my champions," I say. "My children. When the men . . . when they died, I needed them to fight for me.

Alone, I was no match for the Mor. Even with their help, I stood no chance. You saved my life."

"Those . . . were your children? I don't understand," she says, looking back at the smoking gates. She frowns, an expression of confusion, not judgment, worlds distant from the stern look that Brother Ato gave me. I find myself not wanting to see his expression in her eyes.

"It is complicated," I say, gently. "But not unnatural, no matter what the priests say. Some day, perhaps, I will explain it to you. But not now. There might be more of the Mor, somewhere close. We should go."

Lia nods, still frowning. I think of the lightning, the colossal force that brought low the Mor. Such power, to be held in such an innocent vessel; it beggars imagination.

I have heard much, over the years, of the Academies, all little better than rumor, yet still endlessly fascinating to the common man and woman. Tales passed like semiprecious stones from speaker to listener, detailing a secret order.

The tales all agree on the existence of four monastic schools located in the remotest parts of the world, each dedicated to the study of one of the four Aspects. Cold North, house of Earth, Eastmost Water, Southern Fire and, last, the Western Academy of Air: each both temple and school all dedicated to the training of the rare and powerful Elemental Mages.

Never in my life had I hoped to meet one such as Lia, a human trained in the sublime arts of adjuration. Graduates of the Academies, without fail, were said to join the Empire's bureaucracy, taking up residence within the walls of the Imperial Palace, working their magics at the behest of the Emperor himself.

I burn to ask Lia why she is here, why she wanders the Mor-infested roads, alone save for an itinerant priest.

But now is not the time. I follow my own advice and hold my tongue. There will be time to talk, later, when we are far away from here. Away from the place that Jazen Tor met his final death, and where Hollern's ill-placed piety led to so much ruin.

"Brother Ato and I are headed for the City," Lia says, looking around with wide eyes. "I must meet my father. It is very important."

Behind us, Brother Ato falls in line, searching along our back trail. I frown as a thought occurs to me.

"Does something follow you?" I ask him, my voice loud in the still morning air.

"No, I . . . " he says. "I'm just cautious. As you said, there may be more of them."

I glance at Lia, see her frown of worry. "Lying is not a skill that they teach you in the monastery, is it, Brother? You're very bad at it," I say.

Ato begins a sputtered denial, his peasant's face turning bright red, but falls silent when Lia holds up a forestalling hand.

"You are very observant, Kirin," she says. "Brother Ato does fear pursuit. I left the Academy without permission."

"I see," I say. "So, you think they might send someone to fetch you back?"

"It is possible," she says with a shrug. "Before all this, before the Mor, I am certain that they would have, but now . . . " She shrugs. "They have much to do. The Emperor has need of every mage. The Mor are attacking everywhere, or so I hear. Many have been killed. It is said that none who have stood before them have managed to even slow them down."

"I know," I say, images of Gamth's Pass flashing in my mind like lightning. Memories of soldiers, torn asunder like dolls or burned, charred, until their own mothers would not know them. "I've done my fair share of fighting. But that still doesn't explain why you ran away."

"I did not run away!" Lia says hotly, sounding in that

moment very much like the young girl she is. "I did not! But I cannot just sit behind high walls, going to classes and memorizing the seven hundred and seventy-seven names of the lesser zephyrs as if nothing is wrong! My father needs me."

"He needs you to complete your training," Brother Ato says. I can tell this is a familiar argument, one worn smooth through countless revisitations.

"He needs my help! Now! Before the Mor reach the palace!"

I remember the sight of the Mor, dancing as the lightning thundered down, boiling from within as the elemental energy coursed through their bodies, and nod. Such power would be very useful on the battlefield, might have even helped tip the scales at Gamth's Pass.

Idiot! You were defeated before you even took the field, my sister whispers, her voice acid. *Nothing human is a match for the Mor.*

"And yet she killed them. She killed them all. She is the vessel for much power," I whisper back.

"What was that?" Brother Ato asks. I wave away the question, cursing myself for speaking aloud. Ato gives me a long, contemplative look. I do not like the questions I see in his eyes.

"In any case, I have made my decision, and I do not ask you to accompany me," Lia continues, oblivious to our exchange. "I can take care of myself."

Ato turns his attention back to her and shrugs. "I made a promise to see you to the City walls," he says with a sigh. "I no longer have a choice in the matter."

"And you?" Lia asks me. "Will you accompany me? There is much need for skilled hands on the walls of the Armitage, I am told. It is only a matter of time until the Mor finish their attack on the hinterlands, and when they do, the

Imperial City will be all that stands between them and the South."

I shrug, nodding. I have no plans to accompany this willful child all the way to the City, but keeping her near will certainly help my chances for survival. *If you can teach her to stop making so much cursed noise,* my sister hisses. *She moves like a pregnant yak.*

I push aside a chuckle that threatens to bubble past my lips. Lia's grace is anything but yak-like, but her footsteps are much nosier than mine. She could use a bit of woodcraft, if she hopes to avoid future conflicts.

We walk all that day. I head southeast, along the riverbank, where the route is clearest. Just after mid-day, we rejoin the road, and our pace increases further still. The trees make me feel safe and sheltered, muffling sound and hiding us from view.

We stop frequently, to refill water skins and to take meals, but even so I am surprised by Lia's pace. She is slower than a soldier, to be sure, but the vigor of youth is still in her step.

Her curiosity seems to almost overflow her, and she moves from one fascination to the next—a ring of delicate, crimson mushrooms; a cliff overlooking the rushing river; an ancient, weatherworn stone *padu* marker—chatting brightly all the while. Ato and I both remind her repeatedly to speak softly, lest unfriendly ears overhear.

When darkness finally begins to dim the bright vault of the sky, I search for a spot to make camp. I find a dry ledge beneath an overhanging cliff, sheltered from view by thick bushes. The overhang will do much to hide our campfire's smoke.

By the time full dark has fallen, we sit around a small fire. I put my back to the flames, listening for anything out of the ordinary, as Brother Ato prepares a sparse meal of bread and hard cheese. Lia gives a delighted laugh as he produces an apple from his pack.

"Come join us," Lia says to me. "Brother Ato is always telling me how food is not only a necessity, but is also medicine for the soul."

"And I look like one in need of healing?" I say, the words emerging harsher than I had intended.

"You need to eat," Lia mumbles, flinching away from me. "We have a long day ahead of us tomorrow."

The thought of this child advising me about the road ahead amuses me. What can she know?

She knows how to call down the storm, my sister reminds me. *Do not take her lightly.*

I shrug and move towards the fire. Anything large enough to endanger us will make noise coming up the wooded trail. Later, after I have eaten, I will scout out a perimeter, perhaps lay some concealed lines along the approaches to our shelter.

Lia settles herself beside the flames, making herself comfortable, her eyes closing in rapture as she bites into the fruit. Ato smiles indulgently to see her reaction, then turns, reluctantly, to offer me some of the cheese.

Although I am not particularly hungry, I eat the proffered slice. It is dry and sharp, and almost unpleasantly warm, and I find myself envying Lia's apple.

"Eat your fill," he says to Lia, offering the cheese to her. "We don't know how long it will be until we can rest like this again. With the Mor on the roads, we must be ready to travel long and fast if need be."

Lia nods and takes a slice, then frowns. She turns to me. "Do you know why the Mor have come?" she asks.

"I have no idea," I admit. "All I know is that two months ago, give or take, they began emerging from their caves and started burning. They haven't stopped since, not even when faced by five thousand men at Gamth's Pass."

"This has happened before, you know," Ato says. He nods at Lia's questioning look. "Oh, yes, mankind and the Mor have never really gotten along. Our shared history is written in blood. Always has been and always shall."

"Honestly, before Gamth's Pass, I always thought that stories of the Mor were just that—stories." I say.

"That's because they're wont to disappear for decades, if not centuries at a time. But where I come from, even the smallest child knows the old tales. They are passed down, from parent to child, faithfully, lest we forget."

"Forget what?" Lia asks.

"Forget that the Mor have always been man's enemy. The Mor know nothing of mercy, or of compromise. Every time they have ever come out of the dark, the only way to stop them has been to defeat them so thoroughly that they no longer have the means to wage war."

"Where do you come from?" I ask.

He smiles and pokes the fire with a stick, stirring the coals. Sparks rise like a swarm of amber fireflies, swirling into the dark canopy above. "My family lives in a small town called Rudarth. It's a small place, just a few dozen families, high in the mountains north of the great city of Lu," he says, smiling fondly. "They are miners, and have been for generations. Tin, mainly, although I'm the only one in memory that hasn't followed in my family's footsteps. In Rudarth, a man's not a man until they first descend into the black and come back out again."

"And when is that?" I ask.

"Twelve, usually. That's when I—and all my brothers—first made the descent, pick in hand. If the Lady had not called me to her cause, I'd be there still, although by now, I'd most likely be dead. Most menfolk that make their living in the deep black don't live to see their grandchildren grow up, I can tell you that.

"We pass on the tales of the Mor so that we're always ready," he continued, poking the fire more urgently. "Ready for when they come back, as they always do."

"But why? Why do they come?" Lia asks. "What did we do to them?"

"Who knows? All I know is that when our people first came to this land from across the great sea, they thought this land was empty. Oh, there was game aplenty—everything you see that has six legs rather than four was native to these shores— but the Mor, they were nowhere to be seen, at first. They lived in the deeps, you see, and never came to the surface world.

"No, we were all here, our ships broken down to make our settlements, forever land-bound, by the time the first miners discovered the Mor. We tried talking to them, or so the tales all say, but they could not, or would not answer. It was only a matter of time until we came into conflict with them. By then, we could never go home. It was either them or us."

"But they must have some reason, certainly," I say. "They're not immortal. As strong as they are, they can be killed. Why leave their homes to march to war?"

Ato shrugs. "If they have one, they've never told any man. When they come, they kill. We don't even know that they think as men do. For all we know, they might simply be animals."

I think of the tools I have seen the Mor use, of the surprisingly delicate and lovely fittings on their gear, and shake my head. That cannot be the product of simple instinct.

"My father had a book in his library with an image of a Mor in it," Lia says, her eyes heavy and filled with firelight. "It always frightened me as a child. Their claws looked so fierce."

The priest nods. "Aye. Sharp and strong enough to bore through stone as if it were clay. The tunnels they left behind were round and smooth, wide enough for three men to walk abreast and a joy to work in. I admit that, in rockcraft, their wisdom far surpassed ours."

"You should have tried harder to reason with them, then," Lia says. "They would have been useful allies."

"Never!" Ato says, his lip curling. "I would sooner lay down with a demoness than trust a Mor at my back," he says, shooting a look my way. Any lingering doubts I have that the priest does not know what I am evaporate. Oh yes, he knows.

"The power of Shanira will always be my shield against evil," he continues, his eyes never leaving my face, "but the Mor are relentless and unstoppable and altogether inhuman. Those dragged into the depths by them are never seen again. Who knows what torments they inflict on their prey, in the deep, cold black? Even the gods' sight, it is said by my people, cannot penetrate such a weight of implacable stone, and what the gods cannot see, they cannot prevent. Or avenge."

I shrug and turn away, bored by his pious mouthings. Hollern learned just how powerful his god was, calling forth Loran's name under the open sky as the Mor's blade slid through his body. I wonder if, as his last breath was borne aloft on a cloud of steaming blood, the words were a last prayer to Him, and if the Lightbringer found the sacrifice sweet.

Ato falls silent, staring into the coals, his mind elsewhere. Perhaps he is thinking of his long-ago home. I watch Lia's eyes slowly close, hear her breathing deepen in sleep.

Not long after, I uncurl and rise smoothly, silently, to my feet. The fire has died down to bare embers. The sullen red glow illuminates Lia's sleeping face. Behind her, his back to the stone cliff, Brother Ato sits, mouth open in a gentle snore, arms cradling his crosier.

I ghost away from the camp, taking a careful hour to

check the trail. Fitful moonlight dapples through the clouds racing overhead. The smell of rain is in the air. It will come soon, perhaps before dawn.

Satisfied that nothing follows us, I lay a tripline across the obvious trail leading up to our shelter, securing one end to a propped-up log. Anything stumbling into the line and pulling out the support will make sufficient racket to wake the dead.

Only then do I feel comforted enough to sleep. My eyes are closed moments after resting my head on my pack.

THE SOUND OF THE LOG, falling through the rustling leaves, is loud in the pre-dawn black. I spring to my feet, hand on my knife, eyes uselessly sweeping back and forth in the clouded darkness. Behind me, I hear Brother Ato give a sleepy exclamation. Lia's gentle snores do not even falter.

"Wha . . . ?" Ato says thickly.

"Something's down there. Moving up the path," I whisper.

Whatever it is, there is more than one. They are not even trying to be quiet. In the darkness, it is impossible to gauge their size, but they do not sound large.

"Perhaps it is pigs? Or deer?" Ato asks.

I shake my head, forgetting that he cannot see the gesture. Wild animals would have fled at the sound of the falling log; would not be moving relentlessly up the trail into the scent of our humanity and our fire.

"Wake Lia. Gently. Be ready to flee, if I command it."

I grip my knife. I could run down the back trail to safety. I am almost certain that, in the darkness, I could escape. But doing so would doom Lia to whatever fate approaches us. Once more, I am trapped.

There is no place to run. Footfalls scrape across stone as whatever has followed us ascends.

CHAPTER EIGHT

I lingered over Karl's body for hours, tenderly washing at the grime and dirt, as well as the more recent traces of blood, then carefully bandaging the ruin I had made of his poor throat. I knew all of the rituals for the dead from my mistress's books, but I did not choose to follow them, instead making those preparations that pleased me in the moment. I knew that the young man's spirit still lingered, had not been called down into some dark pit to answer for his crimes.

Not yet, anyway. Perhaps he was innocent of the taint that had so infected the likes of Mick and Barrett, but it was too late to contemplate such things now. That he would accompany such men was crime enough for me. Perhaps, when I went looking, his shade would be gone, but I did not think so.

When the body was cleansed and wrapped in my spare blanket, I waited for the stiffness of death to fade from his shapely limbs. I knew the process would take two days, three at the outside, time enough for the others' remains to draw unwelcome scavengers.

I disposed of the other bodies, dragging them unceremoniously to a stony gorge the river had carved and throwing them in. Let the water be their grave, I thought. I hoped their spirits would find no comfort, forever wandering, forever searching for their final resting place.

The first day, returning from my errand, I gathered herbs, then ground them into a paste, boiling it down into a sweet-smelling balm. I rubbed this into Karl's skin, pushing back the scent of decay that had already begun to blossom in his flesh.

On the second, I massaged and kneaded his muscles, helping to break free the rigor that had settled there. I knew that doing so would ease his rebirth, making him more agile, better able to do my bidding. I took care to shoo away the flies that circled him, lest he become the home of unwelcome, destructive visitors.

The third day dawned, and I prepared myself, washing in the icy stream until my skin was numb. My fingernails were a pale shade of shell blue when I reached for my clothes. My hands trembled.

Such cleansing was not required, for the art my mistress had taught me relied not on recited ritual, like the prayers of the priests, nor on invocations and adjurations, such as the elemental mages were said to employ. Rather, it was an act of sheer will. Still, the ceremony set my restless mind at ease, calming my fears.

After I had eaten and my strength was at its peak, I calmed my last, restless thoughts and settled myself. I closed my eyes and, with a breath, I opened my secret, inner eye. Immediately, the darkness behind my eyelids was shot through with traceries of fire. Every tree, every leaf, twig and root, was limned with the light of life. I opened my fleshly eyes, and the traceries remained, glowing faintly.

Amongst this brightness, a dark shadow drifted. As I suspected, Karl's shade was still present, still lingering. He turned his milk-white eyes to me at my command, locking his gaze to my own black orbs. I could feel his struggles, like a fly cupped in my palms, a restless, desperate buzzing, inconsequential and ineffectual. Wordlessly, I commanded him to lie in his discarded shell, and the ghost obeyed.

What rose was not the pale, shining body of the boy I had slain. He did not twitch, then stir, like a man coming awake from a deep sleep, but rather he convulsed, as if the process inflamed his dead nerves, as if I somehow brought him pain.

He flopped onto his stomach, his shriveled eyes opening, weeping pus, spine arching like a cat's, impossibly hunched. A dry rattle escaped Karl's cold, gaping mouth as trapped gas was pushed out like breath from the force of his exertions. His skin split with the sound of tearing silk, parting to reveal crimson bands of muscle and the white knobs of his spine, before what was inside of him ripped itself lose.

It stood there, swaying on its taloned feet, limbs trailing the crimson shreds of its birth cocoon, its gaping, fanged mouth opening, tasting the breeze. Its eyes were opals, shining with iridescent gleams of blue and red and fiery amethyst in the sunlight. Its half-skinned body was all horn-like spurs and leathery muscle, sliding with a gentle sigh under the parchment-like skin. One arm was larger than the other, tipped not with a hand, but with a jagged, hooked blade of bone.

Seeing it, I felt an answering heat in my belly, a force of primal creation that surged upwards, like a bolt of ice and fire, straight to my head. My eyes watered with tears of helpless joy as I looked upon it. My child, the only fruit my womb would ever bear, something at once unique and precious. He had a face only a mother could love, perfect in its imperfection, sublime in its deformity.

My lovely one; my sweetling.

I did not know then, nor did I ever learn, why the same gift that my mistress used to awaken the intact bodies of the dead instead granted me the means to create my dark children. All I knew was that seeing my precious, beloved child struggling free of its cold womb, like a chick breaking through the shell that separates it from the outside world, filled me with such satisfaction as I have never known.

Even my sister, who had known the joys and pains of childbirth, cooed and delighted at my sweetling's arrival, and I beamed at her approval. This would be both our child.

I soon discovered that my beloved's construction made him unsuited to the domestic, everyday tasks that I had hoped he would be able to accomplish. My mistress's servants could be trusted to fetch water, or sweep, after a fashion, or to carry heavy burdens from one place to another. But my sweetling could do no such things; its taloned paw and blade-like arm were too clumsy to hold a broom or a bucket handle, and its mismatched limbs made carrying bundles of firewood or stones from the riverbed problematic.

Finally, after watching it drop a bundle of kindling for the dozenth time, I cried out in frustration, "What good to me are you, wretched thing? Did I not call you to me to be my helper, my companion?"

It paused, listening to my words, cocking its gruesome head at me in a way unlike any of my mistress's dim-witted servants had. Could it hear me? Understand me?

A rustling reached me from the woods, the sound of a deer or a pig, moving through the undergrowth. I recalled the taste and smell of roasting meat, felt the squirt of saliva in my mouth at the memory.

The sweetling took off like a shot, markedly faster than I had ever seen my mistress's servants move, headed like a crossbow bolt towards the noise. Its quarry gave a frightened squeal, followed close by a frightful clamor as the concealing bushes were rent asunder. I hurried forth, curious to see what was happening.

By the time I arrived, it was over, the pig twitching with its last feeble death spasms. It was a boar, a male, two hundred pounds of rock-hard muscle and spine-like fur, snout bristling with ivory tusks that gleamed like sabers. It must have turned to fight, a not uncommon reaction from this erstwhile lord of the forest; not many things in the woods could have hoped to overcome it. I certainly could not have.

The boar lay, its throat torn out, its lifeblood pulsing across the fallen leaves. It had left its mark on my sweetling, the tusks gouging out hideous, gaping wounds from its belly and side, wounds that my dark child ignored. The pig should have run.

That night, I feasted, juices running down my chin as I gorged myself on the sweet, sweet meat. My sweetling watched from the edge of the firelight.

Belly full for the first time in recent memory, I lay on my pallet, indulging in pleasant fantasies of faceless, pale-skinned youths, eager and anxious to attend my every desire. My hands called forth bittersweet joy, moving with increasing urgency until my body finally responded. The release, when it finally arrived, was heralded by my cries.

I turned on my side, sated and drowsy, eyes closing as sleep claimed me. My last sight was of my sweetling, gazing at me from its place in the shadows. It had never stopped watching me. Its opal eyes, full of unconditional love and approval, never left me. I knew that, no matter what, it would never turn on me. Never belittle or humiliate me. Would be my champion, my defender. My silent confidant and supporter.

It loved me.

I slipped into the deep, untroubled sleep of the blessed.

CHAPTER NINE

Lia gives a tiny gasp, and Brother Ato whispers urgently for her to be still. My eyes flick back and forth, searching in vain for any hint of movement. The night is as black as a mine shaft.

The soft footfalls scrape across stone. Whatever they are, they are near. They must hear us. I hear Ato scrabbling at our meager pile of firewood.

Then the light flares as he throws a handful of tinder and pine needles onto the fitful coals. Faces loom out of the darkness, fanged visages with opaline eyes and weeping, broken flesh.

I scream and throw myself forward, even as Ato begins a chant, calling forth the power of his goddess.

"No!" I say. "They do not wish us harm!"

Brother Ato's chant falters, its thread broken. I stand before my sweetlings, arms spread wide, sheltering them with my own body. In the dancing light, I see Ato's eyes go wide with horror. Behind him, Lia struggles to her feet, her arms tangled in her cloak.

"Blessed Lady, it cannot be," the priest breathes. He brandishes his crosier at me, his other hand forming the sign of the Eye, fingers rigid, forefinger and thumb circled. A ward against evil. I have seen it so many times before.

"What's going on?" Lia demands, freeing herself. "Kirin, who is that . . . ?" She squints through the uncertain light, then falters when she sees what is behind me.

"They will not harm you, I swear it," I say, striving to keep my voice calm. Images of the Mor, lying broken and charred, come to me. "They followed me. Some must have been trapped beneath the falling wall. We . . . I left them there."

Three of my dark children have come after me. Their bodies are damaged, their leathery skin ripped and shredded, caked with masonry dust and the black blood of the Mor. Their hands are ravaged, the claws and nails broken and torn away. They must have dug their way from beneath the fallen wall. The stones must have sheltered them from the lightning that consumed the Mor.

One, a sweetling raised from the body of an older archer, Raist I think was his name, looks at me from a skull crushed almost unrecognizable, its lone, weeping eye peering out at me from beneath a flap of dangling hair. Its entire lower jaw has been sheared away, its tongue dangling against its torn chest in a manner that even I find disturbing. It can barely walk; its two shattered knees want to bend in the wrong direction. It drags itself along on its hands, the mangled digits stripped of all flesh. The others must have slowed their own pace so as not to abandon it.

"Time to rest now, my brave one. Well done, oh, so well done," I whisper, tears stinging my eyes. I reach out and caress the terrible face.

A moment later, the sweetling topples back, its body trailing ash as it falls. I see, with my secret eye, Raist's soul flicker away, hummingbird-quick, into the night sky. The sound the departure makes is as soft as the rustle of a wasp's wings.

Behind me, I hear Ato's indrawn breath. Lia curses, a jumble of Harbortown profanity, the words oddly melodious in her mouth. I sit, awaiting judgment, mentally commanding my children to be still, to not move, telling them again and again how very fine and brave I think they are.

Minutes later, I am still sitting. The stone is cold and unyielding beneath me. I look up, and see that both of them are still staring. Ato's face is a blank sheet of granite, obdurate and implacable, the righteous fury of his goddess shining, golden, in his eyes.

Lia's stare, every bit as intense, is softer somehow, filled with equal parts loathing and an unexpected wonder. I frown. I am not used to seeing such a complex expression on one that looks upon my progeny. Usually, their reaction is much more akin to Ato's.

"I had no idea . . ." I hear her whisper.

"They are an offense against Shanira and must be destroyed!" Ato thunders, as if Lia's words have snapped him out of a daze. He strides forth, brandishing his staff. Trails of gold hang in the air like dust as he moves.

"If you wish to harm them then you will have to kill me first," I say, rising. Sadness fills me. Ato, for all his blind prejudice, seems a good man, loyal to Lia. A fellow healer. I do not want this.

"So be it. 'Thou shalt not suffer an abomination to live'," he quotes, his eyes wild with devotion.

"Brother, no!" Lia screams. "There must be an explanation! You cannot kill Kirin! Priests do not kill!"

Oh, but they do, my sister hisses. *Just ask a thousand old women, herbalists and midwives all, taken in the priests' last attempt at purifying the land in the name of their oh, so righteous gods.*

I nod in agreement. I know what this man's kind, if not this man himself, is capable of. His piety, like Hollern's, blinds him to anything outside the narrow boundaries of his faith. It gives him strength along with the desire to use that strength, no matter the cost to others. I ready myself, gathering my legs to spring.

Lia's words have a more profound effect on Ato. He jerks away from them, tearing his eyes from mine to look at her. He stammers out a denial. "I . . . Lia, you do not understand. I must . . . She . . ."

"Is alive. Is a living woman. Brother, you must not do this."

For a moment, I think he will do it anyway. Will call down whatever justice his faith demands for my sins. I wonder if it will hurt, or if whatever force resides in my earthly shell will simply be snuffed out, like a candle flame.

Then he is gone, his sandaled feet skittering across the stone, nearly falling with the urgency of his flight. I hear him, out in the darkness, blundering through the undergrowth, trailing half-heard words; curses and prayers mingled like vinegar and honey.

I look up into Lia's sapphire eyes, and see that this is not over. She has spared me, but she does not like what she sees. A hint of illumination, like the flash of far-off lightning, flickers across her eyes, and I move to put myself in front of my children.

"Shall you finish the job that Brother Ato was too weak to complete, Lia?" I say softly, honestly wondering what she will answer.

The question hangs between us in the still air, as Lia struggles with her answer. I reach out and stroke my sweetlings' faces, awaiting her pleasure, awed once again by the depth of their devotion. No matter what she or the priest decide, they can never take that from me.

THE HEAVY OVERCAST makes the coming of the dawn a slow, dreary affair. The sky is still lightening in the east when the rain begins. Soon, it thickens into a downpour.

I sit in the meager shelter of our camp, while Ato and Lia debate. They have moved off, into the trees, to talk in private, but I can hear the faint buzz of their voices over the rain's restless patter.

As I wait, I clean the worst of the dirt and blood from my children's bodies. It is, I know, a vain attempt to make them more presentable, but I cannot help it. Nothing will change the reality of their warlike forms, or obscure the fact that these are indeed dead things, brought back by my secret power.

You can kill them. Now, while they are busy with their endless arguments, my sister whispers. *Even the girl will not have the power to resist you, once your blood magic is loose in her veins.*

"She would call down the lightning and fry us both where we stand," I murmur, turning to hide my lips.

I do not know why I bother. My guilt is proven in Ato's mind, the evidence sitting on the stone before me.

Why do you not flee, then? They are no match for you in the woods. Even burdened with the children, you could be away before they know it.

It is a good question, one that I have asked myself with growing frequency. I remember Lia, slumbering, as unknown danger approached. Remember her scrambling up, tangled in her blankets, defenseless and blind, and I know.

They need me. She needs me. So many have died. At Gamth's Pass and at Fort Azure. People who trusted me. Lia, despite her mastery of the storm, is only one woman. If the Mor come upon them in force, even she might not have the power to defeat them. All it will take is one knife, one claw.

The thought of her lying in the mud, body torn, her pretty eyes boiled from within and her lustrous hair crisped, fills me with an unexpected rage. No. I will not allow that to happen.

They stop talking, and footsteps approach. I tense; if I am to be punished, if Ato means to kill my children, then I will not surrender without resistance. Deep inside, I feel the first uncoiling of my power, hot and wet and visceral, tingling in my belly.

Lia walks forward, alone. Ato is nowhere to be seen.

"He is very upset," she says, and despite myself, I have to smile. I did not hear every word of their debate, but given his raised voice, the gist was clear.

"Kirin, why?" she asks, coming no closer. She eyes the sweetling, her mouth puckering with ill-disguised disgust. I command it to leave us, and it shuffles off into the undergrowth.

"I don't need to explain myself to Ato, or to you, or to anyone else," I say, meeting her eyes. She flinches from my gaze. Ato has told her what my black eyes mean. "I know what men like Ato believe, what their religion teaches."

"But Kirin, they're dead. Dead, yet they walk. Do you not see what . . . ?"

"I see my children, loyal and brave. I see those that would never abandon me. That would only leave my side when final death claims them."

"Braver than the men that you fought alongside at Fort Azure?" she asks softly. The question gives me pause. I frown.

"Kirin, by calling them back, you deny them their rightful place in the afterlife."

"No, I merely delay it. None can oppose the gods, Lia. If one is chosen to go beyond, then the will of the gods cannot be thwarted."

"That is not what Brother Ato says."

I nod. "I know. And I understand why he believes that. But I believe that he's wrong. My children are—"

"Stop calling them that!" she snaps, turning aside. "They are not children! There is nothing of your flesh about them! Calling them such is . . . " She shudders.

I sit, watching her for the first manifestations of her power. Ato has turned her away from me. I do not want to hurt her, to turn the hungry mouth of my own power upon her, but what choice has the priest left me?

Lia sits on the stone opposite me, weary lines carved in her porcelain skin. Out in the trees, I hear something heavy moving through the bushes.

She looks up. "Go. Flee. Brother Ato's will is strong in this. He thinks he will gain the favor of Shanira if he—"

"I won't leave you. You need my help. The Mor might be near."

"Kirin, please. Just go. I can take care of myself."

That she can, my sister whispers. *Don't be a fool! He is coming.*

I rise, my eyes searching her face. She looks sad, but will not look at me. Wordlessly, for there is nothing more that can be said, I scoop up my pack and slip into the woods. The leaves close behind me like a curtain.

I STRIDE THROUGH THE WOODS, my children moving behind me. One simply forces its way through obstacles, not bothering to seek the path of least resistance. His brother is more crafty, and makes little noise. I am pleasantly surprised. Still, even the racket and the obvious trail that the clumsy one creates would take more skill than either Lia or the Brother possess to follow.

The rain washes down my face, oddly salty and warm, like tears. I scrub them away, muttering a curse.

We do not need them. Leave them to their prejudices and their gods. We are free; that is all that matters.

I nod, knowing that my sister can sense the gesture, but my mind is troubled. Leaving them still feels wrong. Even in the face of Ato's wrath and Lia's disgust, I do not wish to abandon them.

I stop, making a decision, then begin hunting about. In the overcast, I cannot orient myself by the sun, but there are other signs for those with the woodcraft to read them. Inside, my sister growls, ominously quiet in the face of my decision, her displeasure filling my head like smoke.

I swing wide of the road, moving fast. I do not worry about the sweetlings; I know they will catch up eventually. After a spell, I cut left, pushing hard until I see the trees thin ahead. I send out a command to my children, ordering them to stop wherever they are. I do not want them to betray my position.

It will take them time to break their camp, then move back to the road. I must still be in front of them.

I settle back, wincing. My body aches, my limbs and back, even the tender flesh of my chest, pulsing with a sullen pain that throbs in time with my beating heart. I wonder if I am coming down with some malady.

I push aside the greenery to make a window. The road below me is empty, but I know that soon they will be by. I take a morsel of biscuit from my pack and settle down to wait.

CHAPTER TEN

The sweetling I called forth from Karl was my companion for neatly five months, before its time finally arrived. Five glorious months, as summer ripened like fruit into autumn. The woods were always filled with sound: the daytime clamor of the birds, passing along their mindless gossip; the nights a chorus of insects and frogs, all casting about with desperate vitality for a mate.

As the nights grew ever colder, I began to notice my dark child's failing health. More and more, it would stumble across some obstacle in its path, limbs growing clumsy as tissues dried and toughened. A bloom of decay, a delicate, moss-like tracery of rot, began to spread outwards from its opaline eyes and down its sunken cheeks.

The vitality that gave my sweetling its ferocious life and held back the natural process of decay was fading. Soon, I would be alone again.

By the time the trees had begun to shed their cloaks of russet and gold, my child was gone, returned to the dust from which it had come. I mourned then, for those that die a second death are truly gone forever, their souls inviolate and unreachable by any mortal agent.

I wondered then, as I still wonder, if the priests' words were true. If those souls that are called forth to do the bidding of such as I are indeed forever tainted, made unclean and corrupt. Such souls, the priests say, are barred forever from the gentle lands beyond the Vale, and are consigned to an eternity of some vague, shadowy half-existence, cursed to wander the mortal lands until the sun itself goes dark.

Be that as it may, I chose to believe in the wisdom of the gods, and in my fate-given power. I cannot—I *will* not—believe that my sweetlings are nothing more than vessels for unnatural, damned souls. Not them.

I buried my child's ashes under the willow down beside the river, chanting the old rituals faithfully, wishing it well and thanking it for all it had done. Now, at last, it could rest.

I knew the winter would be long; often the snow would lie, thick and white, on the ground for eight months or more. I knew that my cave's minimal shelter, sufficient to block rain but little more, would not protect me from the relentless cold.

But the relatively easy life I had known, coupled with my sweetling's assistance in the hunt, had ill prepared me for what was coming, and I knew it. Without shelter, and without access to the nuts and small animals I had been living on, it would be a race to see if I would freeze or starve in the long, cold night.

The fourth full moon of autumn was still a week away when I returned to the ruined house. The place still frightened me—I knew that whatever killed the family who had lived there might return—but my recent victories had filled me with a sense of competent power. If it were animals that had caused their downfall, I now knew my blood magic would be more than capable of taking care of the problem, and if the threat proved to be human, well, I could always use more material from which to summon my sweetlings.

I buried the remains of the former occupants in a shared grave, four skulls amongst many other, smaller bones, all commingled in the dark earth. Swept clean of debris and dirt, the one-room cottage proved to be sturdy and plain, with a simple elegance that appealed to my newly ascetic nature.

Repairing the roof was a priority, and became the task that took up most of my time and attention. I had watched the men that Urik had hired to replace our cottage's shingled roof, but I lacked the materials and tools to recreate their work. In the end, I decided to repair the existing thatch.

I knew from my wanderings that my neighbors all used the same material, carefully stockpiled in barns and outbuildings until needed. I hoped that they would not miss some, if I were careful. Many nights found me on the roads, the heavy, wrapped bundles strapped across my sweating back, shoulders aching from the rough carry ropes.

Travel back and forth between my new home and those of my neighbors was slow; a single trip took most of the night. I wished my sweetling had endured for a few more weeks, or that I had begun gathering my supplies earlier. My dark child could have made three trips in a single night, pulling many bundles along in a travois.

I came across the carcass of a deer, and, in a moment of inspiration, tried calling forth a sweetling from the remains. To my astonishment, the corpse did disgorge . . . *something* . . . a mass of jangling limbs and bloodied horns, a twisted thing unlike my sweetling's compact, muscled form. When I tried commanding it, it turned its milky eye towards me, dragging itself piteously through the dirt.

The thing's horrific visage and useless body disgusted me, and I swiftly put it out of its suffering. Such a thing would not help me. Discouraged, but without any other choice, I returned to my nightly forays, spreading out my thefts among my neighbors, praying they would not miss a few bundles of thatch here and there.

Weeks later, with autumn declining into the chill of winter, I had the roof nearly done. A pilfered blanket, left forgotten on a line, kept me warm at night as I huddled on a pallet of fresh boughs beside the fireplace. More stolen clothes, a man's thick, homespun breeches and scratchy woolen shirt, helped keep me snug.

The stream still supplied me with ample food: fish mainly, with the occasional bit of sungazer or duck if my aim with a thrown stone was true, but I worried about what would happen when winter arrived. More and more, I saw flocks of migrating birds in the sky. Soon, they were gone. I did not have a garden, and even if I had, nothing would grow in the frosty ground.

I wondered if, when pressed, I would be willing to steal my neighbors' stockpiled grain and smoked meat like I had their thatch. Wondered what might happen if one of them, alerted by a watch dog's frantic barking, tried to stop me one moonless night.

I discovered what my scattered neighbors most needed quite by accident. One night, as I made yet another trip, gathering thatch, I saw a light in the house. A candle. Someone was awake, a most unusual thing for such early-rising folk.

Curiosity got the best of me, and I padded to the window, ears alert for their dog's first warning growl. I peered inside.

There, one of the children lay, face shining with sweat. Her rasping coughs bubbled wetly, and when her mother wiped the spittle from her lips, I saw it was flecked with blood.

The rust cough. Very bad in one so young. I knew that those afflicted, without the proper poultices and teas, seldom lasted a fortnight.

Poultices that I knew how to prepare. Tea made from herbs that I knew where to find, and harvest, and correctly brew.

It was my mistress's game, assuming the role of the wise woman of the hills, trading life-giving skill for sustenance.

I could do it. I could save the child's life, and in doing so, perhaps save my own when the long chill descended.

But how? How to speak with them, when my eyes would so quickly betray my true nature? How to convince them that I wanted to heal and not kill?

Walking back, arms aching from the weight of the bundled thatch, I figured out the way. All it would cost me was one of my precious linen shirts.

"Good morning," I said, lowering my voice into a cheerful yet rasping parody of my usual speech. "Is your mummy around, dear heart?"

The boy, a grubby, luminously healthy three-year-old, peered up at me from where he was playing with his crude wooden soldiers. They were arrayed in drunken lines, parading across a field of dust. Seeing my face, he frowned.

I peered at him through the thin strip of fabric tied across my eyes. I leaned on the walking stick I had cut earlier that morning, probing ahead in a way I hoped they would find convincing. My hair, carefully disheveled, poked in wild, silvery tufts from the hood drawn low across my brow. I hoped that they would mistake its color for the gray of an elder.

The child rose to his feet and ran into the house, calling for his mother. A few moments later, she emerged, blinking, into the morning sunlight.

Her eyes were red-rimmed and weary, deep worry lines gouged deep around them. She had been up all night, tending to her daughter. The rust cough would not, I knew, allow the child to sleep for long. I remembered the same look on my sister's face, the same mix of bone-deep weariness and jumpiness, after many a colicky night.

"Can I help you, grandmother?" she asked politely, peering at me. I nodded, stepping forward and banging into the gate I pretended not to see.

"Good morning to you, my lady," I said, sketching a bow. "My name is Selvina. I wonder if I might interest you in some tea, or some herbal remedies? Something for the monthly troubles perhaps? A nice warming poultice, maybe, perfect for soothing your husband's pains after a hard day's labor? I promise that all my wares are top quality. Try them for free, please do! I shan't disappoint."

"No I . . ." the mistress of the house began. A rasping cough, like wet burlap ripping, floated out from the house. Through my translucent blindfold, I saw her wince. She turned around, casting a desperate glance back into the house, then scanned the fields for her husband.

He was distant, in the farthest field. I had waited for him to leave, watching the house from the forest's edge before approaching. I knew that the mother would grasp at any hope, even that of a stranger, but fathers were more practical, wary of any threat to the household. Best to start here.

"That there sounds nasty, it does," I said. "You've a wee one that's come down with the croup?"

"No . . . it's . . . she caught a chill a few days ago. On the road. There was a storm. She got frightfully wet, helping push our cart out of the mud on our way back from town." She frowned, a tear sparkling in the corner of her eye.

"I think it is the rust cough," she finished, desperation creeping into her tone.

"It may be at that," I replied, matter-of-factly. I patted my herb bag and smiled. "Lucky for you, I have just the thing. Let's go inside and I'll make us, and the lass, a nice cup of tea."

LATER THAT MORNING, before her husband returned from the fields for the midday meal, I left the house. Mistress Johann hugged me when I paused in the doorway, muttering her thanks again and again.

"Oh, now, stop that, missus. I only do what I know how to do," I said, pushing her gently away. "You just be sure to rub that tonic into her chest every few hours, and make her drink all of her tea morning and night, no matter how much she complains about the bitterness. She should be right as rain in a few days."

"Please, I told you, call me Leah. And are you sure that's all you'll take?" she asked, pointing at the small carry sack as if I could see the gesture.

"Missus, a bag of apples and bread might not seem like much to you, but to me it's another week that I'll not have to worry about eating. Besides, you have you and your wee ones to think of, and winter is coming."

In truth, it was a very slight price for saving her daughter. My mistress would have received at least a season's worth of fresh vegetables in repayment for such a thing, or perhaps even a small bag of silver. But she had been well known to the people, not some newcoming, blind stranger. I did not want to ask for too much, too quickly.

"But, where can I find you if she does not improve? What if I need something else?"

I pointed back at the forest. "I came upon a house, back in the forest, a few hours' walk from here," I said. "Someone seems to have been fixing it up, but they must have fallen ill. I found a body, weeks dead from the smell, on the porch. I buried it and moved in. Do you know who it belongs to? I don't want to break any laws."

She laughed at that, a sound that filled me with satisfaction. "Laws? Here?" She shook her head. "Other than in the larger towns, there is no law north of the Armitage save that of the strong over the weak. The house you speak of used to belong to a family, the Marstens, I believe, but they died several winters ago. I wonder who tried to repair it?"

"Well, we'll never know now, I reckon. But I'm glad that whoever it was thought to fix the roof, or most of it. It barely rains inside at all!" I cackled, as my mistress used to do when she found something funny.

As I hoped, Leah frowned at that. "My husband knows a thing or two about fixing roofs," she said. "I'll send him up tomorrow, if you wish. We can't have you freezing come winter now, can we?"

"Oh, don't bother him about me," I said, shuffling towards the gate, sweeping my stick in front of me. I knocked over a stool with a clatter. "I'll be fine, really I will."

"Say nothing more," she commanded. "My mind is set. I'll send him along in the morning. Now, please, won't you take this nice thistleberry pie with you?"

I SAT IN MY HOUSE, belly full of Leah's pie, body warm and languid beside the crackling fire, and laughed. I knew her look; she was already thinking of me as a part of her life.

Many villages supported wise women, even in the face of the priests' displeasure, for the skills of herb gathering and healing are rare and difficult to obtain. Such wisdom was treasured, and those that possessed it were often forgiven for eccentricities that would be frowned upon in others.

I would not be surprised if, by the end of the week, people wouldn't begin turning up on my doorstep, eyes wide, asking at first for the little things: moon tea to ease a woman's monthly troubles and willowbark extract for their teething children. Some might even be bold enough to ask for pennyroyal to end an inconvenient pregnancy. The young ones, girls and boys both, sometimes even their parents, would ask for love charms or for drops that they could slip into their soon-to-be-beloved's beer.

They would bring with them offerings of eggs and ripe summer squash. Apples and bushels of nuts, and possibly sides of meat, smoked and cured. They might even bring coin, if they had any, although probably not until late in the winter, when even the best-stocked household would begin to feel the first pangs of hunger.

I looked about. The cottage was simple and sturdy, but if I were to play the part, I should look it. Still smiling at my own cleverness, I rose to make my preparations.

CHAPTER ELEVEN

Almost an hour passes before I hear them. Footsteps and quiet conversation from the road. Of boots splashing through the mud. I check the undergrowth and nod, satisfied that I cannot be seen.

A few moments later, they emerge from the endless green, one form swaddled in browns and grays, a hooked staff held before him, the other clad in shining white silks under a rich cloak of sky blue.

"Really, Lia, you should put this behind you," Ato insists, his words perfectly clear. "You saw what she called—what she consorts with. Women like her will pay for their transgressions one day, in this world if not the next. When that happens, you do not want to be there to witness it."

I see the other form nod, but she does not speak. Ato waits for a moment, then when no reply is forthcoming, sighs. The pair walk on, past my concealing spot. I can still hear their footfalls long after they disappear around a curve in the road.

When the sounds of their passage have faded, I rise and move to follow. I send out a call to my sweetlings, then wait. Soon, they emerge from the wet greenery.

Of the children I summoned at Fort Azure, only two remain. One was called from the body of Laru, a quiet soldier I seldom spoke to. A Mor hammer ended his first life, staving in his ribs like a strong man would crush a wicker basket, and this injury shows in his reborn form, ribs protruding from his leathery flesh.

The other is none other than Hollern, the man who nearly lead me to my death. The man that, through his incompetence, killed Jazen Tor.

The sweetling I have summoned from his body is larger than most, almost four feet tall, if it ever managed the trick of standing erect. The face is unmarked; Hollern died with a Mor blade in his heart, his life blood boiling from within. The eyes, however, are not the placid opal that I am accustomed to, but rather are a rusty black, filmed with hemorrhaged, congealed blood. It was this one that showed such surprising skill in the wood, earlier. That has somehow managed the trick of moving quietly thorough the green rather than blundering.

The thing that was Hollern watches me, awaiting my pleasure, its mouth half open. The gums have retreated, their tissues already drying and hardening, turning the teeth into yellowed fangs. It shuffles forward a bit, heavy claws dragging in the mud.

"They should be far enough ahead by now," I tell them. I know that words are not necessary, but speaking to them makes me feel a bit less lonely.

I start down the road, the children falling in behind me.

I follow for the better part of the day, ears and eyes alert for signs. Of them, or something else. It would not do to blunder into a Mor patrol.

By midafternoon the trees are thinning; we are coming to the end of the forest. I know this road descends to the rolling foothills that lead to the edge of the great cliff and wall of the Armitage, still three days away. Between here and there, the road passes Fort Jasper.

The last time I passed this way, almost two years ago, this was a fertile land, dotted with settlements and farm holds, the road well patrolled and maintained. Every crossroad hosted an inn, their courtyards always crowded with horses and carriages, their rooms filled with travelers.

Now, looking down across the land, I see the destruction the Mor have wrought.

The rainy air is filled with the smell of burning. Columns of weary smoke rise from a score of places, each marking the location of a burning farmhouse or granary.

I stop at the edge of the trees, eyes scanning for movement, and eventually I see them. Two forms moving along the road, one dark, one light. I wonder if I should just move along behind them and see if Ato and Lia would chose to flee or stand lest they spot me.

I choose to wait for distance to make me invisible. I do not fear Brother Ato's power, nor that of his goddess. I do not even fear Lia's command of the Elementals. All they can do is kill me; I do not know why I hesitate.

Eventually, I lose sight of them amongst the rolling foothills, and break cover. I trot down the road, my children pacing me easily. We could run for days like this. My life, first as a wise woman and later as a trapper and scout, has hardened me in ways I could never have imagined.

The road is a quagmire, little more than parallel wagon ruts filled with rainwater. Without the trees to shelter me from the misting rain, my cloak grows sodden and heavy. My leathers keep the worst of the wet off my skin, but I am glad for the warmth imparted by my continued movement.

Hours later, night darkens the western sky. I hear the sound of many voices ahead. The cries of children, the helpless keening of women newly widowed and the angry shouts of men, make me wary. I command my sweetlings to leave the road, and lie in the ditch beside it, amongst a tangle of fallen bodies.

Hollern, or what he has become, looks at me for a long moment, ignoring the command. His fearsome head cocks as he regards me, his rusty black eyes placid, but somehow challenging. I frown; my children have never disobeyed me before.

I repeat the command, whispering it aloud this time. For a moment, I fear he will disregard me again, but then he drops his gaze, moves to join his brother in the ditch.

When they are settled, I move along the road. The glow of many campfires is bright in the newly minted dark. I look around, wondering if the Mor are nearby, praying that they are not. The glow can be seen for miles, reflecting from the bellies of the overhanging clouds.

I reach the encampment. Refugees. Dozens of them. An impromptu tent city has sprung up around the ruins of a burned-out farmstead.

Many of the inhabitants are women. Women alone, red-eyed and hopeless. Women carrying children, faces haggard, pleading for them to be still, to please, please be quiet. Young women and middle-aged. Very few are old. The old, I know, cannot run very fast, and so are easy prey.

There are only a few men folk in evidence, no more than a dozen, all told. They stand near the fire, talking loudly. Many bear improvised weapons, implements that were farm tools just yesterday, less than useless.

These men must have run away before the Mor reached their homes, choosing to abandon their homes and fields rather than fight. Doubtless, the ones that fought lie, unburied and burnt, where they fell.

Stragglers are still arriving, survivors drawn by the light of the fires. I slip into camp, head bent inside my hood. In the darkness, my deformity will not be noticeable, I hope.

Soon, I come to a tent. Moans of pain and sobbing float out through the open flaps. All around lie the bodies of the sick and hurt, sprawled on the muddy ground. Some lie perfectly still. Others have covered faces.

I peer through the open flap and see Ato inside, hard at work. His sleeves are rolled up, exposing thick hairy forearms. The priest is spattered with crimson from chest to belly, his gore-smeared apron as red as a butcher's. I wonder why he does not just invoke his goddess's power. Why he does not dispel the pain and the terrible injuries with a wave of his crosier. Is he not charged with healing all sickness and injury that come into his sight?

A moment later he moves deeper into the tent, and I cannot see him. I cast about, searching for Lia, but she is nowhere to be found.

Fingers pluck at my leg, and I look down, into the bloodshot eyes of a child. A little girl lies in the mud, her head swaddled in dark-stained bandages. One eye is covered, and on that side I see that her mouth is a split ruin. Her arm lies beside her, twisted.

"Please . . ." she whispers, the word barely heard over the surrounding din. "Water."

Her mother sits beside her, looking at me with empty, hopeless eyes. I move to the table beside the tent, where a bucket sits, ladle out a portion of the water within, then carry it back. She raises herself, grimacing in pain, and sips.

"We need to set that arm, dear heart," I say, setting the ladle aside. "It will make you feel better. Do you trust me?"

The little girl's pain-filmed eye meets mine. I wait for her to flinch away, but a moment later she nods. A ghost of a smile touches those pain-wracked lips.

Delicately, I explore the injury, my wise fingers telling me the story. No bones have been shattered, but her shoulder has separated, the bone floating free from its socket. It must be put back in, and soon, lest the injury swell further and make repair impossible.

I take a blanket from a dead man, exposing his ruined face, cleft in twain by a Mor's burning blade. He will not need it.

"I need your help," I say to the mother. "You have to help me help her." She ignores me, staring at the ground, her face impassive, empty.

My slap fills the air, the sharp sound drawing the eyes of those nearby. I grab her shoulders. "You have to help me hold her. Can you hear me?" The others turn away, lost in their own troubles.

The mother's eyes clear, as she returns from wherever she has been. She puts her hand on her reddened cheek, and frowns. "I hear you," she says.

I wrap the blanket, twisted into a cylinder like a rope, around the girl's chest, and hand the mother the ends. "You must hold her tight. Don't let go, and don't stop, even if she screams. This will hurt her, but it will all turn out all right, I promise. Lean back, and pull as hard as you can."

Mother nods, and grasps the blanket. I wrap the girl's wrist in my hands, gripping it tight. A moment later, it is done. The girl utters one piercing shriek and then falls unconscious.

I rotate the arm, feeling the play of bone and muscle. There will be much swelling, and the tendons feel a bit torn, but she is young, and the injury should heal.

The head wound is another story. Something cut her scalp deeply, the flap of hair falling down in a freshet of blood when I unwrap the bandage. I know that cautery is called for, that the heat will help to drive out the infection already beginning to grow inside her flesh, but I do not think she would survive it.

I settle for stitching the wound closed. I do the best I can, bathing the gash in boiled wine before sewing the angry lips together. I do not have anything I can use as bandages, must content myself with boiling her soiled one in the remains of the wine before winding it back around her head.

Ato might have fresh supplies in the tent, but I dare not enter, dare not ask.

When I have done all I can, I move to the next of the wounded, a woman, blind eyes turned up to the heavens, whispering prayers. A Mor blade has carved a tremendous chunk from her side and belly, the concavity burned black. I do not know how she is still alive. My healing knowledge is useless here.

I help her pass over, my hands covering her mouth and nose, gripping tightly as her body clings to the last shreds of its life. Then she is still, at peace. I open my secret eye, and see her, standing beside her body. She was lovely. Young. Sweet. Like Kirin. Like I used to be. She meets my gaze and nods, smiling, then drifts away like smoke.

The night is hours old when I finally stop to rest. Many have been taken into the Mercy tent, there to be tended by Brother Ato, but many more remain outside, lying in the cold and wet. Some are dead before I can get to them. Others are too far gone for my skills to help. These, I make as comfortable as possible, or help pass over as painlessly as I can.

I am kneeling beside a man, stitching shut the cut on his forehead, when she speaks.

"Kirin . . . why?"

I turn, and there, behind me is Lia.

"Because I can help," I say, turning back to my work.

"No, I mean . . . what you did. In the woods—"

"Is not unnatural, no matter what Brother Ato says. I told you that."

Lia fidgets behind me. Her uncertainty is nearly a physical thing. When I am done sewing the wound, she is still there. I rise, sighing, trying to massage the stiffness out of my shoulders. Dawn is near.

"Where is he?" I ask, and point to the tent.

Lia nods. "He has been tending to the worst of the wounded since we arrived. I helped as best I could, but . . . I tried to . . . there was a woman, holding her child. They were burned. Burned. She died. Before he could even start a prayer;

she was probably dead before they brought her in. Her and the child. When I tried to take the babe . . . it . . . their skin . . . it *tore* away when I . . ." She shudders, her mouth puckering.

Then she is kneeling in the mud, her blood-spattered silks becoming even further grimed, retching. I move to her, automatically, and rest my hand on her shoulder.

She rolls into the embrace, pressing her befouled mouth to my chest. Her sobs deepen into a keening as the last shreds of her innocence float away with her breath. I hold her tight; I know what this feels like.

I wait out the storm. When she has regained a measure of composure, I move back, look into her eyes. They are red-rimmed, sparkling with tears. I brush one aside with my thumb.

"It's hard, I know. But you're strong. You're helping and that's all that matters."

She laughs, the sound harsh, bitter. "Strong," she repeats, her tone disbelieving. Her eyes search the mud, as if some answer might be writ there. I raise her chin, until she is looking at me again.

"Yes, you are."

Lia is looking at me, trying to see if I am lying, perhaps. Her eyes catch the firelight, throwing back highlights that are almost violet. Her brows draw down, as if she is remembering a question she wanted to ask me.

"Bright Lady, be merciful!" I hear a voice cry out. "Lia, get away from her! Guards! To arms! Hold that woman, and, by all that's holy, get her away from the bodies!"

Ato has arrived.

CHAPTER TWELVE

My roof, completed in a single day by Leah's husband and two of his friends, kept me dry all the rest of the winter. There was some grumbling about stolen thatch, but my story about dead squatters seemed to hold fast. The false cairn I raised over the thief's body I had claimed to have stumbled upon doubtless helped.

The men spent a great deal of time staring, open-mouthed, at the trinkets and amulets I had spent the last few nights fashioning. Acorns and beads; a mouse skull strung alongside the teeth of the boar my sweetling had killed; garlands of drying, pungent fall flowers. They were mere decorations, powerless save for their very real influence over the superstitious.

Because they thought me blind, they allowed their eyes to roam over my possessions and my body freely, unabashedly. I was glad to see they did not desire me; I had gone to great lengths to appear decrepit, even going so far as to rub dark black river mud into my hair, lest its sheen betray my youth.

Shortly after they completed the job and departed, one returned, as I knew he would. As he approached, I hailed him from my rocking chair, watching him from behind the thin material covering my eyes.

With much stammering and blushing, he began to ask me about each amulet's power. I smiled, close-mouthed, as he hinted around what he wanted. I let him twist on the hook, enjoying his clumsy attempts to dissemble, then decided to take pity on him.

"What is the girl's name, Nils?" I asked, groping about for his hand. He moved it beneath mine and I patted it.

"Greta," he breathed, his shoulders dropping with relief.

"And why would a strapping man such as yourself need a love amulet?" I asked. "Surely Mistress Greta would be flattered by your attentions?"

"She might, if she knew about them," he admitted, a hot flush making his ears into crimson moons. "I've . . . that is, I haven't . . . "

"You long for her from afar?" I asked, and he nodded, enthusiastically. "Well, then, I've just the thing. A philter of courage. Wear it against your heart, and it will surely help."

Nils stammered his thanks, and I disengaged my hand from his. I opened one of the splintered chests left behind by the former residents, and rummaged inside. A moment later, I drew forth a necklace, formed from crimson holly berries. The cord passed through the center hole of a coin, a hexagonal Imperial farthing. The metal was dull, coated in traces of darkened blood.

"This medallion was soaked in the blood of a mountain prowler," I intoned, slipping the trinket over his bowed head. "Keep it with you always, against the skin over your heart. Let no eye see it, lest its power flee forever. When your true love is near, rub the coin 'twixt forefinger and thumb, and repeat her name seven times. You will feel it working then."

"It . . . it will make her love me?" he said, staring at the bit of junk. He had no way to know that the blood, in fact, came from a hare, caught in one of my snares and cooked up for supper. The symbolism seemed oddly appropriate.

"Love you? Of course not," I scoffed, and nearly laughed as his hopeful expression crumbled. "Such charms can be made, to be sure, but not without great risk. And cost," I said, smiling to myself as his face fell. Thank the gods for men who lusted after women less than they desired coin.

"Start with this," I suggested, tapping my nail against the farthing. "Rare is the woman who can resist a man of your presence, especially when his spirit is bolstered by the fierce courage of the prowler. You'll do fine."

"How much . . . ?" he began. I waved my hands, silencing him with a hiss.

"Such things cannot be bought and sold," I said. "You have done me a great service today, and for that I shall make a gift of the medallion, along with my deepest thanks. If you find it effective, then return, and bring me what little you can spare. A spot of milk, perhaps, or eggs, if you can. We shall help each other, yes?"

I knew from my nocturnal ramblings that Nils's family owned more than three score of dairy cows and their chicken coops were full to bursting. They produced more than enough milk to not only supply them throughout the winter, but to also share with one little old wise woman. I just hoped Greta, whoever she was, would react favorably to Nils's ash-blond good looks and strong chin, once he worked up the nerve to finally speak with her.

Nils departed, fingering his prize through his shirt, stammering thanks. I waved his gratitude away with a smile; he would either have the courage, or he would not. Still, I found myself wishing him well, and not just because I hoped that a happy outcome would benefit me, as well.

I spent the long winter content enough and dry, cozy in my tiny cabin. Before the first snows buried the brittle grass, the surrounding country folk began to arrive, drawn to me by Mistress Leah's stories of her daughter's "miraculous recovery." A week later, Nils returned, bearing clay jugs of milk and a basket of eggs. His radiant smile told me all I needed to know about how things had gone with Greta.

Soon, the arrivals were coming several times a week, mainly for the more mundane cures in my pharmacopeia: willow bark tea, laxatives and soothing balms for fussy babes, and the like. Once, an old woman came down with the rust cough, and the family hurried to my cabin, forcing a path through the deep snow.

After I had given them tea and let them warm themselves at my fire, they asked me to come to her bedside, but I was not sure my disguise would hold alongside the genuine article. I pled a case of gout and sent them on their way with a parcel of my special tea and a bag of herbs, along with detailed instructions on how to boil up the poultices that would help clear the wetness from her lungs.

She, too, recovered, further adding to my reputation. I continued on with my plan of asking little and graciously accepting whatever tribute was offered in return for my services.

It seemed a good plan, and served me through the long cold months. When the spring thaws began, I found myself in possession of a modest surplus of food, something that not every family who came to me for help could boast.

I decided to share my good fortune, a decision that brought me further luck. A few wizened apples, given to Mistress Abuna, the local seamstress, brought me the promise of a new woolen dress. A measure of stale grain, gifted to John Petros, the blacksmith's apprentice, resulted in a fine set of black iron tableware, a stout kettle and, best of all, a sturdy iron gardener's trowel.

The gift inspired me. When the threat of frost was finally passed, I began my planting. Out in the forest, hidden from curious eyes, I turned the rich, black earth and tended my new garden. I knew from my mistress that one should never let a client see one's garden, least they steal seeds or clippings. Let them wonder how an old, blind woman like myself managed to gather the herbs my medicines required.

The month of Rammat approached, and with it the Festival of Blossoms, which my clients told me was held in the town of Mosby. There would be games, they said, and a crowning of a new Maid of the Planting. On a whim, I decided to attend.

I left before dawn, my empty pack on my back and my walking stick in my hand. In the seam of my cloak were sewn the three golden rukhs and eleven silver c'tees I had managed to gather from my clients. I hoped to purchase things my garden lacked from wandering herbalists: seeds, or clippings, or possibly even rare bulbs.

I felt strange as I walked the muddy road. Exposed. Revealed. My time alone had already made me feel more at home when sheltered from observing eyes. Late in the afternoon, Nils and his betrothed rode by in a cloud of feathers, atop their wagon. The back was full of crates, stuffed with squawking, flapping chickens. They offered to let me travel with them, and I accepted with thanks.

We reached the festival grounds just before dark. The sounds of music and revelry floated on the chill night air, spiced with the trill of laughter. Mosby was a large town, a densely-packed cluster of granaries, cattle barns and pig pens mixed with slate-roofed cottages, home to nearly six-score families, or so Nils claimed. The town's main building, a tall water mill, stood proudly at the center of the sprawl. Farmers for miles around brought their harvests to the Mosby Mill, and the town was rich, relatively speaking.

As such, the festival the town fathers sponsored was always lavish, or so I had been told. The road into town, which crossed the river Mos on a proud stone bridge, was lined with cherry trees. Their pristine white blossoms carpeted the road like snow, filling the air with their delicate perfume.

"It's a shame you can't see this, Mistress," Greta said with a sigh. "The cherry blossoms are so lovely."

Nils whispered something to her, and I heard her gasp. Even through the linen covering my eyes, I could see her blush in the lantern light. "Oh. I'm sorry, Mistress Selvina. I meant no offense."

"Oh, don't you mind that, deary," I croaked. "I had years and years to enjoy my sight, and I remember well what flowers look like, never fear. Their scent makes me feel like a young girl again, it does."

Oh, you do lie so prettily, sister, I heard in my head, soft as wind over an owl's wing. *But one day there will be a reckoning, mark my words.* I frowned, wondering what she meant, but she chose not to elaborate.

Greta smiled as blossoms fell into her hair, her plain, moon face transforming into something radiant and lovely. She was a gentle soul, meek and plain. Her looks would never inspire a minstrel, but her smile was another matter, infectious and warm. Nils had done well, and all because of my little charm.

You only fooled him into thinking any of this was your doing, remember, my sister whispered, maliciously. *The risk, and courage, was all his. You're nothing but a charlatan.* I did my best to ignore her; I knew my skill and wisdom had done much good, had saved lives. Nonetheless, her words evoked a quiver of guilty dread all the same.

Market Square, and the festival grounds proper, were just south of town. Many had already arrived, and the field was dotted with tents and wagons. A hundred campfires glittered in the darkness, each the center of a small knot of revelry. The sun would be reborn upon the morn, marking the end of the months-long dark and cold, and the people had come, ready to celebrate.

Barrels of beer and mead had already been breached, and brays of raucous laughter greeted us from most every fire. Children ran hither and yon, in laughing packs, playing at hoops, or at epic games of knight's gambit or chase-the-chasemaster.

"If you need a place to stay, we have room in the wagon," Nils began. I assured him that I would be fine. I knew it would be hard enough to keep my disguise intact, amongst so many new eyes. The possibility of discovery as I slept was an even greater risk.

I slept in a hedge at the edge of the grounds, sheltered from the night mists by a dense wall of boxwood. I rose the next morning stiff and cold; I had grown soft during the winter, sleeping on a straw mattress and beside warm banked coals. I did not begrudge my pain, for my hunched posture and shambling, stiffened gait would only add to the illusion of age that camouflaged me.

I wandered the faire, taking in the sights from behind my translucent blindfold. As I walked, I felt the stares of the passers-by, heard their whispered comments. *She's the one who saved Leah Johann's girl from the rust cough . . . I hear she can make potions that drive men mad with desire . . . Her creams ease the pains of my swollen joints, I've used them myself . . .*

I smiled, groping about with my stick, apologizing when I bumped into people. I wondered if my mistress ever felt the way I did, if the knowledge of her influence on the people of her village brought her the same satisfaction that I felt.

I was still smiling, congratulating myself on my wise plan, when I bumped into the man ahead of me. "Cry your pardon, good sir," I said. He turned, a scowl of irritation sitting upon his brow like a storm cloud.

Even before he looked at me, I knew who he was; the line of his jaw and the thin, sandy blond hair cried his identity, even through the cloth over my eyes.

Urik. My husband. Best friend of Marcus, the man I had killed.

"Watch where you're going, you . . ." he began, then stopped. His eyes went wide. In his hand, he held a scrap of parchment, upon which a rendition had been sketched in charcoal, the face dreadfully familiar.

My face.

Already I was turning, drawing my hood down low to hide my face, but I saw the flash of recognition in his eyes. I heard him, moving behind me, shoving through the crowd.

I slipped amongst the milling throng, threading my way through the densest knots of revelers. "Wait!" Urik cried, trying to force himself through the same crowds I had slipped through. "You there . . . I want to talk to you!"

Then, he shouted my name. My true name.

Despite myself, the power of it compelled me stop, made me turn. I looked him in the face, straightening, the cloak of age I had adopted falling away. Through the crowd, I saw him, saw the flash of certainty that filled his eyes.

He had lost weight during the long winter. The soft, round face I had known was leaner, more angular. Predatory eyes sparkled amongst folds of bruised flesh, over stubbled cheeks.

On his back, the great horn and ash longbow that had belonged to Marcus rode amongst a thicket of brown-fletched arrows. Marcus' leather vest clad his chest, the lacings barely stretched. The Urik I had known would never have fitted inside.

The tableau held for a long moment whilst the faire-goers, oblivious to our drama, passed by. Urik took a step forward. His hand dropped to the hilt of a knife.

I recognized it: the Ulean steel knife I had left beside him in our bed. The bloodthirsty mistress I had gifted to him on the night my sister died.

I turned and bolted, his cries of frustration rising behind me. I did not run, though every nerve and sinew cried out to do so, but I walked faster than any old woman should. I told myself not to turn, to not look back, lest he be right behind me.

In my head, my sister howled for vengeance, screaming defiance and filth at me, calling me coward, over and over.

I implored her to be still. Begged her to stop. I could not hear. All around me, people were looking, their eyes drawn to the muttering, hurried woman with the wildly flailing stick.

I reeled through the festival crowds until I reached the livestock pens at the edge of the field. Then I ran, blindly, dropping my stick when it hindered me. It was only the work of moments to reach the trees, but already I heard voices raised behind me.

I blundered into the thorns and brambles, thrashing wildly, and cast my eyes back the way I had come.

Urik was there, in the company of four hard-looking men, all grim and unsmiling. They bore weapons, things of age-darkened steel, thick with the patina of hard use, carried lightly. Urik pointed to my trail, still clearly visible in the damp, springtime mud.

As one, they started towards me. In their eyes were a flat, cold hunger and a grim amusement. They were enjoying the hunt I was giving them.

But Urik . . . Urik's eyes were the worst. In them was rage and loathing, raw emotion forged into something almost palpable, mixed with something even more terrible.

Love. Hopeless, twisted love. Love enough to destroy the thing that had shattered his entire world, as mine had been shattered.

Reckoning! my sister cackled. *I said there would be a reckoning, and now it has come. It has come!*

Sobbing, ignoring my sister's ravings, I turned and fled into the woods, while, behind me, the hunters took up the trail.

CHAPTER THIRTEEN

The guards, farmers all, take me to the burned farm's stable. I wonder, for a moment, where the livestock has gone. Eaten, most likely, by the hungry refugees. Or killed by the Mor.

The stalls are untenanted, in any event. I am tired, so very tired. The piled straw looks as inviting as a featherbed.

A man stands at the door, a pitchfork in his hands. He eyes me, his expression full of fear. It would be simple, the work of but a moment, to get past him and disappear into the waning dark. So very easy to reach out and pull his life out by the roots, but why?

I am tired. Of running. Of fearing the people that I seem destined to help. Let them kill me while I slumber, if that is Ato's will and that of his close-minded goddess. I sink to the straw, and am asleep moments later.

When I wake, sunlight casts beams of golden light through the open stable door. The guard stands at the entrance to my pen, his rude weapon trained on me. Behind him are others, all men.

I sit up, comb the straw from my hair. My mouth is filled with the bitter gall of not enough sleep and too little food. Nausea ripples through me. The light tells me I have been unconscious for over an hour, perhaps two.

"Brother Ato has called for you," the farmer says.

I nod and rise, then follow my captors out into the sunshine. The early morning light is radiant and lovely, bathing the fields in molten gold, as if the idiot gods have decided to ignore the atrocity all around. The rains have scrubbed the worst of the burning stink from the air.

The camp has swelled further in the night; ten score or more people now fill the yard, a floodtide of human misery. None have escaped unscathed, and all around I see suffering in either body or mind.

The few surviving men surround me, weapons held in white-knuckled hands. I keep my head high, walking slowly, as if they are my honor guard.

Let the blood magic loose, my sister whispers to me, her tone as seductive as a lover's. *They would dare trifle with you? Let slip the magic, and show this priest the true meaning of power.*

"They know not what they do. They are frightened and tired," I reply aloud, no longer caring if they hear. I can scarce make things worse for myself.

The men mutter and sketch warning signs in the air, then steer me towards the blood-spattered tent. Ato steps forth, taking off his butcher's apron and taking up his crosier. His eyes burn, with weariness and the greasy light of fanaticism. Lia emerges from behind him. Her porcelain skin is blotched, face swollen from weeping.

"Do you wish to confess your regrets to Shanira, before I— before *we* pass judgment?" he asks.

"I have no regrets," I say, my eyes alighting on the little girl from last night. She smiles at me from behind her bandage. Her mother is beside her, her face awake and alert. I see others I have helped in the crowd, many just behind the ring of menfolk guarding my escape.

"Y'can't just kill 'er, Brother," a woman says from the crowd. "She's a healer like you."

"Not like me," Ato insists. "I told you. Her power comes not from the pure light of Shanira, but rather from the evil dark beneath the earth. Any she touched should be checked for signs of corruption. I must—"

"She set Jada's arm and sewed her head," the little girl's mother says, stepping forward. The child follows, walking up to Ato boldly. "No other would help, not even you, Brother. Gods only know what would have happened to her, lying all night in the cold mud."

"There were others whose need was greater, good woman. As I said—"

"She set my mother's leg," another woman adds. "She's sleeping right peaceful now, if you feel the need to check on her."

"She made my husband comfortable until he passed," an old woman says, tears running down her face. "She did what she could, but the Mor burned him up on the inside. She . . ." the woman's voice falters. She wipes the tears from her face savagely, shaking her head, then looks straight into my black eyes. "Thank you."

Others add their voices, telling of things I barely remember doing. Limbs set. Wounds sewn. The offer of comfort to the dying in their last moments, or even, for those beyond help, the final peace of the blade, helping them cross over. There are so many of them.

"People . . . good people, please," Ato says, raising his hands for silence. "I do not dispute that Kirin helped you. But that still does not balance the evil things she has done. That she will do again if we allow her to escape. She might go to the Mor and bring them here."

"No!" I say, stepping towards him, and the guards do not move to hinder me. "I would never bring those beasts here!"

"Perhaps. Or perhaps not," Ato says. "But we cannot risk that."

"No offense, Brother, but that's not your decision to make," a man says. "These here are hard times, and, no offense to you or Shanira, but you're only one man. We've got many wounded, and she knows the ways of the Wise Women."

"Superstition and trickery," Ato scoffs. "Perhaps even the power of the infernal. You must not trust her!"

Lia steps forth, into the ring surrounding me, and approaches. She stops. Her eyes stare into mine, searching for something. I see the lightning in them, and realize that here is another judgment I need fear.

"Do you swear that there is nothing of the darkness in your healing?" she asks, softly. "Do you promise those you help will recover, or if they are beyond helping that they will not . . . rise again?"

Who is she to command us? my sister howls. *Insufferable brat! We could raise an army of your children! We could take the battle to the Mor and—*

"I swear it," I say, silencing her ravings.

"Then that is enough for me. Let her go."

"But . . . you musn't!" Ato stammers, his face purpling.

"We've need of her, Brother," the man from a moment before says. "And, of you," he adds, quickly. "Come, let's see if there's anything I can help you with." He leads Ato away, the priest still stammering his outrage, but the man's presence is as implacable as a palisade, solid and impervious. They disappear back into the mercy tent.

As soon as they have gone, the circle of guards dissolves, as the crowd presses forward. Voices reach me, pleas for help for this one or that. Hands reach out in supplication.

"I must help them," I say to Lia. "But I wish to speak with you and to whoever leads these folk. Do you know who he is?"

"I do," she says. "Go. We will speak later."

I allow the crowd to pull me away, towards the lines of pallets, each one supporting its cargo of human suffering. Some, seeing my black eyes clearly in the light of day, sketch the warding sign of Shanira, or sometimes even Lillit, at me, but all are so broken, so weak, that none can put up more than a token protest. Any who do have the strength can wait.

Later, I look up as a bowl is thrust beneath my face. Brown liquid, steaming hot, in which chunks of crudely cut carrots and potatoes float, spots of grease sparkling like jewels on the surface.

I look up, and there is Lia. I blink stupidly; the day has stretched, unnoticed, into late afternoon. The sun is an orb of blood, hanging low in the west. Shadows stretch from the trees and copses bordering the trampled fields, reaching towards the farm like giants' arms.

"She's gone," Lia says, nodding to the child whose hand I hold.

For a time, I thought she might endure, might be able to fight off the infection eating away at her bowels. When her house caught fire, her sister told me, she kept her head, helped her brothers and sisters out the window and down the smoking roof. Helped them drop, one by one, into the garden bushes.

Then, the roof collapsed behind her, falling in a fountain of sparks into the house, showering her with burning embers, lodging chips of fire in her hair. She panicked then, and leaped bodily out into unforgiving space, as if she, in her need, could transform into a raven or an owl.

Instead, she fell, crashing into the split rail fence, her small bones snapping one by one, ribs bending in to puncture lungs and lights. The gods, in their questionable mercy, at least had the kindness to shatter her spine, assuring she felt no pain below the tops of her shoulders.

By the time I reached her, the sickly sweet odor of her death was thick in her chest, wafting to me before I could even bend to smell.

I cleaned away the bloodied pus as best I could, but of course it was hopeless. All I could do was hold her hand as she slipped away from me.

Lia shakes the bowl of stew beneath my nose once more, and despite myself, I feel my body responding. I cannot remember when I last ate, and even horse meat stew smells like one of the mythic feasts that my mother so often told us about.

I close the girl's eyes and drape the body in her blanket, hiding her tiny, peaceful face. Someone will be along shortly to bury her. Or not. I do not know, or care.

Ato could have saved her, my sister spits. *He could have beseeched his Lady to intervene, and yet he did not. Why must this child suffer and die while he heals others? What right does he have to choose who lives and who dies?*

"Kirin?" Lia asks, and I realize, belatedly, that she has been speaking to me.

"Cry your pardon," I say, distantly. "What?"

"I said that, for now, all of the wounded have been dealt with. Even Brother Ato has finally agreed to rest. You should too."

I nod and allow her to lead me away. We sit under the branches of a towering oak, our backs nestled in the roots. The solidity of the wood at my back feels better than a stone wall.

"Do you want more?" Lia asks, and I realize I have eaten the entire bowlful.

I shake my head. "Just sleep, if I need not worry about someone slitting my throat as I slumber."

"Of course not," Lia says, shocked. "Why would someone do that?"

"Brother Ato seems to feel that I'm a witch. That I have dealings with infernal powers."

"Yes, well," Lia says, looking down. She tears at the sparse grass. "But the people don't believe that. You helped a great many of them today. They are in your debt."

"I did only what I could. Less than Ato, I'm sure."

"I am not so sure," Lia says. "Oh, he was wonderful, at first," she adds quickly. "The power of Shanira flowed from him in a golden stream, like liquid sunlight, healing wounds and knitting bones. It was magnificent."

"But?" I ask, hearing the equivocation in her tone.

"But, after a time, the effort seemed to weary him. Before the night was done, he was using other skills, much like yours."

I raise my eyebrow at this. "Your worldly skills, I mean," she adds. "Setting bones. Sewing wounds. Cleaning infection away with boiled wine. He saved the power of Shanira for those that would otherwise have been beyond help."

Like the little girl whose hand you held? My sister's voice is acid in my head, black as venom. *Where was his goddess's power then?*

I shrug, already knowing the answer. Lia has voiced it— he was only one man, despite his goddess's favor. So many times throughout the endless night and day that followed, I wanted to hate him, to blame him for not attending to the people before me, but every time I was moved to rise and confront him, a scream or a moan from the mercy tent would reach me, or some assistant would be helped outside, weeping, or retching, covered with blood, and I knew that Brother Ato had his own price of misery to pay.

"So, what now?" I finally ask, as the afternoon sky deepens into the cobalt of true night.

"I do not know," Lia says, softly. "The people here are lead by Ben Childers, the man who spoke in your defense earlier. I do not know why, but the others all seem to defer to him. We should ask him."

"Whatever we do, we should be away from here. The Mor must know where we are by now. They will be coming. Why haven't they come already?"

Lia shrugs. "There is much talk from those who live to the south that many Mor have been seen on the roads. Many believe the Mor are on their way to besiege the City and the fortress wall of the Armitage.

Besiege the Armitage? A part of me wants to laugh at the idea.

I have never beheld the great wall, but certainly I have heard the stories. A gargantuan structure, running along the great drop of the Northwatch Cliffs, a wall taller than ten men standing atop one another's shoulders, so thick that an entire city was said to lie inside. The Armitage was more than a wall – it was a fortress, running nearly ten-score miles from the shores of Lake Tywyn in the east to the coast of the Sundown Sea in the west.

At its heart, the Armitage guards the vast sprawl of the Imperial City, home to the King of Wheels and his court. The City was said to be vast, home to tens of thousands, a crowded, magnificent place built into and athwart the Northwatch Cliffs, nurtured by the waters of the river Mos.

All traffic between the fertile lowlands below and the highlands had to pass through the City, a never-ending river of food, timber, iron and humanity. If the Mor besieged the City successfully, it would be grave news indeed. It was simply unimaginable that they could ever breach the mighty walls, but certainly they could blockade the walls themselves.

"Then we should flee north and west," I say, "away from the Armitage. Making a run for the City will only bring us closer to the invading army. There are vast stretches of unspoiled forest to the North, enough to hide an army in. I should know."

"Some of the men want to go to the City. Want to join the Imperial Army in its defense."

"Fools," I say, bitterly. My hands are still sticky and stained with the result of these people's laughable resistance. "Their best chance is to flee. To hide, and watch, and possibly harry the enemy from concealment. A face-to-face confrontation is simply . . ." I trail off, once more remembering the way that five thousand men were slaughtered like sheep by a force of rampaging Mor a tenth their number.

"Then you must speak to Ben Childers. You were a scout in the Imperial Army, were you not?" I nod. "Then your counsel should be welcome. I fear that, for all the people look to Childers for leadership, he is still just a farmer."

I nod and make to rise, then gasp as the ground seems to list beneath my feet. Lia grabs me, before I can topple.

"After you rest," Lia continues. "You are exhausted. Come, let us find you a nice place to sleep.

She leads me back to my erstwhile prison cell. She makes a show of arranging the straw just so, as if she were fluffing the covers on a bed. When she is done, she takes my hand, leads me into the tiny stall.

The smell of straw, of sawn wood and manure, is comforting after so much burnt flesh, so much blood. She settles beneath me, guiding me down, until my head is once more pillowed on her thighs.

The song she sings is unknown to me, a lilting melody, diving and swooping like a kestrel on the wing. Her fingers stroke my pale hair, tracing along my brow tenderly, like a mother with her babe. Or a lover.

I sigh, feeling my body growing deliciously heavy, and surrender to sleep's embrace.

CHAPTER FOURTEEN

I fled through the woods, pursued by Urik and his men. All thoughts of subtlety were gone; all my burgeoning woodcraft forgotten. The look of pure, hopeless love that I had seen in Urik's eyes, cut through with such spite, such rage and loathing, had completely unnerved me.

So I ran, blundering through the brush and undergrowth, leaving a trail that a blind man could follow. My breath came, harsh and panting, as I struggled up one rise and then another.

Reckoning! Reckoning! The time has come! my sister crowed, triumphant.

"If Urik kills me, then you, too, shall pass beyond," I gasped.

I was rewarded with her silence, but I feared I had not cowed her with my words. Her quietude had an arrogant feel to it.

Soon I was completely lost. The trees surrounding me grew thicker, the ground hillier. I knew I must now be high in the hills surrounding the river valley. *If I could get high enough,* I thought to myself, *then perhaps I could find a break in the forest. See the sky or, even better, the sprawl of Mosby below.*

I pushed aside a bush and stepped out into space.

Then I was falling, rolling down the hill, my body careening into trees and branches in a cloud of leaves and breathless curses. I slammed into a rock, and the sickening crack of bone reached me. My scream was only silenced by my lack of breath. The world went black for a moment.

I came to rest on the banks of a stream. I woke, my face pressed to the smooth stones. The taste of blood was thick in my mouth.

Slowly, I gathered my hands beneath me, expecting the white hot stab of pain from whatever I had broken. Even prepared as I was, when I made to rise, the agony tore a fresh scream from my raw throat.

I looked aside, and saw the wet, red bone protruding through the flesh of my forearm. Shock had kept me from feeling it until I tried to bear my weight on the useless limb. I curled around my injured arm, water slowly seeping through my clothes as I lay on the sodden bank.

"It came from over here!" I heard a man say, followed by the crunch of sticks and leaves.

I managed to get to my knees, scrambling towards the dubious shelter of a holly bush. My eyes scanned the ridge I had fallen down. Perhaps my pursuers would fall, as I had. My good hand found a rock. The smooth, water-polished weight felt good in my hands.

"Here!" a second voice called out. I saw a face, Urik's, poke through the vegetation. His eyes scanned, back and forth, vigilant, hard as flint.

I wondered where the gentle buffoon I had left had gone, replaced with this implacable hunter. His gaunt face was all planes and shadows, a barbaric war mask, so very unlike the soft, round moon I remembered.

You should have killed him, my sister chortled. *Now he will never rest until you are dead.*

"But, why did he follow? I left him alive, didn't I? Even after all he did to me, I showed him mercy."

Mercy? Is that what you call it? she replied. *Surely he had to explain many things in the wake of Marcus's death. Surely the townsfolk suspected him in his murder, and in your disappearance. And, they were friends.*

"Do you really think you can hide from me?" Urik called down. "From us? Why not come out, where we can talk? We have much to speak of, I think. You and I."

I held my ground, and my tongue, biting back the bitter words that threatened to spill out. I remembered seeing Marcus's bow on his back. He could be holding it, even now, an arrow nocked to the string.

He turned aside, and engaged in a whispered conference with his men. A moment later, he faced the ravine once more. I heard movement, through the trees.

That will be his men, splitting up to cut off your retreat, my sister informed me, her self-satisfaction setting my teeth on edge. *You should just surrender. Urik was your husband, after all. He doubtless means to kill you quick, rather than have you endure the humiliation of rape.*

"Silence, you spiteful bitch!" I hissed aloud, momentarily forgetting myself.

Above me, Urik started at the sound. His eyes swept the bank.

"She's still here!" he called, left and right. "Move in and cut her off!" He disappeared, the sound of his running feet, the crash and snap of the leaves loud in the sudden silence.

I leaned back, just for a moment, and considered listening to my sister. My broken arm throbbed, a sensation that evoked a twinge of raw nausea in my stomach. Surrender would at least, I hoped, be quick.

Then I recalled Marcus beneath me, moaning my sister's name—my name now—begging me to forgive him for killing me. Killing *her*. Remembered the pale limbs in the moonlight, Kirin's sightless stare. Remembered the blood caked on the knife.

A howl of animal fury was torn from both of us. Inside, my sister thrashed like a beast in a cage, the memory dispelling her loathing for me, replacing it with the desire for red justice. I surged to my feet, nearly retching from pain, and stumbled upstream, along the bank.

Thank you, sister, she whispered, her voice as cold as a wolf's howl. *I forgot myself for a time, but now I remember. Beware; they will be close.*

I silenced my footfalls, stepping carefully from stone to stone, wary of snagging branches. With a thought, I reached inside and breathed across the sleeping power of my magic, shivering as it opened raw, crimson petals in my belly. In my mind's eye, the power was like a blood-thirsty plant, all fibrous, veined leaves and wicked thorns, black as the bottom of a well. It thirsted for the men's blood. For Urik's blood.

I heard a sound, a soft curse. One of them was close. I stopped, cradling my injured arm.

He stepped out from behind a tree, a brace of curved daggers held in a loose, knife-fighter's grip, perfect for the close-in work that the concealing foliage would necessitate. He was ten feet away. Close enough to see the whites of his startled eyes.

A moment later, he was screaming, the dropped knives lost in the weeds as he slapped his hands over his streaming sockets. Where his eyes had been were now only twin rivers of blood. The crimson tide flowed around his hands, through his fingers, flying towards me.

It pooled in my upraised palm, my flesh drinking in the fluid, and a bolt of sensual pleasure erupted in my thighs, in my sex. My broken arm tingled, like fire ants crawling beneath my skin.

I clenched my fingers, and his screams were choked into silence. Then I yanked, hard. The sensation of his life tearing free sent a jolt of unrestrained pleasure through me, tearing an answering moan from my lips.

He dropped, bonelessly, to the ground. His face was shriveled, like an old man's. His eyes were two yawning pits, eyeless and empty. Where they had gone, I knew not.

My arm still burned, but when I looked down I saw that my flesh had healed. Where the bone had protruded was now a pale scar. I flexed the hand, gingerly. A childish giggle escaped my lips.

The second man's knife took me from behind, slashing across my back. Suddenly, my legs had no strength, and I was falling, falling. I sprawled across the man I had killed, writhing.

Before I could turn, I felt my attacker drop onto me. His knee slammed down, brutally, crushing down into my lower spine as his fingers knotted in my hair. He yanked my head up, and laid his dagger across my throat.

"Just lay still, *avuna,*" the man breathed into my ear. "You've led us on a merry chase, but you're done now."

The blade at my throat was a deadly promise, and I froze, lest I cut myself with my struggles. The knee at my back was excruciating, and I felt bone grate as he pulled my head back further. He laughed, a sound so full of spite and wicked amusement that it brought tears to my eyes.

I opened my secret eye, and beheld the ghostly face of the first man. His milky eyes pled with me, but my need was greater than his fear. My wordless command sent him drifting back to his mortal shell.

"Urik was right about you, *avuna,*" my tormentor whispered in my ear. His breath was rank and hot against my neck. "Don't fear, I'll not be killing you just yet. I mean to enjoy you before slitting your throat."

"Stop . . . calling me . . . that . . ." I managed to croak. A short distance away, I saw the first man's corpse twitch and stir, heard the soft, tearing sound that I prayed would be my salvation.

"What? *Avuna?*" he asked. "Perhaps you're not a whore, but you will be soon. We'll make you scream, oh yes we will . . ."

His words faltered as the body flopped over, its back twisting, like a crushed snake. I heard the pop and tear of ripping flesh, of tearing sinew.

"Alric?" the man atop me said. "I feared the bitch had killed you. Come, let's . . ."

The sweetling stepped from the undergrowth. Its compact body was mostly skinless, three feet of wetly gleaming muscle. Bone spurs sprouted from its bulging limbs like thorns on a rose. Its face was dominated by a vast, yawning mouth, filled with needle teeth, below a single, madly staring eye.

My dark child paused, sniffing the air, the terrible head swiveling. Above me, I heard my tormentor curse. His fingers slackened their iron grip, and I felt the knife drop away.

I screamed and rolled, pushing him off with my unexpected move. He crashed into a tree, cursing, scrambling forward.

The sweetling moved like lightning, pouncing on his bent back. Long, barbed fingers encircled his throat, squeezing, cutting into flesh. My would-be murderer had time for one brief cry, before his neck surrendered to the awful pressure.

My sweet one let fall the body, staring down at it impassively. I moved to a fallen log, and sat, gingerly. My back was afire, blood running down, soaking my thighs.

There were two more with Urik, my sister warned. I nodded wearily, reaching out to the body with my blood magic. I needed his energy to heal my wound. No answering throb met my anxious probing. He was dead, his blood's vitality already gone. I cursed softly, and opened my secret eye once more.

The second sweetling was awake a moment later, joining his brother at my side. This one was handsomer, retaining most of his fleshy cocoon's features. A set of horns rose from his brow.

"Fetch me Urik's men," I whispered. "Be careful not to kill; I have need of them."

The pair looked at me for a moment, their opal eyes adoring, then, a moment later, they bolted into the forest. I rose and shambled after, the agony in my back tearing sobs from my chest.

I followed the sweetlings' trail through the woods, ripped plants and gouged tree trunks. My children were many things, but subtle was not one of them. The trail led me further upstream.

Within minutes, I heard a scream from ahead, and redoubled my pace. By the time I reached my children, they already had a third man down, his body lying half in the stream. Ribbons of blood threaded the clear water, issuing from a dozen gashes. The horned sweetling was burdened with his former companion's sword, the blade driven clear through its chest. It ignored the inconvenience. Its thorny limbs held him face-down in the water.

"Turn him," I whispered. "I do not want him to drown."

The sweetling flipped him, and the man gasped for air. When he saw me, saw my black eyes, he began to cry. Inside, the blood lust growled like a cat, a sound almost perfectly mirrored by my sister.

I walked to him and pressed my mouth to his, then allowed the blood magic to drive deep into his body. His screams were silenced by my hungry mouth. A second later, his life came up in a hot flood, spurting past my lips. The stolen vitality was like a bolt of liquid fire. I threw back my head, the blood sheeting down my chin and breasts, and laughed.

"Come," I ordered, dropping the empty shell. I rose, my body made whole once more made by the man's sacrifice. The sweetlings followed, falling in behind me.

I knew that Urik and the last man were still out there, somewhere. I headed downstream.

Soon, the sound of splashing reached me. They were not trying to be quiet. Their confidence made me grin.

Fools, my sister purred. *They should run.*

"It's too late for that," I whispered, and sent my children forward. I strolled down the stream, as fresh screams and shouts filled the air. I heard blades scraping on bone spurs, then the flat snap of a bow.

I stopped. The thrumming was repeated, as the archer let loose with a second shaft.

I hurried forward, into a clearing. The sweetlings, both of them, had the fourth man down, their limbs rising and falling like threshing tools, gathering their harvest of rent flesh and blood. The man twitched beneath them, curled tight around his vitals.

Across the clearing stood Urik, Marcus's hunting bow in his hands. They were shaking, and his shot missed the sweetling by feet. It ignored him, intent on ripping its former compatriot to shreds.

"Why?" I asked, and Urik looked at me. He dropped the fresh arrow he was pulling from his quiver. His eyes went wide in his lean face as he took in my blood-smeared body, my blacked eyes.

"I . . . you killed Marcus," he said.

"He killed my sister. He deserved death."

"Not like that," he spat. "What you did . . ." he shivered.

I stood, impassive, as my children finished with the fourth man. Urik watched the process, his horror-filled eyes wide. My sister was right: he should have run.

When his struggles stopped, I opened my third eye, whispered the command to his shade. My third sweetling pulled from its fleshy prison a moment later, joining his brothers. With each birth I felt a small part of me diminish, drained by the effort of compelling the fallen soul.

I looked at Urik. His eyes, when they met mine, were still full of the same defiant rage and apocalyptic love as I had seen before. Even facing the explicit threat of the triplets, he did not run. A thought came to me.

"You wanted this," I said. "You sought me out because you knew that doing so would be your death."

He began to stammer a denial, his face reddening, as I remembered it did when I caught him in some lie. A profound sadness filled me.

Of course he desired death, my sister whispered. *You took everything from him. His friend, his wife: everything that made him important, leaving behind a broken, used up thing. Making such half-formed horrors is your one true calling.*

The words cut deep, sawing across the cords of my raving bloodlust, bringing me back to myself. Urik dropped the useless bow and quiver, then sank to his knees.

"So end it," he said, resigned. "Whatever you've become, the woman I married . . . the woman I loved . . . is every bit as dead as Marcus."

"You're wrong," I said, calling back my sweetlings. "I live, and love, despite your best efforts to kill me. To twist me into some pale ghost of the woman I was."

My children came to heel, arraying themselves behind me. They stirred and hissed; they could feel my rage, and my sister's. They hungered to rip, and tear, and destroy, anything that might harm me.

Kill him! My sister screamed. *Kill! He does not deserve life!*

I walked to Urik's side, reached down and stroked his rough cheek. I tried to remember a time when I was happy with him, when things were different, but no memory came. Still, I had made a vow, sworn in the sight of the gods.

Weak, useless vows sworn under duress, she spat. *The words meant nothing. You have already broken their most cherished laws. You are beyond them.*

The blood magic sang inside of me, threading its obsidian melody through my sister's words. It would be so simple.

"Go," I breathed. "Go, and never seek me out again. If we ever meet again, then one of us will surely die."

Urik blinked up at me, and suddenly there was the man I remembered. Weak. Indecisive. Pathetic. The thought of tasting his blood, of raising a child from his flesh, sickened me.

"Go!" I thundered, my bellow shattering the allure of the music. The cry woke an answering hiss from the sweetlings.

Urik flinched as if I had slapped him. Then he was running, the sweetlings at his heels, nipping and biting. His thrashings faded, slowly, as he fled.

I bent and picked up Marcus's bow. Before that moment, I had never taken a trophy.

CHAPTER FIFTEEN

I am dreaming.

Unusual for me, that. My sister used to have such vivid dreams, visions of elegant people and far-off places. Most mornings, meeting her at our shared garden wall, she would tell me of them, describing every small detail of every phantasm she had met that night. Myself, I seldom saw anything in the black between sleep and waking, or if I did, I forgot.

But now, I dream.

I am in my mother's house, surrounded by her things. The proud clock; the threadbare rug; the good silver that we never used, winking in its locked cabinet. The house is quiet but not still. Somehow I know that there are others here with me.

I look up the stairs; somewhere above me, a baby cries. I start up, surprised to find that I am a little girl again. The steps seem weirdly tall to my child's legs.

The crying comes from the last room at the end of the hall. My old room. Our old room. A woman's voice speaks softly, soothingly, the words indistinguishable.

I pause with my hand on the knob. What if she does not want to be disturbed? Mother was always so adamant that polite young ladies did not interrupt adults when they were busy, and I want so badly to be good.

The sound of the baby's happy gurgle decides me, and I open the door. Inside, our old room is empty. All the toys I remember: the dollhouse with the tiny, gilt furniture; the shelf of porcelain figurines; the hobby-horse beneath the window overlooking the yard; all missing.

The beds and wardrobe are gone as well. Nothing sits on the polished wooden floor save a single rocking chair. In it, a woman with long, pale hair sits, a babe at her breast.

I come around, and look into her emerald eyes. They are white, not black. Certainly not black. She looks down at the babe, a warm smile spreading across her lips, then bends to brush a kiss across his forehead.

He is a chubby little thing, all pale, waving limbs and perfect, pink skin. His pudgy fists grasp a strand of her hair, holding it tight, like a charm.

She cannot see me. This does not disturb me; I am happy to simply watch the exchange between mother and child, to witness this most intimate embrace.

"Kirin," I hear my mother say, as she walks down the hall, "do you need anything?"

"No, mother, I'm just fine," she replies. "We're just fine, aren't we?" she whispers to the child. He smiles back at her, the plump nipple still in his mouth.

A wave of vertigo sweeps over me. Is this really Kirin? Or is it myself? I know that what I am seeing never happened. Kirin seldom visited my parents after Vanessa, her daughter, was born, and Mother never got around to having Father clean out our old room.

I decide that it does not matter. The look of placid, calm love on the woman's face, mine or my sister's, makes all such concerns trivial. The babe's eyes close, slowly, until he is sleeping, his lips still working fitfully at the breast. Kirin's face, my face, is filled with such love. It makes my heart ache, even as it swells.

I lie down on the boards as weariness sweeps over me. Warm sunlight spills through the open window, the golden beam alive with dancing dust. I wish then that I never had to leave this room, to end this moment. To keep that woman in the chair, the babe in her lap, forever.

I wake to the smell of clean hay and animals.

I lie, staring at the roof beams above, tears stinging my eyes. I want to close them, to try to return to that moment, but I know it is gone.

I sigh and roll onto my side. I see Lia, lying on a pallet opposite me, her back to the rough wood wall. Seeing her there, her cheek pillowed on her hands, reminds me of just how young she is. Little more than a child.

She is only a few years younger than you, my sister reminds me. *She may even be older than you were when you married Urik.*

"It's not just her age," I whisper back. "Up until now, she's led a sheltered life, filled with family and school. She knows little of the real world."

Well, she knows now, doesn't she? she asks. I nod, remembering that Lia has helped Ato deal with the sick and the wounded in the hell of the mercy tent. Has tended the dead. Whatever she is now, I know that she will never be young again.

In the delicate, blue light that precedes the dawn, her skin and hair are pale beacons, shining like snow. She frowns, her brows drawing down, as something in her dream troubles her, then turns over.

I rise, wincing at the tenderness in my breasts as I sit. It has lasted for days. As soon as I am upright, a wave of nausea ripples through my belly.

I hurry from the stall, doing my best to be quiet. Others have taken shelter in the barn, many still slumbering on their rude beds of hay, and I do not wish to disturb them. Soon enough they will be submerged in the new day's share of pain and hardship; let them float in dreams for a bit longer.

As soon as I am outside, what little is in my stomach comes up in a heaving rush, spattering the wooden walls. I crouch in the acrid stench, miserable, until the spasms subside.

"Kirin?" a voice asks, behind me. "Are you unwell?"

I turn to face her, a wry smile on my face, unexpectedly embarrassed. "I'm fine, Lia. Just a bit under the weather."

"Well, no wonder. You have had a rough few days. As have we all. Come, we should find something to eat," she says, offering me a helping hand.

The sickness has driven away the last lingering sensations of peace that followed me from the dream. I am fully awake now, fully in the world, submerged in its stink and squalor. I wish I could crawl back into my nest of soft hay. Could close my eyes and return to that sunny, warm room.

We walk through the waking camp, threading our way between the tents and wagons scattered about the yard. The smells of smoke and cooking porridge waft on the breeze. The aroma wakes fresh echoes of roiling sickness in my stomach.

"My nurse always used to say 'The fevered need feeding'," Lia says, oblivious to my discomfort. She looks at me. "Do you have a fever?"

"I'm not sure. I don't think so," I manage to say, swallowing down the desire to vomit. "I can't afford to be sick just now."

We come to a freshly rebuilt fire, ringed by refugees. An iron cook pot hangs over the flames, tended by an aged goodwife in an apron. When she sees me, she waves me forward, to the front of the line.

Several people greet me, genuine warmth in their voices, as I get my breakfast. Many thank me for my help, or for helping their loved ones. I make promises to check on some of those needing bandages changed.

Finally, Lia hustles me away, two bowls in her hands, telling the people that I need to eat. We find a wagon, and sit on the back. Looking at me, she laughs.

"What?" I ask, taking my bowl. At the sight of the porridge, my stomach roils slowly, but I eat anyway. Food should not be wasted.

"Your face," Lia says, answering my question. "It must have been a long time since people were actually appreciative of your skills."

I shrug. All that is in the past. If the people turn on me again, or if Ato finds some new charge of witchery to level at me—I will deal with it then.

Lia watches me struggle with the food, frowning a bit. I gag when I bring a fresh bite to my lips, and her eyes go wide. "How long have you had the sickness?" she asks, nodding towards my barely-touched breakfast. She is smiling now, practically beaming.

"A few days. Don't worry, I never get sick for long. It will pass." Her radiant grin disarms me; it is so at odds with everything that has happened. I wonder what I have said to evoke it. Mentally, I shrug. Who can know why young people do what they do?

"Oh, it will likely pass, worry not," she says, oblivious to my look. "My sister-in-law was sick to death in the mornings for nearly four months with her first. But it passed, eventually. After, she felt wonderful."

"Her first what?" I ask.

Lia gives me a long look, her smile changing to an expression of confusion. "Why, with her first child, of course. I am very excited for you, Kirin. Tell me, who is the father?"

I cannot reply. All I can do is sit, mouth opening and closing, my chest moving air into my lungs, mechanically, despite the growing weight pressing down on them. It feels heavier than a mountain, crushing me down.

Why, her first pregnancy, of course. Tell me, who is the father? Her words echo in my head, repeating over and over. *First pregnancy. Father.*

"Kirin? What is wrong? You are scaring me."

I jump from the wagon, my feet clumsy, and nearly stumble. "No," I mutter, walking towards the nearest fire.

"That can't be right. I must have caught ill, what with all these people crammed together. This is just a sickness."

"Kirin?" Lia repeats. "I did not mean to pry. If you do not wish to speak of the baby I—"

"There is no baby!" I scream, whirling to face her. She stops, her eyes wide, mouth open. "There is no baby," I repeat, shaking my head.

"But . . . the morning sickness. And the nausea at food. It is just like when my—"

"I cannot have children," I say, spitting the words like venom. "I was married, before. We . . . I cannot have children like other women."

I had no trouble getting with child, my sister says. I can almost see the smug smile on her lips.

Has it never occurred to you that we are twins? That it might have been Urik's fault, not yours, that no child quickened in your womb? Women are never supposed to imply that a man is incapable, but you know that sometimes they are. Besides, you and Jazen Tor certainly had enough occasions to make a little one, did you not?

Her words, the unvarnished truth of them, stops me in my tracks. Lia says something, putting her hand on my shoulder, but I cannot hear her through the denials echoing through my head.

It cannot be, I whisper to myself. It must not be. Not a baby. Not mine. Not from my damaged, sorry womb. Not me. Not a baby. It must not be. It must not be.

But it is. You know it to be true.

I walk a few, faltering steps. I have lost all sense of direction. Me, a tracker. Lost and confused.

A pack of children run past, grubby boys and girls in tattered shifts, laughing at some game, their spirits unbroken by the misery about them. Pure, defiant joy is in their voices.

Then, without knowing how, I am kneeling in the mud, weeping, still protesting, pressing my face into Lia's chest as she holds me. She strokes my hair, whispering assurances, her confusion evident in every word.

All I can do is cling to her, like a shipwreck survivor holding fast to some piece of flotsam, struggling with all the strength I have to keep my head above the black tide.

My sister, for once, is silent.

"So, YOU REALLY DID NOT KNOW?" Lia repeats, for the dozenth time. I sigh, and Livinia, the midwife, chuckles.

"It's not uncommon to miss the signs the first time," the older woman says, smiling. "And, to answer your question, yes, deary, you are most certainly with child. May Balasha, the Lady of the Wood, shower her favor upon you."

"Don't let the priests hear you say that name," I say, automatically. "They dislike the competition."

The midwife snorts. "Let 'em dislike it all they want. The people here know who I am, and know my skill. It'll take more than some blowhard in a homespun robe and an upstart, newcomer goddess to scare me." She hawks and spits elaborately into the fire.

I find myself liking this rangy old woman, with her cheerful blasphemy and coarse manners.

The three of us sit beside Livinia's fire. She has built it near the edge of the yard, where we can have a modicum of privacy. Blankets hang from ropes strung between a nearby tree and her wagon, creating a simple wall, hiding my body from curious eyes.

I straighten my clothes, not wanting Lia to see my scars, then laugh at my modesty. Livinia puts away the simple tools of her trade in her purse, chatting all the while.

"There are herbs you'll be wanting to gather; teas that will help with the morning sickness and the thinning of the blood that you may fall prey to. I can help you find them."

"I know them," I say, distantly, my mind still mostly elsewhere.

"Kirin is a healer," Lia says proudly, patting my shoulder.

Livinia nods, and pulls some dried plants from her satchel. "Of course she is. I'm not senile you know. Well, here's some to get you started, until you can gather more. Do you have a mortar and pestle?"

"No, I . . . that is . . . perhaps . . . if I could borrow yours, goodwoman . . ."

"Of course, deary, of course. Whatever you and the babe need, just ask."

The babe. The concept is still so strange to me, so bizarre. I had been so sure that I was barren. That I could never know the joy of motherhood. So sure that my sweetlings were the only life that I could bring into the world—

My sweetlings.

I come to my feet. My fingers fly across the fastenings of my gear.

"What's wrong?" Lia asks, frowning.

"I must attend to something," I say.

The sweetlings. I left them in the ditch beside the road. I think of them laying there, corpses, yet terribly alive and aware, and a gnawing horror swells in my breast. Until this moment, the thought of my dear ones always filled me with a warm glow. Until now, they were my most cherished companions.

Now, the memory of their flayed bodies and ravaged faces fills me with a disgust so profound that, for a moment, it drives the breath from my chest. They must be dealt with. Must be released. Must be destroyed.

I hurry through the camp, ignoring the hails and greetings. Soon, I am on the muddy track leading back to the main road. Lia follows behind.

"Kirin, what is it? Is it those . . . I will not call them your children. Not now," she says.

I nod, then, realizing she cannot see the gesture, say, "Aye."

Unease swells in my breast as I approach the ditch where I left them. I realize that I dread seeing their skinless, horrible forms. Memories of other sweetlings, other men that I have destroyed, buffet me like dark wings.

I think of the dream, of the woman and the babe, so full of light and joy, and the memory fills me with a bone-deep horror. Dear gods, what have I done? What have I brought into this world? No matter that I had good reason at the time; I know better now.

Soon enough, I know I will have to face this strange, new life that the gods have seen fit to serve me. I can bear children, as other women can. I am not broken, not damaged. The thought is huge and overwhelming.

I shake my head, trying to clear it. Time enough to think on that later. For now I cannot, I *must* not, think about it, lest I be turned aside from what I must do.

We round a bend, and I see a form in the road. I recognize its pale, torn skin and bloodied limbs even at a distance. I curse, a chill running through me.

The sweetling has left the ditch where I commanded it to stay. Even before I reach it, I can see that something is terribly wrong.

Its arm drags behind it, nearly severed, trailing in the muck. The other is missing altogether, leaving behind naught but a white stump of bone. Terrible violence has carved gouges in its tough hide, spilling the remains of its entrails to the ground. As I watch, it tangles its feet in the slick, gray ropes, stumbling to its knees.

It looks up at me, beseeching with its ravaged face. Laru, the man who, in his first life, died from a staved-in chest.

Now something even worse has added to its—to his—suffering.

I recognize the wounds at once. Only one thing, save the Mor, has the strength to inflict such terrible wounds. Could have so deeply cut my minion.

Hollern. My blood turns to snow in my veins, cold and thick.

"Oh, gods, Kirin," Lia says, as Laru slips in the wet tangle once more, this time falling on its ravaged arm. The sound of bone grating against bone is indescribable. "End this. Please, make it to *stop*." She turns away, her hand on her mouth.

I approach my swee . . . my minion, and reach out, but cannot bear the thought of touching its leathery skin. The thing that was Laru looks at me, its one remaining eye pleading.

"Go," I croak, turning away, not daring to look as his soul floats free. The thought of what I might see in his face, whether it be love or condemnation, it is too awful to bear.

Behind me, I hear the papery rustle as Laru's mortal shell succumbs. The body gives one final sigh, then all is still.

Lia's sobs reach me. She kneels in the mud, heedless of her silks, head bowed. Perhaps it is for the best; they are already ruined. Nothing will ever get them white again.

"Come on," I say, helping her to her feet. "We have to find Hollern."

She nods and follows, scrubbing at her tear-stained cheeks. Her hand smears mud, black as sorrow, black as sin, across her cheek. The mark is livid, like a brand, or war paint.

Finally, I reach the place where I left them. The signs of a struggle are obvious: the mud is a trampled mess, filled with my minions' taloned tracks. Laru's severed claw lies in the muck, half devoured. Two sets of tracks lead from the pit, one towards the road, a second back towards the dark woods.

"What does this mean?" Lia asks, peering at the tracks. "Where is the other one?"

"Gone. After it attacked its broth . . . after it attacked Laru, Hollern must have headed off in that direction," I say, pointing along its trail.

"Why would it do that?" she asks.

"I don't know," I whisper, the words tumbling into me and through me like icicles. "They have always obeyed me in the past."

Before you decided to betray them, you mean, my sister whispers. *Before you got it into your head that they were abominations, just like the priests say.*

"They are abominations," I reply. "I just couldn't see that before. Things are different now . . ."

Now that you're like every other woman, she spits. *Weak and burdened with a child. Soft and helpless. Easy prey for the next man who takes a mind to having you. Shall you spread your legs for every dumb farmer and cowherd, now that you know they can plant a baby in your belly?*

"Shut up," I say, beating my head with my fists. "Shut up, you hateful, hateful thing. I should never have called you back."

"Kirin?" Lia asks, drawing back, her face full of fear. I barely notice.

You shall be like every other woman, toiling in the dirt to feed an endless chain of crying, hungry mouths. Always taking, taking, never giving. Taking from your body first, suckling until your breasts bleed and sag, then taking your love, like a rushalka, *feeding on your own heart blood. Draining you dry, until there's nothing left. But, you already know what that's like now, don't you dear sister? Why, you're an expert on that red art, aren't you?*

"Shut up!" I scream, my nails scratching at my cheeks, drawing blood, which runs down my cheeks like tears. "Shut your lying mouth! My baby is no *rushalka*. Nor am I! I'll kill you if you say that again!" I snatch the dagger from my hip, stare into the seductive glitter that plays along its edge.

Jazen showed me how to hone a blade like that. How to strop it against the stone just so, feeling for the right angle, until the edge was sharper than a razor, able to split a drifting hair.

The memory of his kind eyes, staring into mine as he moved above me in the half light of the camp fire, closing but never judging as my nails drew blood, like they always did, from his back, is like a cool mist against my fevered mind. My hand goes limp, allowing the dagger to fall.

"Vanessa was never like that," I whisper. "She was never a burden. She was the light of your sorry life, sister. She was all you had to live for. You loved her more than anything. More than even me. She was the only good thing to come from your union with Marcus, and you know it."

Inside, my sister falls still, but I can sense that she is not at peace. I can feel her, coiled, like a snake, nearly trembling with fury.

"I shall not be as other women," I say, louder this time. "No man shall ever own me, not now, not ever. Never doubt that."

I stand and look at Lia. She looks back, the lightning flashing in her eyes. I realize that, had I continued to rave, and tear at myself, she likely would have lashed out. If I say the wrong thing, she still might; she is terrified. The sight of my madness has unnerved her worse than any undead horror could.

"Lia, I'm sorry dear heart, I really am. A madness came upon me, but . . . I'm better now. Really. Lia, please, put your hand down. I would never harm you."

I wonder if I will even feel the bolt as it sears my life away, then realize that I do not care. My only regret is for the babe. The innocent one that will never feel the kiss of the sun against its brow. The joy of a mother's embrace.

Then she is in my arms, saying how sorry she is for what she almost did. I shush her, stroking her dark hair, telling her that it's all right. That the madness has passed. We cling to one another, as if the safety of our immortal souls rests in the hands of the other.

All the while, deep, deep inside, in her secret, black cave, my sister seethes and coils.

Later, when we have regained our composure, Lia and I set off along Hollern's trail. The bright morning is already hot, the pewter sky promising nothing.

Within the hour, we spot his first victim.

The bull must have charged him, must have smelled the wrongness that surrounds him like a pestilent cloud. There is clotted, vile blood on its horns, different from the crimson flood all around. The bull never stood a chance.

The sight of the torn entrails and sundered ribs evokes a fresh wave of nausea, twisting in my belly like worms. I need not approach to recognize the signature of Hollern's barbed hooks.

After killing the bull, Hollern must have tried to eat; there are gobbets of flesh all over, most bearing teeth marks, but this was a token feast. Most of the meat is still here, scattered all about.

"His hunger can never be sated with simple meat," I say, shivering.

"What will appease him?" Lia asks.

"I do not know. Before now, my . . . they always did my bidding without question. The few that tried to eat abandoned the gesture soon after. No, this was something else."

"Murder," Lia breathes. "So much hate. So much pain. Who was he?"

I shake my head. Who Hollern was before he died does not matter. All that matters now is that one of my former children has, somehow, slipped beyond my mastery, and is roaming the forest ahead. The forest that people live in, and near. That shelters them and provides them with wood.

If Hollern finds any of them, they'll stand no chance at all.

It's not hard to see where he entered the wood. Hollern, in death as in life, is a very poor woodsman. A one-eyed child could follow his tracks.

Silently, we enter the trees' cool shadow.

CHAPTER SIXTEEN

The three sweetlings I called from Urik's henchmen were my companions during the first few weeks of my long journey north. I wanted to return to my cottage, to my narrow, warm bed and dry roof and sturdy hearth, but that was unthinkable. Urik must have told someone why he had come, must have informed the authorities of my terrible crimes.

No. They would be waiting for me. Waiting to take me back, to pay for what I had done. Every desperate man from Mosby to the Armitage would want the reward that was doubtless on my neck. My only protection was in movement.

Still, on many cold nights, as I moved higher into the mountains' foothills, I would think about the crackling fire and the fragrant, drying herbs hanging from the rafters. I would remember the small, secret garden and the satisfaction I had felt in planting it, so full of the promise of comfort and healing, and would weep.

Spring in the highlands was wet and damp, full of icy rain and treacherous mud. I was grateful for the warmth of the thick woolen shirt and the oiled leathers that I had taken from Urik's men. Game, at least, was plentiful, the fields dotted with deer in the early mornings and evenings.

I wasted half of Marcus' arrows trying to learn the rudiments of the weapon. Even after I could finally loose a shaft, I soon learned that hitting a moving target, like a fleeing deer, was harder still.

In desperation, I stalked and shot one of the slow-moving *gepar* that were also common in those parts. I had heard that their meat was poison, but my empty belly compelled me. The blood that streamed from its pierced belly was bluish black. I ended its suffering with my knife, gagging in the acrid reek.

I left the kill for whatever scavengers that wanted it. I needed to find a sick, slow deer, or any other animal with four legs. Those I knew I could eat.

I could have easily sent the sweetlings to run my prey to ground, but I knew that one day, not so very far from now, they would not be at my side to defend me. I needed to learn how to use the bow.

It was a joyous day, indeed, when I finally managed to shoot one of the thrice-damned deer in the neck. The animal ran off, my shaft protruding from its throat, but I knew it was done for. I commanded my children to go after it and end its suffering, and they staggered off, limping on their stiffening limbs.

That night, I feasted on roast venison, stuffing myself until I could eat no more. My children watched me while I ate, occasionally mimicking me, putting bones and other scraps into their terrible mouths and chewing, messily, fat and gristle drooling down their chins. Their desire to be more human warmed me, and I did not scold them for their foolishness.

I continued to practice, drawing targets on trees with charcoal and shooting until my fingertips bled and my shoulders burned. Eventually, the wounds hardened to tough calluses. Still I practiced, shooting again and again and again, until four out of every five shafts I loosed could hit a palm-wide circle from fifty paces.

Spring was ripening into summer when I realized that my children's time was near. Their bodies had grown nearly immobile, dried as old leather. Ever faithful, they tried their best to do my bidding, but they were so slow, so clumsy.

Watching them shambling, like old men, brought tears to my eyes.

The trials of the road had depleted all of my hard-won winter fat; my body was lean and tough, my hands the rough, callused paws of a working man. My breasts, never overlarge in the best of times, shrank until they were mere suggestions of womanhood. I did not miss them. What good were they? I would never suckle a babe. They would only get in the way.

On the night of the first summer moon, I sent their spirits on, apologizing to them for my selfishness. I should have released them weeks before, not held them in their decaying shells, watching themselves be reduced from the fierce warriors they had been to such pathetic, shambling things. I scattered their ashes on the wind and continued on my journey.

Summer was short and tumultuous in the North. The days were not the blistering, humid things I remembered from my girlhood; here they were pleasant, almost cool, usually preceding bitterly cold nights as icy winds flowed down the mountains' flanks. Even in the height of summer, when the sun would only dip for a few short hours below the western horizon, the implacable stone teeth glimmered with snow.

Storms would arise, often without warning, as clouds dark as bruises scuttled out unexpectedly from behind the peaks, pregnant with the amethyst flashes of lightning. I learned hard lessons there: how to avoid being crushed in a sudden mud slide; how to read the wind and smell rain from afar. How to read directions from signs graven in the earth and upon trees when no celestial markers were visible.

I never stopped moving during those brief summer months; I wanted to put as much distance as I could between my past and my present. By the time the autumn storms filled the passes with snow, I had already staked out half a dozen likely camps, mainly caves, which I filled with whatever rude supplies I could find.

Even as tough as I had become, that next winter nearly killed me. Lacking proper provisions, blankets or proper winter clothes, I soon fell prey to a constant, wracking cough. I knew my body lacked the resources to sustain me if I fell abed for too long.

As I weakened, my sister grew more and more quiet, until she finally stopped speaking to me altogether. Even then, she still had the power to compel me, when I was deeply asleep. Sometimes, I would dream of her, nightmarish, fever dreams, filled with blood and darkly clotted knives. Upon waking, I would discover that I was outside, in the bitter wind, the cold slicing through my pathetic clothes. As I scrambled back to shelter, I would hear the ghostly echo of her laughter.

I feared that, if I did not do something, one night my sister would take over my sleeping body and walk it off a cliff. Or that she would lead me so far from the cave that I would lack the strength to return.

The nights grew longer, until the sun only showed its face for less than a quarter of each day. My food was nearly gone, and I was too feeble and scatterbrained to remember the route to my other, hidden caches.

"It looks as if you'll finally get your wish, dearest sister," I croaked one night. The last meager scraps of firewood smoked in the shallow pit, throwing off fitful sparks. "I'm only sorry that I've picked such a dismal place to die in. I know you always hated winter, and now here I am, dying in a place where winter lasts for more than a year at a stretch."

Despite myself, I smiled, my chapped lips splitting, blood trickling down my chin. I licked the salty drops, greedily, my body responding of its own volition, as if I could get sustenance from myself.

I do not know how much later it was when I heard the sound. A strange bleating reached my ears from somewhere outside. I opened my crusted eyes and tried to rise. After many attempts, I finally managed to totter to my feet, the effort costing me the last of my waning strength. When I lay down again, I knew I would not rise.

Outside, blinking in the sudden glare of sun on snow, I saw the cause of the ruckus. A gepar, its shaggy winter coat spiked with icicles, struggled a few hundred yards downslope. Two of its six legs were broken, on its left side, and it tottered, ungainly and barely moving, through the deep drifts. The beast's dark, blue-black blood trailed behind, up the mountain, doubtless to the spot where it had met whatever unhappy accident had crippled it.

My eyes snapped to the dark trail, fixing there as if pinned. Blood. Inside, I felt the first predatory tingle, as my power reacted to the sight.

"The flesh of anything with six legs is poisonous," I mumbled to myself, half raving. I draped myself across an icy boulder, too cold to even shiver.

"To eat its flesh is death. Death. Dead death die. But what of the blood? Oh, what of the warm, warm blood? So warm and steamy . . . warmth worth dying for?"

Groaning, I pushed off from my rocky island, praying that I could stagger close enough to the beast before my legs finally gave out.

I DO NOT KNOW WHAT I LOOKED LIKE to the people of the small village, but it must have been a frightening sight. People, gathered together to draw water from the unfrozen warm springs, scattered as I stumbled into the square, I remember that much.

A savage, unearthly vitality sang within my veins, a gift of the gepar's sacrifice. To this day, I do not remember the journey down the mountain; all reason was driven away the moment that the blood magic violated the beast's body, pulling forth its essence. My skin drank in the beast's blood, plunging me into a whirling gyre of rushing noise and purpleblack light. My heart throbbed in my chest, racing, as if I had run for miles, making my pulse sing and my head spin.

Ice and snow covered me, transforming my pale hair into an icy crown. I should have died high above, but with the gepar's vitality in my veins, I did not even shiver. I did not know if something in the beast's venomous blood caused me to black out, or if my lapse had been the result of my extreme sickness, but it seemed as if, for the moment, the worst of the danger was behind me.

All I cared about was that, right now, the deadly cough and pressure that had squatted in my chest for weeks was gone. I did not know if I was destined to lose fingers and toes to frostbite, but at least I would not die. Not today.

I saw a sign, a rude image of a horse that I guessed marked an ale house or tavern, and lurched off down the village's single street. Halfway there, I slipped to one knee on the frozen ground, got to my feet, and then stumbled a second time, this time landing heavily on my side. I lay there, groaning, for some minutes, cursing the timid villagers under my breath. The vitality I had stolen was fading rapidly.

The crunch of footsteps approached from behind, and a moment later a bulky shadow fell across me. "Well now, isn't this a sight?" a deep, masculine voice asked. I flopped onto my back, craned my head to see who had spoken.

He was old, his long, iron-gray hair pulled back in a tail, but moved with the fluid grace of a younger man. His thick beard was crusted with ice. Sunburned skin surrounded pale, gray eyes the color of winter storm clouds. When he smiled down at me, deep lines spread out from those eyes.

His was a face carved deep by laughter, and I found myself, despite the cold and the terrible throbbing in my head, smiling back.

"You'll catch your death, lying in the snow. You know that, yes?" He laughed, a sound that, somehow, was not mocking or cruel, and my smile widened. Dressed in his bulky woolens and furs, with his beard streaming across his barrel chest, he looked like a bear walking on its hind legs.

"Well, then, perhaps you can help me up, since you're so wise and strong?" I managed to reply, struggling to sit up. His large, red-knuckled hands wrapped themselves around my arms, then lifted me, as if I were no heavier than a child.

Perhaps I wasn't. Months of wandering, followed by weeks of sickness, had left me not so much thin as gaunt. Setting me on my feet, his smile faltered just a bit.

"Lass, for truth, are you ill?" he asked, peering at me.

I shook my head. "I'm . . . just very tired. I walked down from the mountains–" I stopped, as his eyes filled with doubt.

"Walked? Dressed like that?" he asked, shaking his head at my tattered woolens. Then a moment later, he turned, addressing the villagers still milling curiously about. "Does anyone know this girl, or her family?" he asked. They shook their heads, averting their eyes. One, a pretty mother, her babe cradled inside her thick, woolen coat, sketched a warding sign at me.

"I do not lie, ser," I said, dropping into the stilted tones I had learned from my mother. "For truth, I have walked far today. I am merely weary, not mad, but I thank you for your kind assistance."

He put up his hands, the smile returning to his eyes. "Oho, 'ser' am I now? I think not. No gentleman am I, lass. I apologize for doubting you, but I can't see how a slip of a thing such as yourself managed the trick of walking so far without so much as a coat . . . " He trailed off, awaiting my explanation.

"I wish I could explain it," I lied, dropping my eyes. "I was very sick, and was sheltering in a cave. I remember wanting to get down the mountain, for my food was gone and I was so very cold. I must have stumbled out into the snow."

Very prettily lied, my sister said venomously. *Shall you tell him you are a virgin, next? The oaf seems to think you're just a girl. Perhaps his tastes run in that direction, and you can seduce away his furs.*

He looked at me for a long while, as if puzzled. Then he shook his head. "Well, however you got here, it's a miracle that you didn't freeze, thanks be to Shanira. The passes are treacherous this time of year, and even the boldest of heart fear to venture too high in such weather."

I nodded, realizing that my bow and knife must still be in the cave. How would I ever find them again? While I stood and fretted, lost in my thoughts, the man spoke again, rousing me.

"Cry your pardon?" I said, snapping back to the moment.

"Hoo, you're an odd bird, I'll grant you that, girl," he laughed, slapping his knee. "I asked if you'd care to be my guest over at the Stallion over yonder." He pointed at the alehouse I had seen before, and I nodded, eager to be out of the cold.

Over a meal of roast mutton and highland greens eaten next to the tavern's roaring fire, Rory, for that was his name, told me his story. While he spoke, I slowly and quite painfully forced the cold from my half-frozen body. At first I was too chilled to even shiver, but soon enough great tremors shook my limbs. I still felt wretched, more dead than alive, but the sensation of food in my belly and the fire's radiant heat convinced me that I would survive.

Rory told me that he was a widower, and had been for almost as long as I had been alive. He, like I, had never been blessed with a child. After the passing of his wife, he had left the house they had built together and simply wandered.

He made a living for a while as a trapper, a profitable vocation for one with his skills, but eventually sickened of the killing of animals simply for their hides. While roaming the highland passes one day, he came across an army patrol, lost in the maze-like channels of a glacier, and led them down to safety. The good fortune was his as well.

"I became their scout," he said past a mouthful of meat. "Their captain trusted me, y'see, and feared to be lost worse than he hated spending his gold, so it all worked out well. When he finally retired from the field, he recommended me to some of his junior officers. I've worked every campaign season since. It's been a good life."

He stared into the fire, sipping from a deep cup of ale, musing over years gone by, or so I assumed. I flexed my tingling fingers in the delicious warmth, holding them, outspread, towards the fire. The same energy that had cured my growing pneumonia must have also spared my flesh from frostbite. Hearing him speak, an idea came to me.

"Can you follow tracks through weather like this?" I asked, gesturing to the shuttered windows. Outside, the wind moaned across the eaves. He nodded.

"Aye. For a time, anyway. But, once the snow starts falling, the tracks will be gone. Why, lass?"

"I left my bow in the cave, along with a knife that's most dear to me," I said.

"You know how to shoot?" he asked, raising his eyebrows. He eyed my corded arms, and I nodded.

"Show me," he commanded, all business now. He rose and lifted his longbow and quiver from the pile of possessions next to the table.

I did not want to go back outside, but I could tell that this was important to him. As I rose, my head resumed its throbbing. I pushed aside the discomfort. As we walked through the door, he draped his cloak across my shoulders. It trailed behind me as we walked around to the back of the tavern.

Rory scribed a rude target on the wall of a barn with a bit of charcoal while I, thirty paces away, strung his bow. It was massive, heavier than even Marcus', but I knew that it was not beyond me. I reached back and drew forth an arrow, fitting it smoothly to the string.

Why are you doing this? To impress him? my sister asked, scorn threaded between each word. I ignored her, focusing only on the small, black circle.

My first shot struck wide of the mark by several inches. My second hit the circle's perimeter. After that, it was child's play to put each shaft into the chest-wide circle.

"Oho, lass, you weren't lying! Well done," Rory said, clapping. He pried the arrows from the wood and walked to me, throwing a heavy arm across my shoulders. "Come. Let's go back inside, where it's warm. We need to retrieve your bow, after all."

"Why?"

"Because, lass, I think you might be able to help me with a most important, and potentially profitable, task."

Arm in arm, we walked back into the tavern's smoky warmth.

CHAPTER·SEVENTEEN

Lia and I follow Hollern's trail for the rest of the day, pausing only to quench our thirst and eat a handful of wild berries. As we crouch beside the first stream, I realize that I have left my pack, and my bow, back at the farm. I curse myself for my haste; I feel half-dressed without the weapon across my back. All the rest of that day, my hand often reaches back for it, probing, like a man with a missing tooth will unconsciously tongue the empty socket.

At least I have my knife, I tell myself, trying not to listen to my sister's laughter at the idea of facing Hollern armed with only a foot of sharpened steel. He must obey me, when I can stand before him and look into his eyes. He must.

Light is still in the sky, reflecting from the clouds in shades of rose and gold, when I finally call a halt. I can still make out Hollern's trail, but I know that this far inside the woods darkness falls rapidly. I want the chance to build a proper fire while I can still count on Lia's help. I am well used to sleeping on the bare ground and eating whatever sustenance comes to hand, but Lia is not like me.

If Hollern comes, *when* he comes, I want Lia well-rested and alert.

My flint is in the pouch at my hip, along with some snares, and soon the fire is crackling in a ring of stones. Lia adds more and more wood, until the blaze is uncomfortably intense, but I do not stop her. True, the light may alert the Mor, but it might also catch Hollern's eye and draw him to us.

As I am showing Lia how to make a bed of evergreen boughs, she turns to me and asks, "Kirin, what shall we do when we catch up to him?"

I pause, considering my answer. Before today, I would have said that all I need do was command the spirit inhabiting my swee— my follower's body to begone, and expect obedience, but Hollern is obviously different from the others. None have ever disobeyed me, let alone slain one of their brothers.

I thought you said that they were no longer your children, my sister hisses self-righteously, *Did you really think that they would tolerate you orphaning them? What did you think would happen?*

Guilt ripples through me, but I push it aside a heartbeat later. Things are so very different now. I cannot allow a thing like Hollern to walk about a moment longer. I cannot summon them ever again. Some things are more important.

"Kirin?" Lia asks, and I realize that I, lost in thought, have not given her an answer. She deserves one. But I do not want to lie. What shall we do, if he will not obey?

"Honestly, I don't know," I finally admit. "This has never happened before."

"But, surely, your master taught you how to deal with such an eventuality? What did he do in such a circumstance?"

"She, actually," I correct her, "and, as far as I know, this would have been beyond her as well. When she would call forth the spirits of the dead, her servants were . . .not like my sweetlings. They were slow, and stupid, barely able to draw and carry water, let alone slay an ox. My servants . . . they are different. Faster. Much, much deadlier. Why, I do not know."

Lia frowns at this, and I resist the urge to explain further. I could not hope to justify a tenth of my crimes, so I remain silent. Let her judge me if she will.

Finally, she nods. "We shall meet Hollern together, then. You and I." Her simple acceptance brings an unexpected tear to my eye. I wipe it away, cursing my weakness. Why must motherhood, even in its early phases, fill women with such useless emotion?

Expect it to grow more difficult as your time grows closer, my sister says, not unkindly. *It's what makes women different from men. The creation of life changes us. Makes us grow. You've never felt that—truly felt that—and will need time to grow accustomed to the sensation.*

I am surprised to hear such wisdom from my sister's lips. Just when I think I have experienced the limits of her cruelty and scorn, she still has the capacity for compassion.

"Kirin!" Lia barks, drawing me out of my reverie. I do not know how long she has been speaking.

"Cry your pardon. I was wool-gathering. What is it you said?"

"Do you take me for a complete fool?" Lia asks, her words dripping with anger. Faint traceries of lightning illuminate her eyes, flickering for the barest moment in the firelight. "You have done this before."

"Do what?" I ask, sudden fear lancing through me.

"Pause, as if listening to a far-off voice. Do not deny it; I can see the signs as plain as day. There is something more to you than appears to the eye, and I think that, after all we have been through, I deserve to know what it is."

Do not reveal me! The priest has doubtless filled her pretty little head with all manner of tales of demon possession. Gods only know what she will do if she learns that I live within you!

"I trust her," I say aloud, and Lia's eyes grow wide. "She deserves to know the truth."

I wince as my sister howls, a sound of pure frustration and fear, then cover my ears in a vain attempt to spare myself as the scream intensifies. The sound fills me to overflowing, and I flop back, writhing. Gods, when did she grow so *strong?*

I see Lia mouthing my name, her eyes filled with panic. Her fear deepens, touching off the lightning slumbering behind her eyes.

"Stop! Stop, Kirin, or she will call the storm!" I scream, momentarily causing Lia to flinch back. She retreats until her back rests against the bole of the fallen tree we have chosen for our shelter, but the flickering blue light does not diminish.

My sister's cacophony subsides. Maybe she has heard me. Or maybe the light, or the rising wind, has finally penetrated her fear. Regardless, I do not mean to waste the opportunity.

"My sister . . ." I pant. "My sister, she was killed. When we were younger. She was my twin, you see. I could not . . . I could not live without her."

Kirin remains silent, thank the gods, and I hurry on, before she can try to stop me again. "My mistress had a ritual. I found it in her books. A summoning for the dead. To call back their shade, and make it live inside the summoner. Forever together. Forever one. I used it one night, beside her grave. I followed all the steps, and her shade came to me."

Lia's eyes are filled with horror, as she comprehends what I have done. I hurry on, wanting her—needing her—to understand.

"She is not in pain," I assure her. I feel a trickle beneath my nose and wipe it absently, noticing that blood slicks my fist.

"True, we do not always get along," I continue with a wry grin. "But, even when we quarrel, I still love her, and cannot live without her. She deserved better than the death she got, you must understand that."

Oh you fool! Look at her. She thinks she knows the limits of right and wrong, simply because she is educated. The young see the world in pure shades of black and white, which they mistake for morality. But she is not your better. Not our better. You must not let her do this thing!

"I trust her," I repeat, ignoring the tickle of fear that the lightning in Lia's eyes evokes. I open my arms, a mute appeal. "I told you that the things I do are not evil. That my powers are natural. Now . . . now I am not so sure."

"Because of the child," she says. I nod.

"I must make this right. Must find Hollern, and make sure that he does not hurt anyone. He must be sent on. His time came days ago."

Lia nods, the lightning fading. "And what of your sister?" she asks. "What about her?"

"I do not know how to send her on," I admit. "All I cared about was having her back. I only learned how to summon her, not release her."

Nor shall you. My work here is not yet done, sweet, sweet sister. Not done. The need is still unfulfilled, and until it is, you will bear the cost of your actions.

"What is she . . . what is she saying?" Lia asks. I must have gone away again for a moment.

"She speaks of her work, as if she has a reason to be here. Some purpose to attend to. But I don't—"

The sound of snapping branches comes from the black woods, and I stop, holding my hand aloft. My warning is not necessary; Lia has heard it too. She, too, looks about, her slender body tightening like a bow string. For once, I find myself welcoming the pale fire flickering in Lia's sapphire eyes.

"Kirin," she whispers, "has he found us?"

I do not know, so remain silent and alert.

Even so, the ferocity of his attack is terrifying. One moment there is stillness, an almost palpable tension in the still air, and then there comes a silent rush of red, red limbs and pale, torn skin. An explosion of leaves as Hollern bursts from the covering bushes. I never would have known that my dark progeny could be so quiet.

But there is no time for thought, or for recriminations, for a second later he is in our camp, leaping over the fire, the light glistening on his exposed muscles, from his burnished claws and terrible teeth. His eyes are like wet, black river stones, filled with bottomless hate.

He rushes past, faster than I have ever seen. Lia screams and crumples, a crimson flower blossoming on her brow as Hollern's claw sweeps across her face.

"No!" I shriek, leaping forward to catch Lia while trying to keep Hollern in sight. He disappears behind a tree even before Lia has finished falling. Then I am kneeling beside her, pulling her into my lap and cradling her, holding her as she held me at Fort Azure.

The blow has taken her in the left temple, the claw laying open her pale skin as cleanly as a scalpel. Yellow bone winks out from beneath the blood which gushes forth in a steady, pulsing stream. For once, the sight of the crimson liquid fills me not with hunger but with sickening dread.

Hollern knows her power. He must. Did he not almost perish the last time she called down the lightning? He knows how dangerous she can be.

But I am not helpless. I have my own ways of dealing with him.

I lower Lia to the ground, hoping that she will not bleed to death in the time it takes me to put him down. I draw my knife and open wide my secret eye. Immediately, the world goes brighter, as if I am seeing the trees' very spirits, leaf, twig and bough wreathed softly in shining, verdant halos.

He cannot hide from my secret sight. I spy him immediately, already half behind me from where he entered the trees, a dark shape, a hunched shadow amongst the life-glow all about me.

"Step forth, wretched thing," I command, the power of compulsion thrumming in every word. I see Hollern pause, see him turn his wretched face towards mine.

He drops to all fours and charges, his claws scything beneath him, gathering speed at an alarming rate.

"Stop!" I scream, and he flinches, but then, with a shake of his shoulders, continues on.

He barrels into me, knocking the breath from my chest, spinning me away from the fire. My hand slaps down on his cold skin, and I let the blood magic loose, reaching with phantom fingers for the core of his life.

Nothing happens. Of course, Hollern is dead. The terrible will that animates him is not life. He does not bleed, and so my power cannot reach him.

I scream in mingled frustration and pain as he disappears into the undergrowth. I can hear him, moving through the bushes, see him with my secret sight, a speeding shadow.

Wetness trickles across my belly and I reach down, tracing the long slice in my leathers with my fingertips. He has cut me, but in the uncertain light I cannot tell how badly. There is blood enough to coat my hand. More runs down, warming my thighs.

His second blow catches me from behind, sawing across the back of my leg as he flashes past once more. The injured limb folds, pitching me to the ground. I roll, towards the fire, towards the light. My knife, the useless thing, is still in my hand.

You are no match for him, my sister laughs, delighted as a child at a festival. *You cannot command his spirit, and you are certainly no match for him physically. Oh, whatever shall you do?*

I ignore her, shaking my head. I must remain calm, focused. I must think about how I can defeat him.

But how? He is dead, but he walks. He feels no pain, no fear. The worst thing that could ever happen to him has already occurred. How has he slipped out of my control?

No time for that now. He is coming. His shadow moves towards me, stepping into the firelight.

With my mortal eyes I see him, see his ripped flesh and raw, exposed muscles. Bottomless hunger rolls from him in waves. His rusty black eyes meet mine, full of a terrible purpose. The wide mouth opens, stretches, thick tongue moving, terribly alive.

"Ab . . ." Hollern says, and my skin crawls, tightening. The sweetlings never . . . they *cannot* speak. The flayed chest moves as he draws a long, painful breath.

"Ab . . . om . . . " he tries again, the words as tattered as he is. I shrink back, the fire hot behind me. Beside him, I see a faint stirring, as Lia moves her hand, ever so slightly.

She is alive. I must not let Hollern hurt her any more than he has. I crouch down, on one knee, my free hand reaching back, towards the near-intolerable heat.

"Hollern, listen to me," I say. "You must pass on. I know that now. You aren't supposed to be here. I can help you to—"

"Ab . . . om . . . i . . . nation!" he hisses through his ravaged throat. The word turns my blood to ice. I do not know if he refers to me or to himself.

He leaps at me, just as my questing fingers come to rest on a chunk of burning wood. My knife will not hurt him; only fire may save me now.

I pull the jagged wood from the fire, my hand blistering, thrusting forward the flaming brand like a spear. He impales himself on the shaft in a cloud of sparks, ignoring the pain of the fire. I hold him at bay, my muscles filled with the strength of desperation, his claws and teeth snapping inches from my flesh. I feel myself weakening only moments later. Sister was right; I am no match for what Hollern has become.

Lia rises behind him. Her face is a mask of blood set with two glowing, flashing eyes. The smell of summer lightning fills the clearing, overpowering even the stench of Hollern's burning skin. She raises her hand, pointing at us, locked together in final combat.

Hollern must sense her, for he begins to turn. No. This is right. This is just. I release the flaming spear and reach forth, grasping him, pulling him closer to me with the last of my strength.

Lia calls down the lightning with a whisper, a tiny sound that precedes the titanic thunderclap. The bolt splits the night, blasting us away like leaves in a gale and scattering the fire.

I do not feel myself strike the ground; my body has transcended pain. I do not know how long I lie there, in the ruddy darkness, but I know I am not dead. I can still smell Hollern's burning reek, still hear the rolling echoes of Lia's thunder, echoing from the distant, invisible hills. My ears feel like they are stuffed with cotton, and a fearsome ringing fills my head. I push myself up, the movement awaking a thousand pains, and look about.

Lia stands in the midst of the chaos, her hair in disarray, blood coating her face. The lightning still flickers in her eyes, but the elemental glow is lower, barely visible. Hollern lies on the other side of the camp, lit by the scattered bits of the fire. He is moving, dragging himself along on his belly with his claws.

The lightning has shattered his spine and blasted great chunks from his animated corpse, but still he moves. As I watch, he pulls himself along another few feet towards Lia.

I stagger to my feet, ignoring the pain that fills me, and move towards him. As I pass the remains of the fire, I reach down, grasping one of the heavy stones ringing the blaze. My flesh sizzles as I heft the burning hot stone, but I scarcely feel it.

"No," I say, almost calmly, as I drop onto his back. His spines pierce my tender thighs, cutting me cruelly, but it is just pain. I raise the stone above my head with both hands.

"No," I pant, swinging the heavy weight down onto the back of his skull. The sensation of splintering bone fills me with a wild elation, mingled with a bone-deep revulsion. Vomit threatens to choke me.

You are killing your son, my sister says. *Is the sensation as sweet as you always imagined?*

"No!" I scream, raising the stone again and again and again, smashing it down on Hollern's skull until nothing remains but a mass of greasy, grayish red mush. Even then, I feel him moving under me, trying with everything he is to exact his terrible justice.

He gives a last shudder and falls still. No sooner does he relax than I feel his body collapsing, crumbling into foul dust. I watch with my secret eye as his shade floats free, his ghost eyes still black, still filled with undying hatred. He mouths something, the words inaudible, some threat or promise, as he passes. Then, he is gone.

I turn aside, surrendering to the heaving in my belly. I sprawl in the mud, the earth softened by my blood, by Lia's blood, lying amongst the scattered embers and blowing gray ash that once belonged to my minion. When I have nothing left to bring up, I turn and look at Lia.

She is still standing, barely, swaying on her feet like a sapling in a gale. Pushing aside my discomfort, I limp to her side. My wise fingers explore the cut on her head, and I sense that the bone beneath is whole.

"Oh, Lia, I'm so sorry. But he's gone now, I promise."

She looks at me, the lightning pulled inside, like banked coals, hidden but not gone. She says nothing.

"We must wash that out," I continue, aware that I am trying to fill the silence with bright chatter, something I never do. Her stare unnerves me. "After, we shall rebuild the fire and I'll stitch your wound. You'll have quite a scar to show your father when you finally arrive at—"

"Do not touch me," she says softly, steel in her voice. I flinch away, then continue my gentle probing.

"But, we must stop the bleeding. Head wounds often look bad but—"

"*Do not touch me!*" she screams. At her cry, the wind swells, transforming in an instant from a gentle breeze to a gale. Limbs whip and flail, and a shower of acorns, leaves and sticks rains down.

I back up, hands upheld, making soft, shushing noises, nearly falling as my injured leg threatens to give way again. Lia looks about, as if the sudden wind confuses her. High above, lightning threads its way amongst the clouds. Thunder grumbles and swells. She waves her hand, negligently, and the wind diminishes. Finally, she sits.

"Let me bathe your face, at least," I say. "You've blood in your hair. Honestly, you look quite frightening."

She stares at me for a moment, as if I've gone quite mad, before a ghost of a smile flickers across her lips. I feel my own tugging upwards in response, and a moment later we are laughing, painfully, almost hysterically. I wince as the movement wakes a line of fire along my cut side and belly, but I cannot stop.

I am alive. She is alive. We are alive. In this moment, that is all that matters.

CHAPTER EIGHTEEN

Rory and I left the inn at first light, hiking though the chill morning air. Up, always up, into the mountains. Luckily, no snow had fallen the night before, and Rory had little trouble locating my trail.

I wondered how he followed my path, even when my footprints left the snow and crossed bare stone. I asked him as much.

"Well, now, lass, that's easy and hard all at the same time, it is," he replied. "Some is signs: a broken blade of grass here, or a footprint. You see? There? That scrape next to that patch of ice?"

I squinted at the spot he indicated, then shook my head. "It looks like every other stone," I admitted.

He moved his mittened hand closer, pointing to a tiny flaw in the ice. "There. Your boot must have slipped, and made that arc in the ice. It is not a natural mark."

I looked at him, impressed. "How do you know it's not an animal track?"

He shrugged. "It doesn't look like a gepar's or a goat's hoof print, and besides, they're too sure-footed to slip on flat stone."

"But, what about following from here?" I asked, gesturing to the broad expanse of stone still before us. The dark rock extended in all directions, bare of snow or even ice in many places.

"That's when you have to think like your prey," he said, grinning. He scanned the rock, then began moving, angling to the right as we went.

"If I were coming this way, I'd take this path," he said, his eyes restlessly sweeping back and forth. "Over on the left, the rocks are more jagged; lots of places to turn an ankle in there. And further yonder," he pointed to our right, "there's ice. Most creatures will walk on stone if they have a choice. Less treacherous. This route leads towards that cleft in the rocks, and I wager that when we get up there we'll see that it's the only easy way down."

We struggled up to the cleft. As predicted, my booted tracks continued on in the snow, leading ever upwards. I congratulated him for his cleverness.

"Don't be too impressed, lass," he laughed, waving aside the compliment. "It's not magic, and it doesn't always work. It's merely paying attention and thinking about where the prey is likely to have gone. Mixed in with a spot of luck from time to time, of course. Now, if only I could get Lady Fortune to look upon me with that same favor at the gaming table, I'd be a happy man!"

We reached my cave by mid-morning. I swiftly gathered my few meager possessions, including my bow and quiver, while Rory rested. Soon, we were headed back down. Rory asked if he could see my bow, and I handed the weapon over.

"Yew," he commented, eyebrows raised. "That's a powerful draw, it is."

"The body is capable of great feats when faced with starvation," I replied with a shrug.

He nodded. He seemed pleased with the weapon, and I asked him again what reason he had for wanting me to recover it.

"The people of the village have a problem," he said. "Something's been coming down out of the mountains to take their goats and sheep."

"They should buy dogs," I said, "and come with torches and spears when they bark."

"Oh, aye, they've tried that. Did no good."

"Why? Certainly the villagers are used to dealing with wolves?"

"They dared not face what's taking their animals. The poacher's no wolf, lass. It's a mountain bear. A male."

I waited, wondering where the difficulty lay. Animals were no match for armed humans, surely? Seeing I did not understand, Rory pressed on.

"The stories say that bears, along with many other beasts, traveled to this land with our forefathers generations ago. The settlers chose their new home well, and all of the beasts they brought with them grew strong in their new home. But the bears, now *they* were special. They didn't just survive; they flourished.

"After a few generations, the bears grew to over twice their original size, or so say the tales. The mountain bear is the king of all bears, the largest and most powerful predator ever.

"I've seen them a time or two, up high, where the snow never melts, or in the deepest, blackest parts of the woods. Believe me when I say that they can break the neck of a bull moose with a single cuff."

I tried to imagine a creature large enough to do what he said, and found I could not. He must be exaggerating, I thought, playing up the tale for a new audience.

"In any case, the villagers have agreed to handsomely reward the man who brings the head of the beast, and I mean to claim it. It's already killed three others foolish or greedy enough to try stalking it on their lonesome. I figured I'd have a better chance of success with someone watching my back, even if it meant splitting the reward. My idea turned out to be a mite more difficult than I planned, though."

"People are afraid if they hunt with you that they, too, will be killed," I guessed. Rory nodded.

"Aye. They say I'm mad to take on the beast, but I think otherwise. And the reward is worth the risk."

I thought over what he had said as we continued down. This was not my affair. These people's livestock did not concern me, and I had little desire for whatever reward so fascinated my guide. Still, the ease with which Rory had located and followed my back-trail showed me he possessed many skills. Skills that would, I hoped, prove valuable to me. If he could be persuaded to teach me.

"All right then," I said, nodding, "I'll go with you. What do we do?"

"Lass, you should know one thing before agreeing," Rory said. "There's a thing that can happen with bears and other meat-eating animals. Once they kill a man, and partake of his flesh, then sometimes the beast grows a fondness for the taste. The bear I mean to stalk has already gone and killed at least three other people."

"Well, then, all the more reason to hunt it down," I said. "It's only a matter of time until it comes into the village or some farm looking for a meal, yes?"

Rory grinned, seemingly well pleased by my answer. He clapped me on the back, and said, "Don't worry, lass. I've hunted bears before. Certainly not as large as this, I'll reckon, but a bear is a bear is a bear, as my grandmother was fond of saying. Once we take its head and hide, and return it to the village, I'll split the reward with you."

"I do not require money; it would only hinder me," I said. "I have something else in mind."

Rory raised an eyebrow, awaiting my proposal. By the time we had hiked back down to the village, we had struck the bargain that would one day lead me into service with the army and, from there, into the arms of Jazen Tor.

THE BEAR'S TRACKS were not difficult to find. Rory picked up the trail before the sun was above the eastern peaks the following morning. By mid-day, we had followed them to a cave, much like the one that had almost been my tomb.

The snow all about the mouth was stained a dingy gray, threaded with red and littered with the cracked bones of countless animals. Rory had explained to me that smaller bears lived in the lowlands, and often ate more fish and plants than meat.

But mountain bears were predators, pure and simple, great silvery-gray mountains of muscle and fur. Our arrows would do little more than aggravate such a monster, unless we struck, and struck hard, at some vital spot.

"Is that a sword?" I whispered, pointing.

"Aye. Belonged to Big Jim Bagget, it did," he breathed back, his eyes scanning the bloody snow. "I recognize the agate set into the crosspiece. Jim was the first to take up arms against the beast, and the first to vanish. When this business is done, we'll return the weapon to his widow."

I nodded, eyes alert for movement, an arrow set onto my string. We crouched in the snow, behind a sheltering boulder, the wind brisk and cutting in our faces.

After a time, I pointed to a new perch, one closer to the cave. "We should move. We might see more from there."

He shook his shaggy head. "No, lass, we'd be downwind there, and the beast's nose is sharp. Plus, I'd like a way to retreat should it—"

A moaning roar sounded from the darkness, cutting off Rory's lesson. We crouched lower, our eyes just above the top of the stone, watching. The roar was repeated, then all was silence.

"He may have smelled us anyway," Rory breathed. "Let's see if he comes out to see who's stupid enough to challenge him."

An hour later, the bear still had not appeared. I shifted my half-frozen limbs, trying to keep them warm and limber.

My fingers were frozen, the sensation in the tips chancy at best. Noticing my discomfort, Rory waved me back, away from the ridge.

When we had gone far enough, Rory indicated I should hold. "The beast is either sleeping and unaware, or is craftier than I'd given him credit for." He scowled. "The question is, which one is he?"

"He has to come out sooner or later," I said.

"Aye, but will we be in any shape to challenge him when he does? The bear is much better suited to waiting than we are. If we're to take him and return before nightfall, we have only a few hours left to make our move."

I nodded. "Then let's waste no more time. We go in, bows ready, and take him. At the worst case, we can always shelter in the beast's cave after the danger has been eliminated."

Rory looked at me and nodded approval. My sister cackled. *Are you doing this for his approval, dear sister? Perhaps you're hoping that he'll reward you with more than his knowledge of woodcraft and tracking? He is very hairy; I suspect that, beneath all that wool and leather, he's more like a bear himself than a man. Perhaps that excites you? Perhaps you yearn for a beast, now? I know that Urik was always a disappointment where such things are concerned.*

I ignored her taunt, even as the cruel barb set itself. Why was I acting this way? Perhaps my newfound powers over blood had made me overconfident. Perhaps I did crave his approval.

All concerns and self-doubts were pushed aside a moment later as Rory started back up the slope. He checked the fit of his arrow on the string, then plunged over the top of the rise.

As we approached the lip of the cave, we split, each taking a side. My eyes roamed across the dark hole, seeking a target. The reek of dead, rotting things, mixed with the pungent tang of the bear's waste, was thick in my nose.

I caught Rory's eye, waiting for his signal to go inside. He nodded, and I rushed forward, the light at my back, sighting along the drawn arrow. A dim tunnel led further back, into the dark.

An ear-splitting roar echoed through the cave. We exchanged a look and moved further in, every scraping footfall and muffled breath echoing from the walls.

The bear roared again, sounding closer now. I heard a clinking, like dead men's finger bones being tapped against the stone, realized that it must be the sound of its claws. The sound grew louder, but still I could see nothing.

The clicking, and the shuffling of its paws, increased in tempo as the beast rushed forward.

"Rory?" I began, my treacherous feet moving me backwards of their own volition.

"Steady, lass. I know you can hit the target when you must."

The bear charged out of the dark, transforming from a dim, gray smudge into a terrifying, shaggy apparition in the space of three heartbeats. Even on all fours it was huge, taller at the shoulder than either of us. Its snarling mouth was filled with ivory teeth, the saber-like canines longer than my forearm. They glittered in the dim blue light.

"Now!" Rory yelled. The bear screamed as a shaft appeared, as if by magic, in its open mouth. I let fly a moment later, then cursed when I saw the arrow protruding, uselessly, from the great shaggy hump rising behind its ears.

I drew a second arrow from my quiver, willing my hands to be still, and took aim again. I would not get another shot before it was on us.

This time my aim was true. The bear stopped, howling, as my second shot struck it in the eye. It reared up, smashing its head on the rocks above. Rory finally readied his second shot and fired, striking the bear in the throat. The barbed head bit deep, burying itself to the fletching in the thick fur.

The beast coughed and turned towards him, incredibly fast for something so large. It dropped back to all fours and moved towards him. Its cuff sent Rory spinning, slamming him into the cave wall. He went down, gasping, his bow flying away into the darkness.

"Rory!" I screamed, nocking a fresh arrow to the string. Time slowed.

With stately grace, I saw the bear's terrible claws swipe across Rory's prone body. Blood burst forth from rent leather, accompanied by his scream of pain.

Blood.

I dropped the useless bow; the beast was too large and too close. My best weapon now was a different kind of attack. I rushed forward, my hands outstretched, as red magic uncoiled in my belly, roused by the scent of Rory's blood.

What are you doing? my sister said, alarmed. *You can't! It will rip you limb from limb. Forget him; it's too late. He's dead already.*

"No!" I yelled again, answering her. I leapt.

I sprang upon the bear's back, hands scrambling for purchase. The beast's fur was coarse and greasy, its musky scent overwhelming. Under the thick hair, I felt the play of unimaginably powerful muscles as the bear turned to see who had dared to assault it.

My fingers burrowed down, through the fetid hair, seeking skin. All I needed was a touch.

The bear rose up again, its head once more scraping the ceiling. Its roar was deafening. With a mighty shrug, it sent me flying. I rebounded from the icy stone wall and fell, sprawling, to the floor.

I scrambled back as the bear's claws scraped across the stones. Panic tightened my chest. I looked into the beast's one remaining eye. The amber orb burned with rage and pain, rolling madly above a mouth full of knives. I saw movement behind it.

Rory, bleeding from a score of wounds, stabbed the bear with his knife, burying the long blade to the hilt in the beast's side. The bear roared again, a whistling note of agony in the sound now.

"Outside!" I screamed. I turned and ran, not waiting to see if Rory followed. In the close confines of the cave, the bear had every advantage. I needed to get above it.

The sound of Rory's footfalls behind me was sweeter than any bard's music as we ran back out into the sunlight. I did not pause to consider what I meant to do.

"Draw it out!" I yelled, cutting hard to the side and scrambling up the rocks that ringed the cave mouth. Fear lent my limbs unexpected agility and strength as my fingers scrambled for purchase.

I looked down, and saw Rory, kneeling in the snow. Everywhere he was crimson, his life leaking away through the rents in his leathers.

I reached the apex of the cave opening, then gathered my legs beneath me. I heard the bear, moving inside the cave, alternately roaring and whimpering in pain. Rory's last cut must have been deep.

We could run. Let time pass, and allow the wound to stiffen. Maybe the beast would even bleed to death.

No. Rory was done, I could see that. He would be running nowhere. And, even it we were to escape, the frigid night would freeze us to death.

I heard the beast moving along the tunnel, the scrape of its claws marking it for me. Just another moment.

Beneath me, I saw the blunt muzzle emerge, then the tips of the rounded ears. My arrow still jutted from the ruined eye socket. The shaggy shoulders followed a moment later.

I dropped, landing on its back with a whuff. My thighs gripped either side of the thick neck desperately. The bear roared and rose up, trying to throw me off once more, but I was ready for the movement, one hand knotted in the coarse fur.

I reached forward, until my fingers touched the wet ruin around the arrow fletching. They probed further, deeper, until I felt the jellied remains of its eye, the jagged hardness of bone.

The blood magic flowed down my fingers, threading itself into the bear's body like hooked lines, twining through veins and arteries. It buried deep, deep, reaching for the mighty heart.

The beast froze, still upright, a tiny whimper passing through those terrible teeth. The hooked barbs found the heart, twisting through the powerful muscles.

I pulled, and the bear's blood came pouring forth in a crimson rush, spilling from mouth, from nose and ears, from even the ruined eye socket, like water from a fountain.

I laughed as the hot liquid sent a ripple of heat and life through my body, the sensation a dozen times more powerful than anything I had ever felt from a man. Only the gepar's life force had been more intense, and that energy had nearly killed me.

Not the bear's. No, the bear's blood was life, raw and unadulterated, hot and bursting with vitality. Again I threw my head back and laughed, my clenched thighs tingling, riding the former lord of the mountains as it trembled beneath me, the sensation somehow more inviting, more arousing than anything I had ever experienced.

Then it toppled forward, its limbs unhinging with the departure of its life force. I tumbled across the snowy ground, rolled easily to my feet. The bear's life filled me to overflowing, thundering in my veins. My head pounded, as if the bear's mammoth heart now beat in my chest. A small noise reached me, and I turned back.

It lived. Despite the terrible thing I had done to it, it still clung to life. Its single eye rolled, mad with pain, fixing me with its terrible gaze. There was no malice there, only a dull, animal rage. It struggled to rise, but its limbs were powerless, flapping things.

I drew my knife and approached. I knew its desire to rend, to crush the life from me in vengeance for what I had done, for that same desire filled me as well, a lingering gift of the bear's sacrifice.

I thought of Urik, and of how I had, at the end, shown him mercy. His gaze, too, had been filled with the same animal hatred. The thought awoke a red rage in my breast.

With a grunt I slammed the knife down into the ruined eye socket. The bear gave one last spasm, as the blade cleft deep, then fell still.

I turned back for Rory. He was still unconscious, his blood staining the snow around him in a widening circle. The bear's vitality still sang in my veins, the blood magic spiraling alongside it in a near-deafening duet. The sight of Rory's blood filled me with a bone-deep hunger.

I struggled, then pushed it aside. No. I would not let him die.

I bent and lifted him, as a mother would pick up her overtired child, so easy to do with the bear's strength in me, and carried him inside the cave.

I would not let him die.

CHAPTER NINETEEN

It is dark once more when we finally stumble back to the farm. We walk down the center of the road, making no attempt to conceal ourselves, yet still our sentries only give warning when we have nearly reached the camp's perimeter. I must speak to Ben Childers about that.

Lia's face is grimed and streaked with crusted blood, and I cannot bear weight on my injured leg. We limp along, clinging to one another like drunks. All the way back, Lia has insisted that the wound Hollern gave her does not trouble her, but the way that she occasionally stumbles and sways worries me.

She will hear nothing of seeing the healers before me, despite my protestations that, besides the injury to my leg and my seared palms, I came to no harm from Hollern's attack. I know what concerns her, so it does not surprise me when Livinia, the midwife, appears.

In the privacy of my stall in the barn, Livinia examines my belly and my female parts, while Lia stands outside, guarding the door. I smile at her dedication. The thought of her, standing out in the barn with blood in her hair, evokes a feeling of warmth deep in my belly.

"And there's been no bleeding, nor cramps, you're sure?" Livinia asks for the third time. "What about a ringing in your ears? Or the taste of metal?"

"No. No and no. I'm fine, Livinia, really. I, too, know the signs of bleeding inside the chest or belly, and of . . . of miscarriage. And I have had none of them."

The midwife nods and gestures for me to get dressed. As I lace my breeches, I hear them, whispering outside the stall door. When I emerge a moment later, Lia's look of worry transforms into a radiant smile. She reaches for me, hugging me tight.

"Thank the gods," she mutters into my hair. "I was so worried about you and . . . about you and the baby. I was so scared that the lightning—"

"The lightning saved us both," I say, awkwardly patting her back. A part of me yearns to return her embrace, but years of solitude and the certain knowledge that my sister is still inside me, watching from behind my eyes, makes me awkward.

Finally, I pull away, and steer Lia towards the stall. "Come now," I demand. "I'm fine, just as I've been saying all day. Let's have a proper look at that cut. Livinia, can you fetch me some water, the hotter the better, and some clean rags?"

"Bandages are rarer than a banker's charity right now," Livinia complains. "But I'll see what can be found."

"No matter, I've extra shirts in my pack that are little better than rags, so they might as well be put to use. The water will suffice," I say, rummaging through my bag for my sewing kit and a length of gut. Livinia hurries out on her errand.

I clean and sew Lia's wound, my bandaged fingers clumsy on the needle. When that is done, Livinia wraps her brow with strips torn from one of my ruined shirts. She shows no signs of concussion, thank the fickle gods, and already her youthful vitality has her on the mend. She will have a scar—I did not lie about that—but she is in no danger.

Lia and Livinia finally leave, in search of food, and, at last, I can rest. I lay back and am asleep moments after my head touches the clean straw.

"No, THAT WON'T DO AT ALL," Ben Childers says, peevishly. "Surely that's not the best answer you can give?"

I hold his eyes with mine until he drops his gaze. "It is, Mister Childers, I'm sorry. I've spoken with the refugees that came this way from the south, and I believe that the Mor are headed to the Armitage. Many were seen moving along the road. We cannot move towards them; the danger is too great. Nor can we stay, for we are too exposed here. These people have heart, I grant you, but they're not soldiers. The farm is indefensible if we are attacked."

We sit around the main fire, a dozen landowners, those whom the people have come to look on as leaders, and I. Lia is with Brother Ato. I wish she were here; I have no talent for pretty words and compromise. I know what these people must do if they want to survive; the trick will be to convince them.

"But what of our wounded?" Ben complains, the same argument he has been making for an hour. "What of the children and the old folk who cannot go any further? Should we just abandon them?"

Yes, he should, my sister says. *Best to leave behind those who would perish on the road. The Mor will linger; will take the time to put all of the infirm out of their—*

"We shall leave none behind," I assure him. "We have wagons enough to carry the injured and the sick."

"But few animals to pull them with," he says. It had not taken long for the hungry, scared people to turn to their beasts of burden for sustenance. Now all were gone, save for a few precious horses.

"People can pull wagons just as well as animals," I say. "And they must, or else some must remain behind. That is something I will not tolerate."

Childers ponders this, then nods. "Aye, it might work," he allows.

"But, begging your pardon, m'lady, there's still the issue of where we'll go," a goodwife says. Days of hard living have melted the fat from her face, leaving her with bulldog jowls and bruised eyes.

"I still say we stay here!" another man says. He has voiced this opinion often. "We can, I don't know, build a wall or something. Plant stakes. We've plenty of able-bodied folk here to do the work."

I bite back the laugh that threatens to burst from my lips. Build a wall? Against the *Mor?* And out of what? Why not try barricading a storm with a wattle fence?

"I know you've lost everything, Massers," Childers says, calmly. "We all have. And I know it took you and yours four days to walk here."

"Almost five," Massers says, brandishing his spread-fingered hand. "My littlest one . . . my littlest one died of her wounds on the way. I've three other children to think of, Ben!"

"All the more reason to flee," I repeat, for what feels like the dozenth time. "You cannot build a wall out of timber that the Mor cannot breach. They are masters of fire and flame. And even if you managed to get these people organized and willing to work, it will take weeks to build a proper post wall, weeks in which you are vulnerable, and exposed."

"So goodwife Jordan's question is a good one. Where shall we go?" Childers asks.

"Fleeing south is no good," I say, then hold up a hand as Massers tries to interrupt once again. It seems as if no idea I have is good enough for him, the fool. "Fleeing south is no good, I say!" I shout over him. "The Mor are sure to be on the roads, and as we get closer to the Armitage, there will be more of them. We must go in another direction."

"But what if the army comes, looking for refugees?" Childers asks. "Shouldn't we stick close to the road, so they can find us?"

I think of Gamth's Pass, think of the bodies laying strewn across the trampled ground, limbs missing, heads gone. The burns, and the smell of charred horse and human flesh.

The unearthly keening of the Mor as they invoked the fire slumbering in their weapons; the sound of their thundering feet as they pushed forward in a wordless rush.

"The army has other priorities at the moment than looking for refugees," I say, pushing down the horror the memory evokes. "I fear that they will not come, not for a while in any case. Until then, we must care for ourselves."

"So where shall we—" Goodwife Jordan begins.

"West, into the mountains," I say, pointing at the snow-covered peaks. "There is an abandoned manor up there, beside a lake. I remember it from before, when the army passed through the highlands. It's remote, but it does have a wall. There was fresh water and game aplenty, if memory serves."

Childers and the others ponder this. "I know the place you speak of," Ben says finally, nodding. "In the spring and autumn, I hunt for deer near there, as do many others. The manor though," he shakes his head, "is a ruin, abandoned for years, with tumble-down walls and a rotted gate."

"I know the place as well," Massers says, scowling. "That's where Martin Dupree once lived. That's no good at all. The walls were broken by the Emperor's troops thirty years ago. My family used to have relations with the Dupree family, but when they began to give shelter to rogues and highwaymen, well my father told my mother that they—"

"You were ready to build a log palisade with your bare hands a moment ago," I interrupt, shaking my head. "Surely a thick, stone wall in need of repair is better than no wall at all? Surely a rotted gate is better than no gate at all? We will be safer there than here, in any case, and the manor is far from any road."

Fort Azure had thick walls as well, my sister reminds me. *They did you no good. Or have you forgotten that already?*

"Lia was not at Fort Azure," I mumble under my breath, the words lost in the babble.

Ben Childers allows the argument to rage for several minutes, then holds up his hands and waits until the voices subside. When all have fallen silent, he says, "I know that I can't speak for you and yours, but I think Kirin's plan has merit. I mean to go to the Dupree manor and all who care to follow me are welcome to do so. We shall hold out there until the King's army can push back these invaders. Who will accompany us?"

It is as simple as that. Childers's quiet confidence and decisiveness seem to spread, like fever, to all sitting around the fire, and soon most are nodding and smiling in approval. A few, Massers among them, leave the firelight unhappy and unsmiling. I will need to watch them.

Childers approaches, and takes my hand in his, steering me gently away from the fire.

"You're sure about this, Kirin? You're sure the Mor haven't beat us there?"

I blink, surprised he has only now thought to ask me this. "I can guarantee nothing. But the Mor have shown no interest in any human concepts of shelter, save in their desire to burn them to the ground. Since you say it is abandoned, it should be clear. But I will scout ahead, of course."

"But, you can't!" he says, shocked. "What of the child? You should ride in one of the wagons, and leave the trail blazing to the menfolk."

I give him a long, lingering look. He seems serious. Then I laugh.

"Pregnancy, despite what you may think, isn't a disease, Ben. I'm quite capable of doing my job. If the gods are kind, we will be sheltered behind stone walls long before my belly forces me from the road."

"Then let us pray that the gods are indeed kind," Childers says.

I RISE BEFORE THE SUN, gathering my things in the feeble moonlight that penetrates the clouds. Lia walks me to the horses. Before I mount, I grasp her hand in a silent promise. She nods, then pulls me into her arms.

She is warm and soft, and smells of smoke and clean skin. The aroma of sunshine still lingers in her hair. The embrace steals away my breath. Her lips brush my cheek, and she whispers something in the impossibly beautiful language of the air elementals. Then she is gone, hurrying away towards the mercy tent.

I watch her go, then swing astride my mount. Soon, I am alone, cantering across the fields. If my maps and my hazy memories are accurate, I should be able to reach the valley and the manor by mid-day tomorrow. As I travel, I watch for impediments that will slow the refugees: bogs that might trap the wagons; groves that could conceal an ambush.

Always I am alert for traces of the Mor. The signs of their passage are everywhere. Where they have walked, their heavy, clawed feet have churned the earth into muddied tracks, which stand out, stark, against the grass. They do not seem to know how to walk softly, to conceal their movements. They do not know, or they do not care. Most of the tracks are days old, but a few are very fresh.

I pass two other farms, both burned. One is deserted but the second is littered by the sad, sorry bodies of the family who once lived here. The crows and other scavengers have left little to show who they were.

I almost open my secret eye, to see if their shades still linger, but stop myself. Nausea twists in my belly, and I wonder if the sensation is simply morning sickness or my body recoiling viscerally from what I almost did.

I cannot. Never again.

My instinct is to press on, but my horse needs rest and food and I find that I cannot leave them there, exposed to the unforgiving sky. I drop to the ground, wincing at the pain in my leg and lacerated thighs.

There are tools aplenty in the shattered barn, and I find a shovel that has not been too badly damaged by the blaze. I chose a likely spot, on a hill overlooking the valley that they had made their home, and begin to dig.

Afternoon is deepening into night when I am finally done. My wounded leg and blistered hands ache, the dressings spotted with fresh blood. I limp towards the row of mounds, my hands clutching something soft and wet.

I lay the charred doll atop the last grave, final resting place of a girl who could not have been more than four or five. The fire that killed her reduced her to a small, shrunken thing, almost weightless when I picked her up and laid her in the shallow pit. The doll sits on the stones I have piled on top of her, a sad, broken guardian, soaking in the mist and rain.

I cannot stay; the shades may still be here, clamoring soundlessly for someone to avenge them. I swing back into the saddle and ride west. An hour later, the blue dark is thick. The horse stumbles on an unseen rock. I cannot risk it twisting a leg, and decide to wait for the dawn.

A fire would help push back the damp and the chill, but the Mor may be near. I sit and shiver, wrapped in my damp woolens, thinking of Lia. I wish she were here, but she would only slow me down. Still, a kind word, or one of her smiles, would doubtless warm me better than even a hot meal.

In the morning, I make better time, despite the morning sickness that plagues me and the burning ache in my thigh. I ride at a brisk canter amongst the scattered scree and boulders that litter the mountains' skirts, stopping occasionally when the nausea threatens to overcome me. The overcast endures until mid-day, although, happily, the rain does not return.

Later, the sun breaks through the clouds, warming me, casting its radiance over the peaks and valleys.

I remember when I came here before, with Jazen Tor, not so very long ago. He went on endlessly about the glow from the chill snows high above, about the dance of sunlight on this stream or that. I remember he made me a necklace of flowers and laughed when I told him that I did not wear such things.

"Yet," he had said, plucking a fallen blossom from the grass and tucking it behind my ear. "You do not wear flowers yet."

But you did. You wore them for him eventually, did you not? On the night you first gave yourself to him, yes? my sister asks. The sound of her voice in my head sends a fresh spike of nausea through my viscera.

"You will not speak of him," I say, shaking my head. "What Jazen and I shared—"

Was the rutting of animals. Passionate, true, but nothing more. You know that you did not love him. He was a convenience; a pair of strong arms to hold you through the long night. To warm you when the darkness grew too lonely and too cold. Do not let the fact that he happened to fill your belly with his seed change what you know to be true.

I ride in silence for a time, framing my denial, but inside I know she is right. I desired Jazen. Sometimes, too often perhaps, I even yearned for him, but I did not love him. Does that mean that I cannot, that I will not, love the child of our union?

Lost in thought, I almost miss the fact I have arrived. I stop at the crown of the rise, my breathing labored in the thin air, and gaze at the valley laid out before me.

It is long, its far end blue with distance, a narrow cut, nestled between towering peaks. A lake sparkles at the valley's center, the water so deep blue that it is almost black.

A river snakes its way along the valley floor, a pale line of glimmering light amongst the verdant greenery. Beside the river runs the ghost of a road, long abandoned but still visible to the eye that knows what to look for.

Thickets and copses dot the valley floor. As I watch, I see a herd of deer, almost a score of them, emerge from the tree line. They begin to graze, cautiously, never straying from the security of the shadows, watched over by an attentive buck.

Near the valley's far end the manor sits. It is the same pale gray as the surrounding stones, the only clue to its existence the unnaturally geometric shapes of its towers and battlements. From here, it is impossible to judge its fitness.

I sigh and start down the slope. Shadows have already begun to pool in the valley floor, but if I hurry I should be able to make the walls before full darkness falls. The abundance of water and the sight of the deer fill me with hope; this would be a good place for the survivors to shelter.

The deer raise their heads, alerted by my far-off presence, then meld into the shadows. I stop my horse and swing down from the saddle, then take down my bow and set the string into its notch. I push aside the pain in my leg, trying to move quietly despite my limp. Gods willing, I will feast on hot meat behind stone walls tonight.

Smiling, I move to stalk my prey.

CHAPTER TWENTY

Eight days after we left to stalk the bear, Rory and I returned to the small, nameless village. I grinned when I saw it below me, and tightened my grip on the travois.

"Not long now," I panted, struggling to pull Rory's bulk over a patch of stone.

"Thank the gods," Rory replied, his voice barely a whisper.

I looked back, over my shoulder, at where he lay. All I could see of him was his wan face, the skin red and blotchy in the biting wind. He had lost a frightening amount of weight. He lay beneath the bear's skin, shivering. Taking the hide was the first thing Rory taught me, after waking from his fever.

I started down the long slope, hoping that someone would see us against the snow and come to help. The afternoon was almost gone, the dark of night pooling in the mountain's folds and valleys. Lights glittered with the promise of warmth below.

"Not long now," I repeated, heading down.

We were nearly to the village's single street before someone saw us. A herdsman, attending to his flock, started as he came out of a barn, nearly colliding with me. He scrambled back, his eyes wide.

"Go get help," I commanded. "He's been sore wounded."

He blinked at me for a moment, then nodded. He pelted off, his feet splashing in the muddied road.

Free of the snow, the travois bearing Rory became too heavy to pull, so I waited, breathing hard, as voices floated

to me. Soon, we were surrounded, as the villagers came out
to see the source of the commotion.

Hands reached out, stroking the bear's soft, gray fur,
muttering talismanic prayers to this god or that. I was
pushed gently aside, as other hands took the poles and began
pulling Rory away. We walked, a tiny parade, towards the
sign of the horse.

RORY CUT INTO HIS THIRD MEAT PIE. He shoveled the bite,
steaming, into his bearded face and rolled his eyes comically
with relief. Good-natured laughter filled the smoke-filled
tavern.

As news of the bear's demise spread, others arrived at
the inn, filling the room with a mass of boisterous, laughing
faces. The bear's hide hung on the wall, so large that the rear
paws trailed across the dusty floor.

I sat in the corner, a bowl of stew before me, sipping the
thick, brown sauce. It was delicious, even more so after a
week of eating nothing but tough, fire-charred bear meat. I
bit into a carrot and closed my eyes as a sensual ripple went
through my body.

I did not care that Rory's story of the fight with the bear
was wrong. He did not cut the throat of the beast, as he was
telling the pretty bar maiden and the rest of the onlookers,
nor had he delivered the killing blow that had laid the bear
to rest. In fact, the only time that he mentioned me at all was
when he spoke of his convalescence.

"Aye, the bear clawed me deep," he said to the lass,
raking his hooked fingers down his side to illustrate. "My
juice was leaking all over the snow in a red stream, it was.
After the bear finally dropped, I followed, near to swooning.
Kirin there," he pointed at me, and the many heads of his
audience swiveled to face me, "Kirin, she patched me up
right pretty. Kept me from freezing to death with the warmth

of her own body. A not unpleasant fate, lads, let me tell you!" He winked and the crowd laughed.

I shrugged. It was true. I had lain beside him, as the fever coursed through his veins, his body shivering uncontrollably, rank with fever sweat. I dared not leave him that first night, even long enough to gather firewood, lest the shock stop his heart. Together, we lay in the bear's cave, on the freezing stone, until morning. If not for the cave, we both would have certainly perished.

Let Rory have his ribald fun, I thought. We both knew who had slain the bear, as we both knew he had been far too busy struggling against death for amorous advances. Let these oafs clap him on the back and wink, and leer at me if they liked.

"What of Jim Baggett?" a voice called from the back of the room. "Did you find any sign of him?"

I turned, along with all the others, and saw a small woman at the door. She pulled down her muffler, her eyes wide and beseeching.

Rory coughed, dropping his eyes, and muttered, "Goodwife Baggett. Aye, I found him. Lass, can you fetch my pack?" he asked me.

I nodded, rising and walking to the meager pile of goods that had been brought inside. I drew out a long bundle, and walked to her.

I saw her eyes flick up and down what I carried, shaking her head in denial of what she already knew to be true. When I flipped aside the covering, exposing the rusted hilt set with agate, her face crumpled.

"I'm so sorry, mistress," I began, then stopped as her keening wail split the air. She crumpled, slowly, to her knees, reaching out for the ruined blade. I put it into her hands and she held it to her breast, like a lover.

I resumed my seat, awkward, wanting to say something to salve her grief, but I did not have the words. The room watched, looks of triumph changed to embarrassment, as Jim Baggett's widow cried for her dead husband.

WE SHELTERED IN THE TAVERN FOR TWO WEEKS, as Rory healed and recovered his strength. On the fifteenth day, he met me in the common room downstairs. He was still a trifle thin, and wan, but plentiful food and drink had done much to restore him.

"Top of the morning to you, lass," he said, blearily, gesturing for the tavern maiden to fill his cup. The night before, like too many others, had seen him drinking until he was too unbalanced to stand. I frowned; I did not care for his habit of taking mead, or even wine, in the mornings. Marcus and, later, Urik, had done the same.

The lass looked at him as she poured. Her eyes were as red as his, but for different reasons. Her face was blotchy and swollen from crying.

"I think we should talk about leaving soon," I said in a low voice. "Your wounds are nearly healed and I know you can walk when you—"

When he's not staggering from the effects of wine, my sister hissed, venom dripping like acid from the words.

"When you want to," I finished.

"Aye, we'll leave soon enough," he said. "I think I've taken the measure of this town." He looked at the maid for a long moment, a leer splitting his thick lips. She turned away from him and hurried to the end of the bar, busying herself with wiping down the already clean counter.

"But, like it or no," he continued, "I was wounded in service to these people, and they owe me compensation."

All true, my sister whispered, spitefully, *but that does not give him license to take what he likes.*

I nodded, agreeing with her. Rory had indeed been difficult to live with over the past several days, with his never-ending demands for this or for that. At first, the people had been eager enough to reward their savior, but as the days wore on, and Rory's demands increased, I watched as their open smiles turned to something more forced, their open mouths more snarls than grins.

Any who hesitated were treated to yet another rendition of Rory's brave deeds, of his terrible mauling. This had worked, so far, in weakening the dissenter's resolve, but I could tell that the villagers' patience was wearing thin.

The bar maid walked over to refill his empty cup, shooting him a look of mingled spite and longing. Rory had taken her into his bed on our third day back, pulling her under the covers one evening as she helped him to his room. She was young, barely old enough to bear a child. Seeing her beside Rory, watching his eyes roam freely over her body, filled me with a gut-deep chill.

All men are beasts, my sister said. *Animals. Give them the barest scrap of encouragement, and they show their true faces. This one showed promise at first, true, but he is like all the rest.*

Rory drank deep, his hairy throat working, then sighed deeply in pleasure. I looked over to where the maid, matron now, I supposed, was tending the bar. Her father, the proprietor, stood behind her. His face was full of sick rage.

There were others in the tavern, sitting in groups of two and three, unusual for such an early hour. These were working folk, not the type to frequent drinking houses in the morning. I realized that almost none had food before them. They exchanged glances with one another, from table to table.

"We must go," I said, pushing aside my plate and rising. Something felt wrong. Years of gauging people's looks, of watching for peril in the eye of an overly pious zealot, had made me alert to such things, and now that instinct told me to get out. Now, before whatever the townsfolk were planning could come to pass.

"But, lass, I've not yet had my meat and eggs. Even if we were to leave today, I can't set out until I've eaten."

"We can and we must," I hissed, bending so that only he could hear my words. "Come outside with me. Now. I mean it."

As I said these words, I felt something warm and slippery shift inside me. Rory opened his mouth to protest, then stopped as his eyes met mine. He sat, mouth working, for a long moment, then nodded. Like a man in a dream, he rose and stumbled towards the door. I gathered our packs and our weapons from their place by the door and followed after. Whatever we had left in our rooms would stay there.

The whole town was outside the door, waiting in the freezing rain. Some looked worried, or near sick with guilt, but most had the same look of hard anger in their eyes. I heard men moving behind me, following us out through the door.

The village elder walked forward, a small leather purse in his hand. He looked scared, but resigned, as he approached. Rory, still befuddled, blinked at him.

"We appreciate all you've done, but now you must go. We've our own families to feed. Here's your pay, just as we promised."

He put the sack into Rory's paws, then backed away. The hunter scowled at it, blinking, as if he did not know precisely what it was. He looked at the elder, and I saw Rory's waking resentment and anger, struggling to break through his lethargy. I stepped forward, putting a restraining hand on Rory's arm, praying that whatever I had done to him would last just a few moments longer.

"We thank you for your hospitality," I said, pulling Rory along the street. There was nothing more to say. We walked down the mud street, the town's residents watching us as we went.

I did not fear them. I knew that, should they be foolish enough to attack us, they would run, shrieking, at the first signs of my blood magic. Any resistance would be swiftly eliminated if I should call forth even a single sweetling. But I did not want to hurt these people. They had done nothing save show their displeasure at Rory's impositions, a displeasure I myself shared.

As we approached the street's end, a figure walked into the road. She had a long bundle clutched to her breast. Goodwife Baggett.

She looked at us, at me, her face filled with some unnamable emotion. Her eyes were sunken and red from weeping, her lined face even more pinched than the day we had arrived. She stood in our path, blocking us. I stopped before her.

"Mistress Baggett," I said. "I wanted to tell you again how sorry I am about—"

She spat in my face.

Her action seemed to serve as a signal. A moment later, the air was filled with stones and flung mud. A chunk of icy slime splashed against my back as I turned to grab Rory. The big hunter roared as my tenuous control shattered. He reached for his knife.

"No!" I screamed into his face. "We did not almost die killing the bear to slay these folk! Run!"

A rock bounced off my shoulder, the pain flaring bright, then dulling into aching numbness. Rory looked about, as if seeking someone to attack, his teeth bared in a savage grin.

I dropped my hand and ran, leaving him. Let him be dragged down by the furious townsfolk if he desired; it was no concern of mine.

I ran. Ran until the breath burned hot in my chest, until the sounds of furious pursuit had dwindled to silence. I stopped and turned, and was surprised to see Rory running along behind me. There was blood on his face, a crimson trickle which ran down from his wounded brow.

The sight of the red life awoke a pang in my belly as the blood magic responded. My sister growled low, like a cat with a mouse in its jaws. I felt her hunger and her rage.

All women would benefit from that one's death, she whispered. *He used that girl abominably, I'm sure. She was young enough to be his daughter. His granddaughter! It would be the simplest thing to—"*

"I still have things to learn from him," I whispered back. "I will not kill him."

Rory ran up, laughing. If the blood in his eyes bothered him, he gave no sign.

"Well now, that was indeed a bracing way to spend a morning, eh, lass?" he laughed, blowing hard. "Who would have thought they'd be so upset over a few stolen caresses and casks of wine?"

I bit back my reply, that any thinking person would have seen it plain. I reminded myself that, despite Rory's misogyny and his other questionable scruples, I still needed him.

THE WEEKS FLEW PAST as we wandered the highlands. Rory, away from the bottle's influence, was a generous and patient teacher. He showed me, over and over, how to best set a snare, or to back trail an animal to its lair. He taught me how to bait a proper hook and to properly dress and skin a deer. I picked up his skills swiftly, and soon no animal, no matter how light-footed, was able to elude me.

Our solitude was pleasant enough, but I came to dread those times when our travels brought us near a town or village. Inevitably, Rory would find his way directly to the local alehouse or tavern, and soon would be reeling. When he drank, the gentle, patient man I knew was eclipsed by something else, something that lived inside of him, some spirit or devil, woken by the first few sips of liquor.

The sight of his weakness sickened me, and, when we returned to the road, I took no pains to conceal my displeasure. His apologies seemed earnest enough, but all I could hear was Urik's voice, mouthing the same empty explanations and promises.

I admit that I hid from him during those times, not because I feared him, but rather because I feared *for* him. If he were ever to succumb to the liquor's call, and come after me . . . I knew only one of us would survive such an incident, and I knew who that person would be.

I shall never forget the night I killed Rory. Such a waste. Such a stupid, stupid waste.

We had just left the town of Ravenshire, headed west along the skirts of Mount Aden. Rory was ill-tempered, suffering, as usual, from the aftermath of too much revelry.

I was simply happy to be back on the road. It had been a bad visit, and I had spent the better part of three days either in a hay loft, shivering and wanting to be away, or in Ravenshire's small market square, selling our stock of pelts. Hunting had been good, and the furs were of excellent quality. Business, at least, had been brisk.

On the fourth day, with all our skins finally sold, we departed. Rory, as usual, had drunk the better part of our profits and gambled away the rest. I did not care; I meant it when I told him that money and riches would only serve to slow us down. Truth be told, I was beginning to loathe the sight of money; it gave Rory the ability to buy more liquor.

I went to sleep that night, secure in the knowledge that, now that Rory was away from all that, I'd have back my wise, generous mentor. Until the next town, the next tavern.

There was nothing more that I could learn from him, I knew that, but the rootless, wandering life we shared appealed to me. Soon enough, spring would arrive and with it new campaigns. He would re-join the army that he spoke of so often, but for now I was content. All I cared about was my next meal and my next dry camp site, and I had both. I slid into dream.

I awoke to his hot breath in my ear, to the sensation of his rough hands on my body. The stench of wine was thick in the air.

"Rory, what . . . ?" I mumbled, already knowing what was happening, not wanting to believe it. He moved behind me, pressing himself into me.

"Shhhh, lass," he drawled, wine fumes reaching me as he breathed across my neck. "You're so fine you are, so very fine. I've dreamed of you."

My blood became cold as winter river water. He would not betray me so, not after I had saved him in the mountains. He must not.

"Rory, you're drunk. Stop this," I said, despising the weakness in my voice. Inside, my sister writhed and snarled, wordless, enraged.

"Shhhh, now lass. It will be so sweet. The two of us. I've seen you looking at me. I want this, too. It will be all right," he mumbled, his hands clumsy, pawing at my breeches.

"Rory, no, please stop this. You are my friend. Don't make me . . . Don't make me hurt you."

He pulled back and I rolled over. He looked down at me. In the dim firelight I could see his tousled hair, his stubbled cheek. Fresh wine stains splashed across his shirt. He must have brought the bottle with him, in his pack, when we departed.

"Hurt me?" he said. Then he laughed, as if the very notion was somehow comical. He bent his head and, still laughing, covered my throat in rough kisses. His hand reached down and roughly stroked me, the sensation barely felt through my leathers, but still painful and humiliating. "Gods, Kirin, the sight of you! It makes my blood burn, it does."

The sound of his laughter breathed across the coals of my blood magic, fanning the power inside into bright, crimson flame. My sister's growls of outrage shifted into a throaty chuckle.

"Rory, look at me," I said, the words pregnant with the power of command. They pierced deep, lancing through his stupor and his lust, dragging his head back. His whiskers scraped across my throat's tender flesh as he pulled back. His eyes met mine.

I could feel the hungry tendrils of my power reaching for him, probing at eyes and nose, wanting to be inside of him. I grasped them. Despite his weakness for women and for drink, Rory was still my friend. I did not want to see his blood splash across me, see it absorbed into my skin. Did not want to see him convulse and die.

"Your blood runs hot, does it?" I said, marveling at the sound of my own voice. It was deep and rough, filled with alien passions and lust.

"No . . ." he said in a tiny, choked voice. "No, Kirin I—"

The blood magic clamored for his life, as did my sister. Their mingled cries ascended in my head, swirling and spiraling like birds. Somehow, I resisted them, held them back.

"If your blood is so hot, then perhaps you should cool off," I finally managed to say through clenched teeth. He needed to be away from me, now, lest the temptation overwhelm me. "The stream at the bottom of the hill should do. Go there and sit in the water, until your ill-advised ardor passes."

Mute, he lifted his bulk off of me, staggered to his feet. His eyes were sightless and glassy, his jaw slack. Whatever light was in him was subsumed in the tight grip of the blood magic's compulsion.

He disappeared into the darkness. A minute later, I heard a splash as he dropped into the icy water.

I lay back, trembling from the effort of holding back my power. My sister crooned in my ear. *Well done, sweet one. Well done. He'll be so very miserable in the morning. Oh, so well done.*

She continued to sing to me, a lullaby, until I slipped into exhausted sleep.

I found Rory the next morning, submerged to the chest in the stream. His open eyes were two frozen, gray stones. His lips were two ice blue crescents framing jagged brown teeth set in gums the dark, bruised color of berries.

His blood is not so hot now, is it? my sister purred, then cackled. I sank to my knees, unable to tear my gaze away from his confused, lost face.

Even dead, his gaze pierced me like a blade.

CHAPTER TWENTY-ONE

One hundred and eighteen refugees set out on the long trek to Castle Dupree. For the three days that they travel I do not sleep. Instead, I constantly patrol, riding in widening spirals around the vanguard of their advance, always alert for any signs of the Mor.

At midmorning on the fourth day, the refugees finally reach the valley. By the time they crest the valley wall, six have perished along the road, mostly the very old, as well as one woman whose wounds made the prospect of her journey dismal at best. A seventh, lying in one of the crowded wagons, looks like he will not last the day. His belly wound has been torn open by the conveyance's rocking and swaying, and his bandages are streaked with black blood and ominous yellow pus.

I am weary, and sore, but I cannot stop, or rest, until I have led the people to shelter.

Even as tired as they are, the refugees send up a cheer when they finally arrive at the manor. Many have fear in their eyes as they take in the state of the walls and the fallen gate, but none complain. Even as the wagons are being unloaded, I am riding through the people, Ben Childers beside me, organizing the work parties that will be our best chance at salvation and safety.

When I was last here, I scouted out the things we would need. I have already drawn a map for the stone masons, leading them to the quarry that the original builders used. There was cut stone aplenty there, extra blocks and formed stones that they must have been saving for repairs.

Next, we will need wood for the gate. I take a group, seven women and two men who claim to have knowledge of woodcutting, and ride out. "Aye, this will do right nice," the leader of the woodcutters says, eyeing the stand of timber I have led them to. He is leathery and squat, as tough as an old stump. His knuckles are thick and swollen from a lifetime of gripping an axe. There are nine of them, with only six axes between them, but it will have to suffice.

"Are you sure that you'll be all right out here?" I ask. "You must not become so focused on the work that you stop watching. The Mor—"

"Don't fret," a second woodcutter says, testing the edge of her axe with a thumb. "We'll be sure to hide if they come. We'll split up and make our separate ways back." She says this with admirable calm, although I cannot help but see the way her eyes dart along the tree line. I recall that she was the wife of a woodsman, before the Mor. That she has left three children back at the manor, in the care of the community. I empathize with her desire to be with them, but the work must be done.

I nod, gathering their horses and roping them together. The animals must follow me back; the scouts will need to remain mobile. I feel a pang of worry and guilt at leaving the work party out here, all alone, but push it aside. We are all at risk while the walls remain broken and the gate open.

I return to find the refugees swarming the manor. Children run through the uneven courtyard, running in and out of the sagging main doors, or clambering up the uneven stairs leading to the ramparts. I recognize the game they are playing: the Ogre and the Maiden. The sight is bittersweet. Even amongst so much pain, so much horror, they can still laugh.

I breathe deep, loosening the tightness that has settled across my chest. I commandeer some of the old folk, those too infirm to help with the unloading, and tell them to man the walls. Better their tired eyes on the lookout than no eyes at all.

I feel better when I see my new sentries' silhouettes. Nodding, I head off, in search of likely scouts.

MORE DIE THAT FIRST WEEK. The man with the belly wound. A goodwife who, after losing her husband and four children, simply stopped eating and talking. No wounds mark her, yet the journey to the valley proves to be her undoing. A man tumbles from the roof he is attempting to repair when a rotted tile breaks, pitching him to the courtyard.

Ben Childers proves to be an efficient and tireless leader, always at the front of any work party, always selfless in his praise. He leads through example and not by intimidation. It is not the military way, but these folk are not soldiers.

Any strong enough to assist with repairs are put to work, carrying stones to the top of the walls, or shaping the rough timbers brought out of the woods into something resembling a gate. Most of the refugees are women and children, unused to such hard labor, but the work proceeds.

Those who cannot help with the work, the very old or the very young, are sent out in groups to gather nuts and wild berries, or to try their luck with hook and line at the lake. Soon, every nearby tree and bush is stripped to the bare limbs, but still it is not enough.

I spend much time away from the castle, hunting. There are so many mouths to feed. I am used to leading men trained to forage as they travel, not a collection of refugees. The highlands are wild and untamed, grudging of sustenance.

Luckily, game is plentiful and my aim is still as true as ever, and I return in the evening of most days with a fresh kill across my horse's withers. The herds are not large enough to sustain us indefinitely, but Ben is optimistic about the gardens that have sprung up outside the walls.

I see Lia only occasionally, usually at night across the community fire. The trials that have left some gaunt and weary seem to agree with her. She has been working outside, as has everyone, and her skin has darkened to a rich nut brown. It seems to glow in the ruddy firelight. She has replaced her tattered white silks with simple homespuns. Her elegance and beauty shines through her rough garb like the sun through clouds.

After the evening meal, I often find the presence of so many people around me uncomfortable. I walk then, through the nearly-completed gates, to the edge of the graveyard. Calling forth my sweetlings would ease the refugees' work, and would give a measure of security, for they need no sleep, no rest. But, I cannot. The thought of summoning them sickens me now.

I caress my gently-rounded stomach. I can still get into my leathers, but I can tell that I will not be able to for much longer. My breasts are increasingly swollen and tender. Morning sickness still assails me every day, bouts of nausea that sometimes last for hours. Between the miserable retching and the scarcity of food, I have lost weight, not gained it as I should.

A small noise reaches me and I look up, my hand dropping to my knife's hilt. From across the graveyard, Brother Ato stares at me. He, too, has lost weight since we first met. The merry, round face I remember has shrunken, becoming harder, more angular. Bruises ring his weary eyes, beneath a haystack of unkempt hair. He leans heavily on his staff as he stares at me.

"Kirin," he says, deceptively mild, "fancy meeting you here. Come to do some work this evening, have you?"

Even in the dim light of the watch fires I can see his eyes, sparkling dangerously. I bristle, and my sister growls, softly.

He has power, too, don't forget, she whispers. *For all his foolery, he is a priest, and his goddess is with him.*

"Brother Ato, I . . . I do not know why I've come," I answer, honestly. "I think it is because I find graveyards peaceful places. Here, the dead can finally lay aside their burdens and rest."

"Death is a failure," he spits back. "A lost opportunity. The Lady grants me the power to mend broken flesh and spare lives. To hold death at bay."

"And yet all things must die. It is part of life itself," I say. "Surely the gods know when a man or woman's time has come. How can that be a failure?"

He regards me for a time, his fingers clenching and unclenching on his staff. His mouth is hard and uncompromising.

"I know why you worship death, witch," he finally says, his voice soft, yet flinty. "Do not try to confuse me with your lies, as you did with Lia. They will not work. I know that you serve the dark powers. That those that you call your children are abominations, the reanimated corpses of those that should rightfully have passed beyond. I will—I *must*—oppose you."

I nod, dropping my eyes. Not long ago, I would have argued with him, would have reminded him that I have saved many lives since my arrival, possibly more than even he. Would have railed at him for speaking ill of my sweetlings, for denying me my only chance to experience something akin to motherhood.

But things have changed now. Now I know what it feels like to shelter a growing life inside my belly. Now I know the sweet, sweet pain as my body changes, readying itself for what is to come. Soon I will know the searing, delicious agony of childbirth.

I have changed so much, but I cannot tell him that. He has made up his mind about me, and I can sense that nothing I say will change his opinion. Even if I were to save a thousand lives, ten thousand, I would still be a broken, evil thing in his eyes.

"Do what you must," I say, ignoring the demands that echo in my head, my sister's shrill calls for his blood. "I will not try to stop you from claiming the justice your goddess demands."

"I . . . I would not hurt the babe," he says with a scowl, seemingly surprised by my reaction. "For all of your crimes, it, at least, is still an innocent, despite its bastardry."

The word lances through me, surprisingly painful. Of course the child will be a bastard. I will never marry; never be owned by a man, ever again. The babe will never carry his father's name, or share in whatever inheritance he might have from him or his family.

I feel something on my face and brush at it. My hand comes away wet.

Tears. I am crying.

The realization shocks me. My sister falls silent, her surprise mirroring mine.

Then I am sobbing, bending slowly to fall to my knees. I lean forward and grasp the loose soil of a refugee's grave, clenching it, holding on as if I fear the earth will shake me into the sky.

Gods, what is *wrong* with me? Why does the memory of a man I barely knew, a man that doubtless sheltered his own inner darkness, like all other men, fill me with such sorrow? The babe cannot miss what it never had. I know this.

Nevertheless, the sobs rip through me, turning my legs to water. Ato regards me, a satisfied smile, the first smile I've seen on his face in weeks, turning up the corners of his mouth.

"Yes, Kirin, that's good," he says. "Do not try to hide from the Lady's righteous judgment. Embrace the pain, and in doing so, transform your sinner's soul." I look up as he approaches. He holds his staff before him, not as a weapon, but in benediction.

Is this the source of the pain? Am I truly damned? When I knew I was alone, when it was just my soul in jeopardy, I scoffed at such notions, but now I have another soul to worry about.

Do not do this thing. I can read your heart, and I tell you that this is not the answer. Please, as you love me, do not—

"I do love you. More than anything. But what if he is right?" Ato flinches back as I speak, his eyes darting to and fro, as if expecting to see one of the infernal lords of the abyss materializing in the darkened graveyard.

I look deep into his eyes, seeing his fear, his indecision. I see no otherworldly energy there; no lightning, no glimmers of power. The might of his goddess is not with him, or if it is, then I cannot see it. Maybe this is what the priests mean by needing to have faith.

Do not! Do not do this! This is wrong! This is not the answer! Do not! my sister keens, but her voice is already fading, dimming, like a crying child being lowered down a deep well. Soon, it is gone. Again, I am alone. For the first time in years, alone.

Never breaking my eyes from his, I sigh deeply and say "I desire forgiveness, brother. Tell me what I must do."

I AM HAPPY IN THE WEEKS THAT FOLLOW. The meat I bring suffices for the refugees until the crops they have planted sprout and grow tall in the summer sun. As soon as they are harvested, they are planted again.

The second planting is still in the ground when the days begin to shorten, as the season begins its months-long slide into autumn. There is still time enough for a second harvest, or so the farmers say. I hope there will be; even with the extra food and the rationing, it looks to be a lean winter.

Soon after, my burgeoning belly persuades me that riding is no longer safe. I spend my days tending to the sick and injured and training those with aptitude in the use of the bow. Even with one harvest gathered and a second on the way, the meat my hunters will gather will be crucial to our survival.

When I am not on the archery range, I am with Lia, drilling the refugees strong enough to hold a spear or a knife in the rudiments of combat. Gods know that I watched the army train enough times; I may as well at least try to impart some of that same skill.

Winter will be hard, but at least I will have someone to keep me warm, I think, stroking my belly's growing swell. Livinia tells me that I am heading into my third cycle, and the baby will grow rapidly now. Already, I have felt its first stirrings and kicks, sitting beside the fire and grinning like a fool at Lia's beaming smile, basking in the sensation of her warm, delicate hands on my belly.

"He will be strong, like his father, I can tell," she says. "Such kicks!"

"He, or she," I correct her gently. "I do not care which. I just want the baby to be healthy."

Following my conversion and the lengthy confession of all my sins, things improved markedly between Brother Ato and me. His newfound approval seemed to dissolve the last of the refugees' lingering reservations, and everywhere I went, all I saw were approving glances and warm, open smiles. My eyes remained as black as ever, but it did not seem to matter.

I know that every welcome has an ulterior motive. I realize that all here have come to rely on my hunting and my healing, on the herbs I still gather and render into vital medicines, but I do not care. It has been so long, so very long, since I saw smiling faces.

After that night in the graveyard, my sister has remained silent. I do not know if the power of the Lady has driven her away, as Brother Ato claims, but I sense that she is still with me. Still watching over me. I imagine the scowl she would have on her face hearing me repeat my daily prayers, and I laugh.

I still cannot work in the mercy tent. I do not know how Ato stands it. So much blood has stained those simple walls. So many screams have echoed inside; the fabric seems impregnated with them. No, I prefer to do as I have always done, and visit those who need my help directly.

The refugees are too numerous for the manor, even as large as it is, to contain them all. Attempts have been made to make the manor's out-buildings – the stables; the forester's cottage; some simple structures that may have been used for storage – into habitable homes. Others pitch tents, or build round-houses of wattle and daub. Soon the people have scattered, searching out every scrap of shelter.

My duties take me all along the length of the valley. Livinia tells me that walking will help ease my labor when it arrives, and I plan to stay on my feet until the very last moment.

I am outside the manor walls, headed for one of the storage buildings, when I hear the commotion. Someone is yelling. A woman invokes Loran Lightbringer, raw panic in her voice. Curious, I approach, wincing as my steps wake fresh pain in my lower back.

Whoever was yelling has gone by the time I arrive, riding off in a cloud of dust. One of our sentries. A chill runs down my spine, a premonition of ruin. "What is it?" I ask a scared goodwife.

"Gods above save us!" she says, tears in her eyes. "Oh, Gods, no! We must flee!"

I stare for a moment, already knowing what the sentry said. Only one thing could frighten these people so. Why now, with the babe's arrival so close? Surely the gods do not hate me so much?

I shake my head, walking off as fast as I can. The people here will only know what they've been told. Panic begins to sweep through the household as the news spreads from person to person. I hear screams and sobs.

I must get to the castle. Ben Childers will know what's happening. The walls and gate have been repaired. There will be safety there.

Unbidden, I recall Fort Azure. I see in my mind's eye the Mor, burning their way through the fort's defenders, implacable and unstoppable. Remember the sight of hard, chitinous limbs grasping glowing blades, rising and falling like threshing tools, harvesting human lives. Remember their opaline eyes, shining behind expressionless bone armor, so very lovely yet so very inhuman. So filled with hate.

"Oh, gods, do not do this thing," I pray, turning my eyes up to the sky. "Surely you do not so desire the sight of blood, Lady Shanira, that you would let the Mor slaughter these people? High Lord Loran, please, if you are indeed merciful, as Brother Ato claims, please do not do this thing."

The sky does not answer. The vault overhead is the perfect cerulean of early autumn, studded with storybook clouds, which shine pale orange in the afternoon light. It is incongruously lovely for such grim news, as if the gods are smiling down at the sight of this, their latest jest.

When I reach the manor, all is chaos. People run hither and yon, gathering supplies. Already scuffles are breaking out in the courtyard, as frightened people turn on one another over food, or a place on a wagon.

I push through the swirl, one arm cradling my belly protectively, the other outstretched. Soon I reach the keep's main gate. A guard stands there, Bey Rathcliffe, a dairy farmer before the coming of the Mor. He wears a sword, one of the three the refugees brought with them, on his hip. A helmet sits atop his peasant's head. The sight chills me.

"Let me in," I demand. "I need to speak to Ben Childers."

"M'sorry, mum, but I have my orders. None are to—"

"Stand aside," I say. Something hot shifts inside of me.

My eyes bore into his, as something almost palpable reaches between us. Rathcliffe stares, his mouth hanging open, his eyes glassy. Then, a moment later, he steps aside, woodenly.

I sweep through the gate and up the stone steps, headed for the empty library that Childers and the other leaders have adopted as their meeting hall. I hear voices, raised in heated argument, from the top of the steps. As I approach, words resolve themselves.

"We must flee, Ben! You know it is the only way!" a woman's voice says. Other voices join it, clamoring for attention, agreeing or disagreeing, it is impossible to say.

"No, no, no!" Childers thunders over the babble. The voices fall silent. I mount the steps, hissing as the motion stabs painful daggers into my back. I haul my ungainly body up, huffing with effort.

"We have worked hard to repair the castle's defenses," he continues. "Trust them, and the training that Kirin and Lia have labored so hard to give us. We all know what to do. If we try to flee, the Mor will pursue and eventually catch us."

The cacophony resumes, the words indistinguishable. I reach the top of the stairs and hurry towards the door. Ben tries again to speak above the clamor, but they are no longer people to be reasoned with. They have become a mob.

I reach the threshold and look inside. It is as I imagined: a knot of frightened humanity, circling their leader, arms outstretched and beseeching, fingers equally ready to grasp at hope or curl into a fist. Childers tries again to speak to them; I see his mouth open as he tries to be heard, but they are not listening.

"Enough!" I shout, the heat in my belly filling the word with the essence of command, slicing through the din like a sharp knife. They turn, as one, their individuality erased by the power of the mob. Their eyes roll, wide and filled with panic.

"Ben is right!" I say. I know I have but moments to make myself heard. "Make no mistake; any who leave will be slaughtered. Your only chance is to stay here, behind high walls, and fight!"

"But . . . the Mor will—" a goodwife begins. I cut her off with a sneer.

"The Mor will chase you like hounds after a lame fox. When that happens, when they run you to ground, they will burn you alive, from the inside out. Your children's eyes will smoke and steam, and fly from their skulls. Their tongues will blacken and their hair will crisp as they scream for you to save them. Is that what you want?"

The goodwife's mouth flops open, shocked and speechless. Better. Inside, the hot thing unfolds vermilion petals, like an enormous flower. I bite back a laugh of pure exultation.

"Lia and I have done what we can to prepare you for this. Now they have found us. If they are but few, we still might live to see a new day. We have weapons and a strong wall. And, we have Lia's power; the power of the storm. It is a fearsome thing.

"But all of us, if we want to live, must fight. None can flee, for that path leads only to death."

The mob dissolves, I see it go, turning back into a collection of frightened people. Its shadow still lingers over the room; it can return at any moment, but for now, they are focused, are in control of the crippling, fatal fear.

"The people look to you to lead them," I say to them, gently now. "So lead."

As one, they shuffle out, their eyes glazed, shocked. I know that they will do as I bid them, at least until the first sight of the Mor. Then, who knows?

Ben Childers approaches, and waits until we are alone. He, too, looks at me with painful hope, an unspoken plea graven in his face. "We're not going to win, are we?" he asks, his eyes begging me to tell him that he is wrong. "They're going to kill us all."

I take his hand and grasp it tight, then shake my head. "Not this time, they aren't. Before today, I had nothing to live for. But now—" I stroke my belly "now, I cannot, I must not, believe that. Now I have a responsibility greater than myself."

The memory of Lia fills me, the simple recollection of her, looking down at me as I lay in her lap, singing. The sun making a corona of her hair.

For months I have run. Months of blood and pain and tears. Months of fear and desperation. But I am done with running. It ends here, for good or ill.

It ends here.

CHAPTER TWENTY-ONE

"Quiet now, lads," I whispered, checking the fit of the arrow on the string. "Don't move from this spot."

Behind me, Jazen Tor breathed something to the rest of the hunting party. The men remained motionless and silent. I stalked forward, eyes scanning the ground for dry leaves, or sticks, or anything else that could make noise.

Across the glen, a group of deer grazed at the edge of the trees. Their hides blended almost perfectly with the lush browns and greens around me. They were cautious, as deer always were, never bending all at once to eat, their graceful heads constantly swiveling to scent the air.

The breeze blew into my face, carrying my scent away from my prey. The long grass sheltered me. I was close, almost close enough to take my shot.

Behind me, one of the men made a sound, a tiny thing, but the deer heard it. Every head came up, then turned as one to face the place where I had left Jazen and the rest.

The deer gathered themselves to spring away, and I rose and drew the feathers back to my ear. My mind was calm, quiet.

My shot caught a doe in the throat as it bounded forward, bringing it down in a tangle of spindly limbs. The men rose, baying like hounds, and pelted through the clearing, headed for the place where the doe had fallen.

"You'll scare away all the game for miles, fools!" I hissed as they ran past. They either did not hear or did not care. Moments later, they reached the place where the animal still thrashed and struggled. I saw a knife flash, and its struggles fell still.

"Well shot," Jazen Tor said, stepping behind me.

I turned, a smile playing across my lips. "Thank you, sir. I'm just happy to be of assistance."

Jazen grinned and sketched a brief bow, then moved past, headed to where the men were gathering up the kill. I watched him as he walked away, my eyes lingering across his wide shoulders and narrow hips. His hair, worn long in the style of the northern hinterlands, was pulled back into a horse's tail tied with a blood red cord.

I had guided this, the third ranger company of the Imperial army, for almost a month, blazing trails and bringing down game. Rory's name had earned me an interview with the leader of the Empire's scouts, and my skill with my bow had earned me my position. The commander had been disturbed at first by my black eyes — most people were — but the five arrows I grouped in the center of the range's furthest target seemed to dissolve his concerns swiftly enough.

Even after five weeks in the field, Jazen, their sergeant, was still a mystery to me. At first blush, with his coarse demeanor and wild hair, he seemed like many other inhabitants of the untamed borderlands. But, on the occasions where we had spoken, around the fire after a meal, it swiftly became apparent he was better educated than the usual settler's son. We talked of art and religion, and of the fickle nature of the gods, and for the first time in years I was thankful for the education Mother had forced us to endure.

Their Captain, Hollern, however, was an open book, one that I had been forced to read countless times. Pious. Mistrustful. Tentative. A man ruled and defined by his fears: fear of dying, fear of the afterlife, fear of judgment and of being found lacking. A man whose understanding of the world was limited to what he could see and touch, and whose comprehension of the deeper mysteries went no further than the closest priest.

Watching Jazen supervise the men, expecting respect rather than loudly demanding it as Hollern often did, only served to make him that much more attractive. Unbidden, I thought of the way his hair, unbound in the evenings around the camp fire, would catch the firelight, throwing it back in shades of chestnut and ruddy bronze, the dark spill framing his angular face and curling beside his muscled neck. Even then, I wanted to bury my face in that hair, to see if the reality of its scent matched my imagination. Wanted to knot my fingers in it and pull back his head; to watch his eyes close in ecstasy as I devoured his throat with kisses.

I cannot, I told myself. I will not. Jazen, for all of his fair looks and commanding presence, was just a man, with a man's weaknesses. True, he did not look at me like a hungry wolf eyeing a haunch of meat like many of the men, even as they sketched the sign of Loran or Shanira behind my back — *Hypocrites! Cowards!* my sister hissed at this thought — but he would doubtless show his true face soon enough.

The men returned, grinning and laughing, with the deer slung across a pole. The animal would make an excellent meal. Jazen nodded and smiled as he passed, brushing against me as he did. My skin tingled at the contact, as if his touch were charged with gentle fire.

I shook my head and moved to follow them. The camp was not far, just over the next ridge. Our sentries had reported nothing of note in days, so I allowed my mind to wander as I walked, constructing pleasant fantasies even as I derided myself as a weak fool for doing so.

Gods, look at you, mooning over him like some witless pig farmer's daughter, my sister said with a snort. *If you want him that much, please, by all means, take him and be done with it.*

"Hollern hates me enough as it is," I whispered back. "Fraternizing would only make things worse. Jazen says that

Hollern has been looking for a way to have me reassigned since the first day I joined them. I tell you, when he looks at me, I could swear that he knows."

Hollern may be a captain in the Imperial army, but despite his rank he is still just a jumped-up peasant's son. He is not educated; he is ignorant and superstitious.

"Exactly. He takes every opportunity to speak with the priests, and to unburden his soul of his sins. When he speaks of me to them, who knows what they tell him?"

She remained silent for several minutes, then said, *What does it matter if they tell Hollern that you can speak to the dead? Will they command him to abandon you out here? No. He has his orders, and they say that, like it or not, you are his scout. His kind never have the courage to think for themselves, or to disobey.*

Besides, there's only one man's opinion that matters to you. Isn't that right? She laughed as she said this, the sound, so full of lascivious glee, echoing in my head. Even then she knew, as did I, I suppose, how this would play out.

I thought of how Jazen's sword-callused hands would feel on my skin, his fingers so strong and sure as they stroked my face, my breasts. Dreamed once more, as I often did, about the taste of his mouth, about the scrape of his whiskers across my belly as he moved to give me pleasure.

The thoughts kept me warm through the long, cold spring night.

"Kirin! The tree line!" Jazen called, pointing. His sword was naked in his fist, the bright steel stained with blood. Around him, men screamed and struggled. I followed his gesture and saw the fleeing figure.

Without thought, I shifted my aim, raising the point of the arrow to adjust for the wind. The figure ran for the trees, as if his life depended on their shelter. It did.

With a breath I let loose the shaft, watched it rise, gently, curving gently right and down as the wind pushed it. It struck the runner in the back of the thigh, knocking him sprawling, scant yards from shelter. The men, Jazen at their van, ran down the slope in pursuit. In a moment, they had seized him.

Tracking the highwaymen had not been difficult; they lacked true woodcraft, and did not know how to properly conceal their trail. The actual ambush had been more of a challenge, for the patrol, clad in jingling mail and heavy boots, did not move lightly or quietly. It was fortunate that the bandits had taken a cask of wine in their last raid; it had made them slow and sleepy and incautious.

Jazen walked up to me, the men following behind. They half dragged, half carried their wounded captive. The bandit groaned as they returned him to the clearing.

"My thanks, mistress archer," Jazen laughed. "If he had escaped, he would have reported back on our position. I wish every eye were as keen as yours," he said, eyeing the company bowmen. They shifted, refusing to meet his gaze.

I kept my face neutral, even as something inside of me warmed at his praise. My sister sighed.

The soldiers ransacked the bandits' meager camp. Besides the now-empty wine cask, they found bolts of fine cloth and a small cask of coins. I reached down, when none were looking, and picked up a small comb, an enameled butterfly with teeth made of tortoise shell. It disappeared inside my vest. The merchant whom they had killed for these spoils would never miss it.

At the clearing's far side, Hollern bent, whispering threats and demands. The bandit shook his head. Hollern gripped the protruding arrow shaft and yanked, and the man's scream floated up on the chilly air.

"How many men are inside?" Hollern demanded. "How many swordsmen? How many archers? Tell me, and I swear by the Lightbringer that your suffering will end."

I moved to the edge of the trees, my eyes, as ever, alert. When I was alone, I touched the comb through my leathers and smiled. It was lovely, and delicate, and refined. Everything I once was. Having it against my breast made me feel different and special. Made me feel like a woman.

I looked up at the sound of footsteps. Jazen and Hollern were walking towards me. Behind them, the bandit sprawled, unconscious or dead, I did not know. Fresh blood stained the grass around his body. Jazen's eyes, usually smiling and warm, were cold and hard, like flint, above the bloodless gash of his mouth.

"We have the information we need, scout," Hollern barked. "Sergeant Tor will get the men ready. Go ahead and blaze their back trail clearly. Clearly, do you understand me?"

I nodded, resisting the urge to curl my lip. If the bandits' trail were any more obvious, it would be on fire.

I moved out, stopping at intervals to bend down a marking branch or to scuff a symbol in the mud. The trail was very fresh; the tracks were only hours old in many cases, moving back and forth through the dense brush.

Not long before dark, I located our goal. An old tower, rising like a stone fang from the surrounding trees. Its roof was tattered and jagged, half fallen in. The walls were rough and uneven; the neglected stones had shifted over the years. A sentry's silhouette moved atop the roof.

Even half-ruined, the tower was a formidable structure, its summit studded with crenellations. Even a small number of competent archers could pin down a superior force under such cover. I had seen the results of the bandits' skill at arms at the site of over a dozen robbed, burned wagons and merchant caravans, all bristling with broken arrows. They had skill enough to worry me.

Night was gathering in the sky; it was too late to try and plan an attack at this hour. I turned back. Jazen would need my report to plan our next move.

I touched the comb hidden in my vest and smiled, imagined wearing it for him, the bright colors sparkling in my pale hair. The thought warmed my cheeks.

As I moved along my back trail, a distant horn blast split the gathering gloom. An Imperial recall. I paused, head swiveling, fixing the position of the summons against the mountains' backdrop. When I was satisfied, I broke into a run.

We would need to make haste. As it was, I doubted we would be able to reach the source of the call before night fall.

WE MARCHED AS THE SKIES TURNED BLACK, then marched still more, pausing neither for the evening meal nor to let the men rest their weary legs. The soldiers grumbled and muttered; usually they would be in their bed rolls by now, dreaming beside the watchfires, guarded by their sentries. The darkness made the men clumsy; several tripped on unseen obstacles. After the third such occasion, Hollern called me back and railed at me for choosing such a poor trail.

"This isn't her fault, sir. The men can't see. We should make camp until dawn, then start fresh," Jazen said.

Hollern shook his head. "The recall was an order. We'll press on," he insisted.

Eventually, we reached the road, and our pace sped considerably. Ahead, the night sky was lit with the glow of many fires. The road was rough with recent foot and hoof prints. An hour later, we crested a rise and saw the army encampment below. The men gave a ragged cheer.

Hundreds of men had bivouacked in the revealed fields. Scores of campfires pushed back the darkness. Tents sprouted like enormous pale mushrooms in jagged lines. At their ends were improvised hitching posts where lines of horses were tied.

I turned, and saw that Jazen was as perplexed as I. Why had so many men gathered here? He shrugged and adjusted his shield's straps, settling it in a more comfortable position on his back.

"Only a bit further, you worthless lay-abouts," Hollern said. "Quit your belly-aching, or I'll tan your hides, I will." For him, it wasn't a bad attempt at motivation.

The company reached the outermost sentry picket, and I drifted away, soft as smoke. The men no longer needed my skills. I would watch from the cover of the trees, as I always did.

JAZEN CAME TO ME when dawn was a suggestion of blue in the east. I heard him before I saw him.

"Kirin?" he whispered. "Where are you, woman? I brought you something to break your fast."

I waited until he had passed, then swung down from the tree that sheltered me. Soundless, I ghosted across the forest floor. When I was a few scant steps behind him, I said, "You should be more cautious. I might have been a bandit."

He stopped and turned, seemingly unconcerned. He shook his head. "I would have heard a bandit. Only you could move so softly. I've brought food, and wine," he said, proffering a small sack and a nearly-empty skin.

I thanked him and accepted the food, tearing in with gusto. I had not eaten since the afternoon before, and my belly was hollow with hunger. Jazen smiled as I ate, his eyes alternating between watching me and scanning the dark trees.

"Did you find out why the recall was sounded?" I asked, after washing down a few mouthfuls.

"Aye. It's bad," he admitted. "It seems that the Mor have chosen now to re-emerge from their caves. The commander has reports of them moving south, burning as they go. They think they may be massing for an attack."

I stopped chewing, and searched his face for signs this was a jest. He looked back, unsmiling.

"But, why now?" I asked. "The last time the Mor attacked was generations ago. Half the people in my village thought the Mor were nothing more than tales meant to scare little children."

"Unfortunately for us, they're very real," he replied. "They've already swept through the outlying farms in the hinterlands, from what we hear. They attacked Mosby in force a few days ago and killed every last man, woman and child there, then decimated the bridge garrison. Only a handful of riders managed to escape to bring the warning."

I scowled. I remembered Mosby well; Urik had found me there. Many families had lived there. Many children had played in her streets. I felt a warm flush of anger in my chest.

"So, what now?" I asked.

"We are to move out and assemble at Gamth's Pass," he said. "We shall join forces with an expedition that was dispatched from the Imperial City. All told, we should have no less than five thousand men to guard the Pass by week's end."

The easy way he said this reassured me. Jazen was an experienced soldier and a sergeant in the Empire's army. He was well trained in the arts of warfare. Surely he knew how to gauge the threat posed by this dimly remembered enemy.

"You look worried," he said, then laughed. "Fear not. We shall have more than enough strength to break these monsters. Reports say that as fierce as the Mor are, they have only a fraction of our numbers. Plus, we have cavalry. And archers, as wretched as they are."

I shrugged. I was a scout. I would not be called upon to fight in a battle. My responsibility ended when I led my charges to their destination.

Jazen strode to me, and I looked up, startled, as he wrapped his arms around me. I began to protest, and his lips found mine.

A warm shock seemed to spread down from my burning face, and I felt my mouth opening beneath his, my tongue flicking out to brush against his. Jazen breathed in, drawing my breath into his body, and the tingling spread further still, evoking a fluttering shock in my belly. A moment later, he pulled back, smiling bemusedly, as if even he were surprised by what he had done. His eyes caught the growing dawn, shining pale blue in the chancy light.

"Kirin, I apologize. I don't know what—" he began.

My arms reached up, twining around his neck. My powerful archer's fingers cupped the back of his head, pulling him against me, hard. Once more, our mouths met. When I finally pulled away, I was breathless, my heart fluttering in my chest.

"You have to get back," I said, releasing him. "Hollern will be looking for you."

Jazen looked at me for a long moment, then nodded.

"We shall speak of this again. Soon," he said. I nodded, saying nothing, unsure if my voice would tremble.

He walked away, back towards the camp, and I let him go. As soon as he had disappeared, I sank to my knees.

"Gods, that was unwise. Unwise, unwise, unwise," I chanted to myself. "Hollern will soon lead us to war, and this is what I choose to think about?"

Inside, my sister chuckled, but said nothing more.

CHAPTER TWENTY-THREE

I stand on the manor wall, facing west. The last precious rays of the lowering sun shine with dazzling brilliance, orange and gold, over the tops of the distant peaks.

Ben Childers, along with the members of the refugee council, stands beside me. The walls are thick with frightened refugees. More crowd the manor courtyard in a milling, frightened mass. I stare into the setting sun, my eyes casting about for any hint of movement.

A smudge appears on the horizon, a cloud of dust. A moment later, a small figure can be seen; a horseman, riding hard. "Scout returning!" I shout in reflex. "Make ready the gate!"

My hunters, the most trained of the refugees, pull back the stout bar and swing wide the gates, just as the rider gallops into the courtyard. The horse, confronted by the people thronging the courtyard, rears, before calming hands quiet it.

"What news?" I call down. A moment later, the call is picked up by the rest. A hundred voices clamor for information. The scout answers, but his words are lost in the din.

"Get him up here," I tell Childers, "along with as many of the archers as you can find."

He nods and hurries off, fording the frightened tide of humanity.

"What should I do?" Lia asks.

"Go and make sure that Ato has all that he needs in the mercy tent, then return to me. I'll need you at my side."

She smiles. "I will not be long, and then we shall show these monstrosities the folly of their ways, yes?" She smiles. The look in her eyes, an expression brimming with unquestioning hope, stabs at me like a blade. I nod, hoping that my own expression does not betray my fears.

The repaired manor walls are thick, and tall. The gate is complete, remade from stout timbers reinforced with what iron we could salvage. But I remember, all too clearly, the awful strength of the Mor. If there are more than a few of them, even the repaired walls will not guarantee our safety. When they come, as I know they will, we must kill them; they cannot be allowed to leave, lest they summon more of their brethren.

In the end, it will come down to the training I have strived to impart to these people, coupled with their untested courage. Even Lia's considerable power can only do so much. If they breach the walls . . .

I wrap my arms about my belly as a wave of despair washes over me. *Oh, gods, no . . . not my child. Anything but that. Do not give me this gift only to snatch it away.*

The scout finally reaches the top of the wall, Childers in tow. The expression in Ben's eyes tells me all I need to know.

"How many?" I ask the scout anyway, already knowing that the news will not be good.

"It was hard to count; I fled as soon as they noticed me, as you ordered. I saw more than a score, though. Perhaps twice that," he pants. Several of the people around us wail at the figure, or offer up prayers for deliverance to the Lightbringer.

The taste of ashes is bitter in my mouth, but I force myself to say, "Well done." Two score. Against a hundred peasants, mostly women, armed with three swords, some woodcutting axes and a score of bows.

At the yard's far side, our precious horses are tied in a group, the riders stroking the nervous animals. At Gamth's Pass, the horses charged into the Mor again and again, until the enemy's burning blades finally broke the charge, but those were war horses, bred and trained for battle, not farm nags. I pray the mounts will not panic at the first scent of the burning or the blood that will soon come.

My eyes seek Lia's slender form, but she is nowhere to be seen. I wish she were here, at my side, squeezing my hand and telling me with the infuriating confidence of youth that all will be well. That we will live to see the sun rise in the morning.

"I see them!" a child shouts, pointing west into the last of the blood-red light. On the horizon, a larger cloud rises, as dozens of taloned feet churn the road into dust. People scream, and pray even louder than before.

Once again, just as they always do, the Mor have come.

"WHAT ARE THEY WAITING FOR?" Lia asks. The Mor have stood beneath the manor walls for over an hour, their stone gray bodies slowly melting into the gathering gloom. All that remains, all that we can see, are the glowing, emerald points of their eyes, watching us.

"I do not know," I admit. "Darkness, maybe. When we fought them at Gamth's Pass it was like this as well. The men, five thousand and more, waited for the Mor charge at the top of a long, broken slope. It was a good plan; the advantage of the high ground would blunt even the swiftest cavalry charge."

"What happened?" Lia whispers.

I lower my voice so that the sentries around us will not hear. Why discourage them? "Eventually, the men, embold-ened by the enemy's seeming hesitation, took matters into their own hands and charged. We outnumbered them ten to one, and as fierce as the Mor appeared, our commanders assured us that victory would be ours.

"It wasn't. The Mor withstood the charge. Though outnumbered, they held their line."

Lia nods, but says nothing. In the darkness, the sapphire flashes that cavort in her eyes are bright, heralds of the lightning that I know is hers to command.

The night deepens. Clouds roll from the west, drawing a charcoal blanket across the stars and the moon. A chill breeze rides in their wake, threading icy fingers into cloaks and hoods. I huddle in my cape, rubbing myself for warmth.

The baby is active tonight, twirling and kicking, as if it wants to be free of this place. I hug myself and hum a snatch of a lullaby, telling the baby to rest.

Why are they waiting? They did not hesitate to attack at Fort Azure. No sooner had they arrived than they surged towards Hollern's hastily erected barricade. If they have ever felt fear as we understand the emotion, I have never seen it.

Even at Gamth's Pass, even when they waited for us to bring the fight to them, I felt no fear in them. Why did they wait?

An idea occurs to me, and my blood goes cold. I turn to Lia.

"What if they are waiting for more of them?" I ask her.

"Why would they?" she replies, frowning. "Do they not already have force enough to attack?"

"The Mor always kill every human they encounter. Burn them and tear down their homes and dwelling places. We always thought that it was because they hated us for reasons we didn't understand, but what if the reason they attack isn't hatred, but rather fear? Then, might they not wait for as many of them to come as possible before committing to an attack?"

Lia frowns, considering the idea. Finally, she nods.

"It makes a certain kind of sense, I suppose. But what should we do about it?"

"Attack," I say, trying to sound certain. "Once the Mor commit, they never retreat. If we send out a force, then draw them back inside the walls, the Mor will doubtless pursue."

"But, Kirin, sending the people out there—"

"We'll send the riders out for a single skirmish, then pull them back as soon as the Mor counterattack. They'll retreat past our archers."

"Some very well might die if they go outside the walls," she whispers. "What if you are wrong?"

"We always knew the horsemen would have to get outside to be effective," I say. "The only difference now is that we pick the time. And, if the Mor are indeed waiting for reinforcements before attacking, I'd rather fight this smaller force first and then deal with the others later, rather than trying to defend the walls against all of them at once."

She nods, the lightning spiking in her eyes. "I shall tell the leader of the scouts. Give us five minutes."

I clap her on the shoulder before she can leave. She stops at the touch of my hand. Then she is in my arms, hugging me tight, so tight that for a moment I cannot breathe. I feel the slide and play of her muscles under her linen shift, the hard smoothness of her body pressed to mine.

I breathe in the clean smell of her auburn hair, my eyes shut tight. She kisses me on the cheek, and whispers something in the wind-like language of the zephyr spirits.

"What was—" I begin.

"Ask me again, when the battle is won," she says, then draws away. As she turns, I see the sparkle of tears in her eyes. Then she is gone, hurrying down the steep steps leading to the courtyard.

I turn away, to face the leader of my archers. "Ready your strings," I say. "Be ready to shoot on my command."

The woman nods, grounding the tip of her bow behind her heel and bending the stout yew shaft. She slides the looped bowstring into the notch, then checks the pull. The other archers, nineteen strong, mirror her movement.

I string my own weapon, then check the bag of arrows propped against the low stone railing, filling my quiver. "Don't waste a single shot," I remind them. "We only have a few score shafts apiece, and the Mor's armor is thick. Aim for the eyes, or the joints. Even if you do not kill them, you will slow them, and slowing them might be enough."

In the courtyard, the horsemen mount their beasts and turn to the gates. The crowd parts for them. Voices rise in a babble of questions.

"Stay together," the leader of the scouts shouts over the din. "One pass, and one pass only, then retreat to the safety of the gates!" The riders nod and fidget, their eyes full of fear. Their anxiety is picked up by the animals, who stamp and circle nervously.

Lia stands beside the gates, looking up at me. I catch her eye and nod. She barks a command, and the refugees shoot back the bar. The gates swing open, accompanied by the riders' desperate battle cry. The thunder of hooves fills the yard.

The horses shoot across the smooth grass in a jagged line, headed straight for the Mor. I cannot see the enemy, but I hear their eerie, piping voices, raised in alarm, or consternation, or perhaps simple amusement, I cannot tell. The dim light glints fitfully from their burnished carapaces as they shift to meet the new threat.

Each rider has been armed with several short spears, fire-hardened sticks little longer than javelins. I have trained them, every day, in their use, riding them past hay-filled dummies until they can skewer the target four times out of five. Before they ride past the ring of our firelight, I see the spears brandished in their fists.

The charge meets the unseen line with a crash of splintering wood. Men and women scream battle cries; to Loran; to Ur, the red-handed god of battle; to the distant Emperor. I see inhuman knives flashing in the darkness, long, serrated blades shining with laval heat, rising and falling. A horse screams, then a second, and I hear the sickening sound of breaking bones, chillingly clear over the mêlée's din.

"Fall back! Fall back!" the scouts' leader shouts. I hear the horses, still galloping, see the indistinct black smudge that marks the mass of riders, sweeping left, then circling back. Occasionally, a horse goes down, whinnying, as it stumbles into some unseen hole. Behind them, I see a larger mass, moving like a black spear in their wake, pursuing. The enemy swiftly silences the fallen horses' and riders' screams.

The Mor, it seems, have taken the bait.

"Archers ready!" I shout, plucking an arrow from my quiver and setting it to the string. The riders are a hundred yards away, galloping as fast as they dare in the darkness for the gates. The Mor are close behind, as implacable as the tide.

"Draw!" I say, pulling the feathered end back to my ear. Instinctively, I raise the tip, then shift to the right, into the rising wind. Below, the horsemen thunder into the firelight, then through the gates. I hear the boom as they are slammed shut and the bolt replaced. "Steady, now! Steady!" I call.

The Mor are fifty yards away now. Forty. Thirty.

The first form swims out of the gloom and into the firelight, the ruddy glow reflecting from polished, bone-like armor. I see the glare of emerald eyes, fixed on the fragile gates. See the massive, clawed upper arms, strong enough to rend mail like paper, to pluck a man's limbs from their body like a child pulling a weed. The smaller, lower limbs clutch braces of weapons, square hammers or sullenly glowing knives as long as swords.

"Shoot!" I scream, aiming for the lead monster's face. Beside me, I hear a slithering whisper and a thrum as twenty bows sing out their subtle war cry. The darkness is filled with the whistle of death.

Below, a Mor screams as a shaft finds a vulnerable place. Then a second, unnerving wail splits the night. I see a Mor warrior, staggering, its lower hands reaching up to clutch at the shaft sticking out of its ruined eye. My heart thrills at the sight.

My hand reaches back and draws a second shaft, fitting it to the string, pulling and loosing all in one smooth movement. "Make every shot count!" I yell. My second shot is still in the air as I ready the third.

The Mor surge forward, into the firelight. A rain of arrows bounce and skitter off their armor with a sound like stones hurled against slate. Several have shafts protruding from the softer joints, limping with pain, but still they come. I see one go down, an arrow jutting from its face shield, maybe the one I saw hit before, perhaps a second, I am not sure. The rest of the Mor trample it into the dust.

They reach the door, upper limbs booming against the timbers. I lean down, searching for a vulnerable spot, but from above, all I can see is the smooth dome of their shoulder armor and the tops of their helmet-like heads. Around me, the archers rain down shafts, all of which bounce away harmlessly.

"Save your arrows! Save your arrows!" I scream. "Help me with this!"

I hurry to one of the piles of stone the masons have laboriously carted up onto the wall. The pile is secured by planks of wood, tied with rope across a five-foot breach in the stone rail. I pull out my knife and start sawing at one of the ropes.

An archer, Natalie I think her name is, a young girl who already shows much promise with the bow, draws her own knife and attacks the other side. A moment later, the rope parts and the wooden slats tumble out, followed by a rain of jagged stone.

The debris falls, a deadly hail that even the mighty Mor cannot withstand. The tiny avalanche crushes several of the inhuman warriors to the earth in a cloud of dust. The archers send up a ragged cheer as the Mor pull back.

I wince as the baby kicks, hard, driving the breath from my lungs. I reach down and pat my belly, absently willing it to be still. It thrashes inside me, as if frightened by the din.

Below, the rubble is piled four feet high before the scarred gates. Armored limbs protrude from between the stones, some still, others twitching. The stones shift, and I see with horror that several of the trapped Mor are already moving, struggling to free themselves.

"Kirin!" Lia screams. I look over, and there she is, striding through the archers, lightning flickering in her eyes. I feel the hairs on the backs of my arms rise as the glow is reflected in the skies above.

"Sssssath al'wazul, d'ssth kal tum!" Lia shouts in the language of the wind spirits, her arms upthrust, beseeching her elemental allies. The air is filled with the sharp tang of summertime lightning.

A bolt of dazzling, amethyst fire lances down like the finger of an angry god, striking the mass of buried Mor. The thunderclap sounds in the same moment, stunning the ears of all present into silence. Even the Mor, usually implacable in the face of the worst that men can throw at them, flinch away from the bolt.

Lia calls out again, drawing down a second, then a third stroke. In the dazzling brilliance, I see Mor scattering, flying through the air amongst a hail of stones and small boulders.

When my eyes can once more focus, I see the pile below, glowing sullenly. Six of the Mor lie still, their armored flesh split and steaming. Others move, feebly, obviously sorely wounded. The archers give a cheer, which is swiftly picked up by the refugees in the courtyard.

Even as the shout is echoing from the manor's stones, the Mor surge forth again, clambering up the stony slope to resume their assault on the gate. Their talons gouge chunks from the timbers and their fiery blades pry into the uneven cracks.

I command the archers to let loose with our second and last rock fall. Again, the stones rumble down. This time, however, the Mor are prepared, and raise their powerful upper arms above their heads like shields as the rocks fall. Some go down, but many others are merely staggered as stones large enough to crush a man in an instant are pushed aside.

Lia once more begins her chant, her arms reaching for the clouds. A fresh stroke of lightning pierces the night, scattering the Mor like leaves and tumbling them from their feet.

I look over, and see a dark smear on Lia's face. A freshet of blood streams from her nose. She pants in exhaustion, leaning forwards against the stone rail. Below, the Mor stir once more, unburying themselves. More than a dozen lie on the ground, almost half of the attacking force, unmoving, hopefully dead, but more, so many more, are even now struggling to rejoin the fight. Gods, what will it take to finally stop them?

"Archers, keep shooting!" I shout, putting action to my words. Shafts flicker out, seeking Mor blood but only occasionally finding it. I move to Lia's side, grasp her arm.

"What's wrong?" I hiss in her ear.

"Calling down the storm . . ." she pants, pawing at the blood on her face. "It is so difficult. My allies . . . demand so much . . ."

"How many more bolts can you summon?" I ask.

"A few more," she says, looking up at me, resolve shining in her eyes. "I shall do what is necessary, worry not. The Mor will not harm you or your child, I swear it."

I nod, her vow drawing stinging tears from my eyes. I look over the wall. A Mor looks up at me, and, without thinking, I draw a shaft and shoot. It shrugs aside at the last moment, and the shaft ricochets off its face plate.

My blood magic curls and twists in my belly, woken by the sight of the Mor's eyes boring into mine. *Blood,* it sings. *Eternally blood. Blood, and death, and power.*

I frown and push the desire aside. Using the blood magic on the gepar in the mountains saved my life, I remember, but the alien quality of its life force nearly overwhelmed me. There is no telling what the blood of a Mor warrior will do to me.

The Mor press against the gate once more, their claws booming against the planks, a sound like huge, infernal drums. A moment later, the barricade gives a last shuddering groan, then splits with a sound like a giant handclap. Clawed hands reach forth and grasp the edges of the breach, striving to tear the entire gate aside. Inside, people wail and scream, near panic at the sight of the timbers buckling.

I look over, and see Lia struggling to rise. She once more begins her chant, but it is ragged and weak. I must do something, or they will come through. That cannot happen; Lia's power cannot be used, under any circumstances, while the enemy is amongst the refugees.

"Look at me!" I scream as, inside, the blood magic shifts, somehow gargantuan, hotter than blood itself. The Mor, compelled by the power threaded into my words, look up. I lock my gaze to a set of glowing, opaline eyes.

The first Mor dies, screaming, as my power flows into it. The blood magic rampages through the inhuman body, spread with every beat of the thing's mighty heart, exploding veins and arteries one after another. It staggers aside, black blood streaming from every joint and opening in a dark, jetting tide.

A second Mor meets my gaze and jerks as the power hooks it. It has time for a single, piping gurgle before I stretch forth my hand. A river of black blood springs from its eyes and mouth, flying back to me, splashing against my alabaster skin and soaking through my shift.

A moment later, the foul substance sinks into my flesh, leaving my skin pristine and pure once more.

I laugh as the Mor's strength pours into me, setting my nerves afire with mingled ecstasy and pain. Inside, the baby jerks in time, responding to the influx of savage vitality, but compared to the enormity of the black tide, the sensation is a distant, feeble thing that I barely notice.

Again, I reach out and thread the tendrils of the blood magic into a set of Mor eyes, relishing in the sensation of my power twining through the very root of its life before yanking it out, viciously, in a spray of midnight blood.

All around me the archers are screaming and running, many covered with the same blood that now sings inside my own veins. I wonder what they see when they look at me, my black eyes shining like coals, clothes soaked with the blood that, even now, sinks without a trace into my body. I laugh at the idea. They do well to be afraid. Let them fear me, even as I save them.

A fourth, then a fifth Mor jerks and falls before the mass of inhuman warriors begins to realize what is happening. They pull back, their visored faces swiveling upwards, seeking the new threat. A sixth warrior's strength flows into me with its blood, then a seventh. I am so strong now. I could rend their armored flesh like paper, if only I could get my bare hands on them.

The idea sings to me, so appealing, too tempting, that I actually step forward, intending to step out into the air and fall amongst them. Distantly, I hear Lia scream my name, the sound insignificant compared to the blood tide thundering in my head.

Inside, the baby thrashes and kicks, desperately. I scarcely notice. Then, a moment later, it gives a last, mighty push, and falls still.

Instantly, a pain greater than anything I have ever felt rips through me, outwards from my belly. My legs twist, every muscle cramping at once, pitching me to the cold stones. I feel blood splash across my thighs as something inside of me lets go. I scream.

Lying on the stones, I am suddenly myself again. The madness whirling behind my eyes withdraws. The power of the Mor still rages inside of me, but the terrible pain has, for the moment, pushed it aside.

I look up, and see Lia beside me. She is splattered from head to toe with black blood. She says something, maybe my name, the words lost in the raging tumult.

Then the pain returns, worse then a barbed sword, worse than fire, a sensation like claws rending my flesh from the inside out. I scream, scream until I taste blood in my mouth from my torn throat.

The baby is still. A moment ago, it was thrashing and moving. Now, it is motionless.

Motionless.

"Oh, gods, what have I done?" I whisper. I meet Lia's eyes, and beg, "Save it. As you love me, save the baby!"

Once more, the pain stabs through me, and all I can do is scream once more.

CHAPTER TWENTY-FOUR

Jazen Tor came to me on the first night of our journey to Gamth's Pass.

As always, I camped apart from the men. He followed the light of my fire. Normally, I would have banked the flames, made them difficult to see, but that night, I made the fire a beacon in the darkness, drawing him to me.

He had flowers in his hands, a rude bouquet of the tiny, sky-blue wildflowers that grew beside the road. I laughed to see them, imagining him gathering them, furtive, in the dark.

We wasted no time with words. Our bodies, our hands and fingers and other, more sensitive things, spoke for us. The bouquet fell to the ground beside the blankets I had laid beside the fire. I yearned for him, for his touch, hurrying, almost tearing at his clothes and mine. I tugged down his breeches with fingers made rough with urgency.

I turned, pushing him down, and stripped off my own leggings. I swung astride him and lowered myself onto him. The sensation of him entering me, filling me, made me shiver.

Jazen reached up, stroking my face, my throat. I growled and grasped his wrists, forcing them over his head and pinning them to the ground. I lowered myself and devoured his mouth with mine.

He moaned, the sound traveling through our mingled breath into my own body. I pulled back, gasping for breath, then bent again to lick and nip at his throat. Soon my climax swept over me and I screamed, not caring if any man or beast heard me.

It had been so long. Gods, so very long, since someone had held me, had touched me with desire, let alone tenderness. I collapsed on top of him, Jazen still moving beneath me, seeking his own release. I let go his wrists, felt his powerful, swordsman's fingers grasp mine. When he stiffened beneath me, breathing hard and whispering my name, a second shock rolled through me.

I rolled off him, then lay beside him on our mingled blankets. The mountain air was chill, the fire a warm, welcome presence. I tasted the salty musk of blood in my mouth, and looked at Jazen. During our lovemaking, I had bitten him on the shoulder. The wound still bled, sluggishly, from the double crescent my teeth had left.

"I'm sorry. I hurt you," I whispered, tracing the wound with a fingertip.

"It was worth it," he murmured in reply, nuzzling me. I shivered as his lips brushed across the soft hairs on the back of my neck. I reached out and gathered up the scattered blossoms, twining them absently together into a princess's diadem. I remembered the times when Kirin and I had woven flowers into each other's hair. I sensed her, smiling inside of me, at the memory.

"Besides," he continued, pressing himself against my back, his arm tight and strong across my chest, "we northmen are hardy, not like those soft creatures of the lowlands. It will take more than a love bite to hurt me."

I rolled away from him, onto my back, then pulled him on top of me, relishing the feel of his weight. I put the flower diadem on my head, watching Jazen look at me. His expression, so warm, so tender, a secret look so unlike his usual confident, challenging gaze, re-ignited the coals of my lust. I pulled him down.

Once more we kissed, mouths opening, tongues sliding and tangling. Soon I felt him stiffening once more between my thighs. This time, the lovemaking was slow and purposeful, as we each strove to fulfill the other and ourselves.

He stayed until dawn was a dim, blue promise in the east, then slipped away after many farewell kisses and caresses. I put out the fire and gathered my things, placing the wilted diadem carefully into my pack. I spent the day trying to do my job. To not think of his face, of the sight of his body moving above me.

We took every opportunity in the four days that followed to be together, spending the long spring evenings at each other's side, sharing food and drink before slaking our other, more base, appetites. Every night, Jazen brought me more of the delicate blue flowers, and every night I wove them into a garland for my pale hair.

"The men must know about us," he said one night as he lay beside me, still breathing hard from our last passionate tussle. "They're covering for me; the small japes and jests they've let slip are obvious enough. They're good men, gods love them. Better than a commander like Hollern—Captain Hollern, I mean—deserves. Still, he is our superior and so is deserving of our obedience."

I frowned at Jazen's tone of respect, then mentally shrugged. Loyalty such as Jazen's was the granite foundation upon which the Empire had been built. It was a good trait in a soldier, I supposed, no matter how undeserving one's commanding officer was of it.

"You do not agree," he said.

"I . . . I think that you do yourself proud by your loyalty," I replied. "The men are lucky to have you watching over them."

"And what about you? Do you feel yourself lucky?"

Our mingled sweat stood out on his deep chest, sparkling in a thick mat of hair. In answer, I leaned forward and licked a salty drop, then moved my attention to his tiny nipple. His breathing roughened as the flesh stiffened under my tongue.

"I don't want to talk about the men, or about Hollern, or anything else right now," I whispered. "Right now, I have other plans for that oh so loyal tongue of yours."

Jazen laughed, twining his fingers in my hair and rolling over. He laid me on my back on the blankets, moving over me, then sliding slowly down the length of my body. When I felt his hot breath against my thighs, I moaned, softly, in anticipation of what was to come.

Soon, I surrendered to the feelings growing in my sex, allowing myself to submerge in the sensation like a blood-warm tide. Inside, my sister purred in shared ecstasy, murmuring wordless approval at my choice.

As always, he stayed afterwards, lying beside me until the small hours just before dawn. I watched him as he slept, his rugged face just visible in the starlight.

I did not join him in slumber; I needed little sleep. As the stars slowly spun overhead, my eyes searched the darkness for any threat.

I shook him when dawn was imminent. "You mustn't be late," I said when he protested, pulling the blanket over his face. "Hollern must not discover where you have been spending your nights."

He frowned as I said this, as if he meant to protest, but I shook my head. I knew that Jazen saw nothing wrong in what we did. I, being a scout, and so outside the chain of command, was not bound by the army's rules concerning such things.

Still, I had my reasons, even if I did not feel like explaining them; let my mere desire be good enough for him. He shrugged and rose, wriggling into his leathers, before departing with a last, lingering kiss.

That morning, before the early morning fog had fully lifted from the valley, we reached Gamth's Pass and saw the Mor for the first time.

I CURSED AND KICKED MY HORSE'S RIBS, urging the animal into a quick trot. The ground was treacherous with stones and unexpected holes, concealed by the waist-high grass. I felt nervous and exposed out in the open, and wanted nothing better than to complete my mission and return to our lines.

The Mor were not difficult to find. The creatures filled the northern end of the valley, a carpet of slate gray flesh and waving claws. They were huge, much taller than a man and almost twice as broad.

In appearance, they resembled a knight in armor, heavy shoulders protected by curving plates of burnished gray armor. They framed a blunt, wedge-like skull, featureless save for a narrow eye slit. Their legs were short and stout, thick pillars of armored muscle, supporting barrel-like chests.

The Mor had two sets of arms. The inner pair were small and delicate, tipped with graceful, four-fingered hands. The upper were very different, huge and powerful. They terminated in four thick claws, each almost a foot long.

No sooner had I stopped to begin my count, than they began surging forward. I finished my task, striving to remain calm as they began their advance up the valley's slope. As soon as I was done, I turned my mount and started back. Behind me, the Mor's strange war cry filled the long, narrow valley. The sound, like pipes, or like the whistle of wind past a rooftop eave, sent a chill through my blood.

Some of the men, those who had families that worked in the deep places in the earth, had been telling stories of the Mor for days. Of how their claws could rend armor like cloth. Or of how their shamans could harness the heat of the earth, breathing it into their stone weapons.

Most laughed at what sounded like such obvious exaggerations. Never Jazen. He watched, and listened, drinking in every detail as if his life, and those of his men, depended on it.

I supposed that they did. After all, Hollern certainly could not be bothered to learn about the enemy; he was far too busy receiving the Lightbringer's blessings and the priests' assurances of victory to bother with the mundane details of war. In his mind, the battle was already won.

Behind me, the Mor that I had outdistanced turned back and rejoined their fellows. I rode back, up the long slope leading to our position at the southern end of the Pass. I felt their eyes on my back, a dull, malignant pressure.

"Scout returning!" our sentries called out as I approached. I guided my mount towards the red and blue striped tent of Lord Mermond, commander of the Imperial Expedition and warlord of the assembled companies.

"What news?" Hollern said, grabbing my horse's bridle. I swung down and gave him a withering look.

"I suggest you come inside and hear my report if you want to learn more. Sir."

Hollern's ruddy face paled as I said this. Behind him, I saw Jazen standing with the men. He shook his head minutely, his eyes warning me. I ignored it.

"Why you . . . " Hollern began. "You're under my command and I will hear your report. Now."

I leaned forward, pitching my voice so that only he could hear.

"You pompous fool," I hissed. "Find some other way to curry the favor of the Lord Commander. This news is not for the men's ears. The army has seen fit to make you the leader of these men. Act like it."

Hollern pursed his lips, and I saw the muscles in his jaw jump as he ground his teeth together. I turned away and headed towards the tent door.

It was crowded with officers; captains all, with their aides in tow. My arrival triggered a chorus of demands for information. Hollern trailed in my wake, his impatience pressing against my back like a shove.

I ignored all of them and walked straight to Lord Mermond. He sat behind a camp table upon which a map of Gamth's Pass was spread.

Two priests, one of the Lightbringer and a second of Ur, attended him, standing a respectful distance behind the Commander. I frowned to see them; they had no place here.

As I walked forward, the priest of the Lightbringer sketched a warding gesture in my direction, his gaze fixed on my eyes. I favored him with a long, unbroken look until he turned aside with a curse. Inside, my sister growled a wordless warning.

I stood until Mermond looked up. He frowned.

"What news?" His voice, like the rest of him, was hard and rough, the result of decades in the field.

"They are assembled in the north end of the valley, just as we hoped," I said. "I saw nothing resembling mounts; I'm not sure how that rumor began. All of them are on foot.

"Our cavalry will be hard-pressed to set a proper charge, however," I continued. "The ground is very broken, with many stones and hollows."

"That will hinder the enemy as well," Mermond said, then addressed the captains. "We shall hold this position atop the rise and receive their charge, not rush down to meet them."

He turned back to me. "How many did you see?"

"I counted them as you told me, and figure they have no more than five hundred, all told," I replied. Judging their numbers had been surprisingly easy, thanks to Mermond's advice: look at the enemy and divide them in two, then divide again, and again once more, only then counting individuals. Of course, only someone with schooling could multiply the final number by eight, but thanks to my mother's insistence on education, I was such a woman.

Mermond looked at me levelly; perhaps my answer had been too quick. Then he shrugged. No doubt the other scouts would verify my figure.

"Good work," he said, turning back to his map.

I saluted, as I had seen the men do, even though I technically did not need to.

Outside, I rejoined Jazen and the other men. His eyes were serious, so different than they had been last night. "How many?" he asked.

"About five hundred," I told him, softly. "The way I figure it, we outnumber them ten to one. Perhaps Hollern is right this time and the gods are smiling down on us."

"*Captain* Hollern has prayed long and hard for our safety," Jazen replied, a bit louder than was necessary. "If the priests say they are on our side in this, then you can believe it."

I frowned, but something in his eyes kept me from replying. I shrugged and moved away. When he was with the men, there were times that I did not understand him.

He does what he must so that they will keep following Hollern, my sister whispered in my head. *You should not contradict him, or speak ill of him in front of them.*

I shrugged but did not reply. I knew this, even as I knew that it sickened me to see a proud man such as Jazen Tor the follower of such as Hollern.

After a time, the captains emerged from the tent, then dispersed, headed for their companies. Hollern, red faced, strode towards us.

"Assemble your men, sergeant," he said to Jazen with a swagger. "The Lord Commander has given us our place in the battle line. Together we shall show these beasts what it means to cross the Empire."

"Very good, sir," Jazen said, then turned to shout orders at the men. At his command, squads and companies formed up, moved into their lines.

I had never before, nor would I ever again, see so many armed men, all moving with such grim purpose. Seeing the sheer number of them, arrayed under the fitful sun, the light gleaming from their mail and their sword pommels as if from a vast, metallic glacier, made me shiver.

Certainly, even beings as singularly puissant as the Mor were no match for such a force.

I moved back, further up-slope, to where the archers were assembling, and waited for the coming battle.

"HOLD THE LINE! HOLD THE LINE!" Jazen screamed, riding along the rear of the formation. His sword was brandished high above his head, shining in the sun like a flame-red banner. His cloak, the midnight blue and silver of the company's colors, streamed behind him.

I took careful aim at the enemy, then loosed a fresh shaft. It would not do to strike our own men in the back, and with the Mor lines merging with ours, the danger was great. I cursed as the shaft, like many before it, bounced harmlessly from the enemy's armor.

Below, the screams of dying men mingled with the Mor's keening wails. Burning blades and stout hammers rose and fell. Mighty claws ripped and tore, each blow reaping another life. Step by step, the Mor were doing the unthinkable.

They were pressing us back.

Even though we had the advantage of numbers, they overmatched us in sheer strength and ferocity. Even my untrained eye could see that the soldiers, so sure of victory a scant hour before, cocky to the point of arrogance, were faltering. I had to do something.

I broke from formation, leaving the other archers behind. Ahead, I spied Mermond's blue and red tent. There was only one way that I could help them, help Jazen, even though it meant exposing my forbidden knowledge.

Ahead, on a tall rise, Mermond and the rest of his officers stood, overseeing the battle. I tried to approach, but the guards blocked my way. "But I have a way that we can aid the men in their fight!" I protested. I pointed to the piles of dead already heaped outside the army's mercy tent. "Do not let their sacrifice go to waste!"

One of the guards looked at me, deciding if I were a madwoman, I suppose, then turned and hurried up the slope. He spoke to an aid, then pointed down at me. The man scowled, but walked down.

He looked annoyed at the interruption, and hesitated to listen, even when I promised him that I could help with the battle.

"You must come with me and see for yourself," I said, as the blood magic twisted in my belly. His eyes went slack, just for a moment, and I knew he would follow. I strode to the mercy tent.

I picked a body, a man cut from groin to chest by a Mor blade, and opened my secret eye. All around, the specters of the dead wandered, their white eyes burning, lusting for revenge. They turned to me, a mute wall of supplication, translucent arms outstretched.

"Soon," I whispered.

I gestured for the ghost of the slain man to step forward, then a moment later the body began to twitch and jerk as the spirit sank back into its former flesh. My sister crooned a welcome as my sweetling tore itself from its former shell, blinking in the dazzling sun.

"Gods!" the aide exclaimed. "What foulness is this?" He drew his sword and my dark child hissed.

"Abomination!" someone called. I looked over, into the wildly rolling eyes of the priest of Loran Lightbringer. He held his staff before him, the lambent flame of his god's power crackling at the tip. The call was swiftly picked up by the men.

"No! You do not understand!" I screamed. "Herein lies our salvation! My sweetlings are relentless in battle. They feel no pain. They can help. Please, do not do this! *The men are faltering!*"

"Lightbringer, protect us!" the priest boomed, swinging his staff in a two-handed strike. The blow struck my sweetling in the head. Power surged, and a moment later my child crumbled to dust.

"Restrain her!" the aide called out. Rough hands gripped me. I wailed, protesting the death of my sweetling, but a madness had overcome the men. I saw fear written in each face, shining from every eye.

"Do that again, witch, and I shall order them to kill you where you stand," the priest said. "Take her away."

"Should we restrain her?" the aide said, his sword still in his fist.

The priest eyed me, then shook his head. The screams of the battle below floated up to us. "No. We have larger problems, and cannot spare the men. But mark me, and mark me well, witch; when this is all over, if I ever see your face again, then there shall indeed be a reckoning."

I nodded, understanding his words. The men hustled me away from the camp, then released me. I strode off, headed back down-slope, back for Jazen and the others. As I turned, I saw Hollern, watching from his position at the rear of the company. He had seen the entire exchange. A satisfied smile turned up the corners of his mouth. His eyes shone with a fanatic's hungry light.

I was almost back to the lines when the trumpets sounded. My blood ran cold. The horns signaled a full retreat. Ahead,

I saw the colorful mass of the soldiers' cloaks splinter, like a shattered rainbow, breaking apart as spikes of seething gray rent the tenuous lines.

"Retreat! Retreat!" I heard, over and over. Below, the cavalry rode into the Mor flank, heedless of the treacherous ground. The action slowed the Mor, somewhat, allowing the bulk of the men to disengage.

"Jazen! Jazen Tor!" I screamed, trying to make myself heard over the din. I looked and there, near the left flank, I saw a knot of silver and blue.

I breasted the line of fleeing men, the sound of battle growing louder with every passing moment. Soon I saw them ahead: the tattered remnants of the company. Jazen stood with them, his sword rising and falling. All around, the bodies of fallen men littered the grass.

"Jazen! We must withdraw!" I screamed, coming up behind him. The Mor were there, right there, grappling with the men. Up close they were even more terrifying than I had realized, towering mountains of stone-hard muscle. Their knives glowed with heat that I could feel even from afar.

He looked back at me, then nodded. "Retreat! Fall back" he shouted. Just as they had been trained to do, the men compacted, overlapping their shields. Maintaining formation, they walked backwards, up the treacherous slope. Hollern came up behind me, in time to observe the last orderly retreat. All around, broken men ran and screamed, all semblance to an organized army gone.

Below, the Mor surged forward, irresistible as the coming of the tide.

The battle of Gamth's Pass was over; now all that was left was the slaughter.

CHAPTER TWENTY-FIVE

Lia helps me down the steps to the manor courtyard as the battle outside the gates rages. The terrible pressure in my belly slackens abruptly, and I feel a fresh surge of hot, sticky wetness flowing down my thighs. The pain is immense and indescribable, robbing my legs of strength, nearly pitching me to the flagstones.

All around me, women and men are shouting, animals are screaming, the cacophony threaded through with the ululating piping of the Mor. The gates shiver as mighty limbs slam against them.

Refugees surge forward, armed with rakes and staffs and other improvised weapons. They beat at the taloned paws clawing at the splintering wood. A red-hot blade flickers through the gap, and a goodwife reels back, screaming, her shift and hair afire.

A second, then a third refugee falls, the victim of claws or burning blades. Terrified people scream as the Mor crowd the widening gap. Soon the wood will fail. Soon the defenders will break. Then the Mor will be inside, and it will all be over.

"You have to close the breach!" I scream at Lia. "If you cannot, you must scatter them, or all is lost! There are fewer now. Maybe you—"

Lia looks down. "Your water has broken," she says. "We have to get you inside."

"It can't have broken. I've weeks to go . . . It's too soon . . ." I protest, weakly. "Lia, please, they must not get inside! *Help the defenders!*"

"The gates will hold long enough," she says.

Inside, the red tide of my blood magic, coupled with the otherworldly vitality that I stole from the Mor, sings in my veins, filling me like a chalice near to overflowing. I feel as if I could run, could dance and twirl like a young girl. That I could leap from the stone walls and be gone from this slaughterhouse in a twinkling.

The pain drives a fresh blade of agony into me, turning my legs to water, and this time I do fall. Lia grunts as I become dead weight in her hands.

She calls out for help, and a moment later rough hands grip me, lift me. Two men hurry me away, towards a familiar, blood-stained tent.

Inside, men and women lie, their life leaking away in rivers of scarlet, moaning, screaming. Without meaning to, I open my secret eye, and see that the living are surrounded by the spirits of the dead. They turn their white eyes towards me, mouths stretching in supplication, pleading for me to help them, to avenge them. To allow them one last minute of life.

"I cannot be here!" I scream, shutting both my mortal and supernatural eyes tight. "I cannot bear it!"

"But . . . Ato can help you to . . ." Lia stammers.

"Take me out!" I howl. I know that if I remain, I will open my inner eye again.

The men turn me, and a moment later I am outside once more. "Find Livinia. She will know what to do," I pant, as a fresh wave of fire tears through me. My belly is a stone, a dead weight, dragging me down.

Lia commands one of the men to find the midwife and takes my arm. He dashes off, calling her name. Lia and the man half carry me towards the main hall. Inside, women and children are huddled in a frightened mass.

"Stay with her until the midwife arrives," Lia commands the man. He nods, his eyes round and wide. He looks at the black blood that coats me from head to toe and swallows, as if holding down his gorge.

Lia grabs my face, forcing me to look at her. "We shall live through this, you and I. And the baby. We shall endure. Do you trust me?"

I nod, weakly, wanting desperately to believe her, and try to smile. The expression twists into a grimace of pain as a fresh contraction ripples through me.

"Go. Please, go now. The gates—"

She nods and hurries out. All around me, people move forward, murmuring comforting words, leading me with gentle pressure deeper into the manor.

Then I am finally lying in a bed. My back screams in protest as they lower me, but even that pain is a pale shadow of what I feel down below. I paw at my dress, sliding the sticky, ruined thing up. The garment smears the Mor's stinking, black blood across my drum-tight belly.

My body absorbs the blood in an instant, leaving my pale skin clear. A woman breathes a prayer, or a curse, I cannot tell.

Darkness beats at my face like blackbirds' wings. A face swims out of the murk. Livinia.

"Something is wrong," the old midwife says, her hands stroking my belly. A moment later, her fingers slide inside of me, the sensation tearing a scream from my lips. I look for Lia, but she has gone, returned to the fighting.

"Your time is very near now," she says, bringing her face close to mine. I close my eyes, every fiber of my body screaming at me to push out the thing inside of me. A moment later I feel her hands on my cheeks, pulling my face back to hers.

"Kirin! Do not push yet! Listen to me, Kirin. Not yet!"

I nod, eyes still clenched tight, striving to master the agony. Years of study have taught me that labor is indeed painful, but nothing could have prepared me for *this*.

"It is too soon . . . too soon . . ." I moan. "Please, Livinia, do not let my baby die."

"I have seen babes survive such an early birth," the midwife says, clasping my hand in hers. "Just concentrate on breathing, as we talked about."

The thought of facing this agony with naught but a few breathing exercises would almost be amusing, were I not in such pain. I bite back the curses I yearn to fling at the old woman; she means well.

"Hold her knees," she commands. I feel women's hands on me, people I do not know. They spread my legs wider. I feel no shame; am beyond caring about anything as trivial as exposing myself to strangers.

The increasing spasms drown out the noise of the battle raging outside, obliterate every other sensation. Throughout it all, the baby is still, motionless. Waves of pain come and go in a nightmare progression, heralded by Livinia's demands that I not push, that I breathe.

How long I lay there, I do not know. Minutes and hours lose all meaning. My world narrows to my bed of white-hot fire.

"I see the head!" Livinia finally crows. "Push now, Kirin! Push!"

I bear down, my muscles trembling. The strength of the Mor has faded. My body is so very weary, lacking the strength to do more than offer up a token effort.

"Again! Push again!" the midwife calls, her hands busy. I feel something hard, stretching me, sliding past flesh and bone. Livinia grunts as she twists and pulls.

A final push, and the baby slithers out. Instantly, the pain is gone, clean as a knife cut. My torn and stretched flesh still aches in protest of the abuse it has endured, but compared to the overwhelming pain from before, it is easily borne.

"You have a lovely son, Kirin," Livinia says. I hear the concern in her voice.

The babe is tiny, a scarce double handful, slicked with bloody residue and creamy white mother's wax. It kicks, feebly, in the midwife's hands. It does not cry.

He does not cry.

"Give him to me," I say, something hot and visceral entering into my voice. Livinia begins to protest, then a moment later nods, stupidly. Never taking her eyes from mine, she lowers the baby and places it on my breast.

It is so tiny. So light. Certainly not more than three or four pounds. Its weight on my chest is at once barely noticeable and crushingly immense. The thick, dark cord running from its—from his—tiny belly snakes between my thighs. Both it and the baby are feverishly hot.

Still, he does not cry.

My son looks at me. He has Jazen's eyes, large and dark, fringed with thick lashes. His head is crowned with a mass of thick, wet hair. I count fingers and toes, then laugh at myself for doing so.

The midwife steps back, shaking her head, muttering. She seems dazed, confused.

"He's beautiful," one of the women says, and makes a sound, half laugh, half sob.

Lia strides into the room, her face streaked with grime and blood, her hair in disarray. The flesh around her eyes is bruised, as if someone has struck her, again and again. She sways with weariness.

"Kirin?" she calls, her voice rough with exhaustion. She sees me, sprawled on the bed, and a look of relief floods across her face. "Oh, Kirin . . . I missed it."

The baby frowns, his expression almost comically serious, the tiny brows drawing down, just as a man's would. His mouth opens, a silent, dark "O." I see something, the barest hint of movement, in his face.

I stare, horrified, as roses of blood blossom in my son's

eyes, unfurling crimson petals outwards from the orbs' periphery. He gasps, and a tear of blood runs down his cheek.

I know then what has happened.

"Oh, gods . . . no. No. Nononono . . . *No!*" My scream tears from my throat as I struggle to rise. My flaccid muscles betray me, and all I can do is flop back into the bed.

"A knife! Give me a knife!"

"Kirin? What do you   " Lia begins.

"Cut the cord!" I howl, fingers scrabbling at the slippery rope. It flexes . . . *pulses* . . . under my hand, horribly alive, like a snake, hot and tight. My nails can find no purchase.

Without hesitation, Lia grabs the midwife's knife from the bedside table, begins sawing at the tough, dark cord.

"It must be tied first!" Livinia cries, finally seeming to come back to herself.

The razored edge parts the cord, and blood cascades forth. So much blood. A river, an ocean, gushing across the sheets, coating my thighs. Far, far too much blood.

The babe's eyes roll back, the orbs now pools of deepest red. Crimson streams trickle out from his nose, from his ears, as he struggles feebly. I see tiny, dark spider webs tracing across his lovely cheeks, as the delicate veins there burst, one by one.

He opens his mouth and gives his first, and only, cry, the sound coming swift before a gout of black blood. It splashes across my breasts, running down my sides, coating us both. The reek of the Mor wafts from it in waves, a smell like charred fish and hot iron. Horrified, I see the dark liquid sinking slowly into my skin.

My son's blood. Absorbed by my skin.

My scream is primal and wordless. It drowns out all light, all sound. All I can see is him, my baby, my son, struggling for life.

Livinia finally manages to tie a knot in the cord, stopping the torrent. His face is black now, like a strangling victim's, his tiny tongue dark and swollen.

He sprawls across my breast, lifeless, motionless.

Dead.

I STAND OVER MY SON'S BODY. The sounds of battle fell silent hours ago. I am beyond caring. We must have won, otherwise the Mor would have come in and torn us, burned us, long before.

I would not have tried to stop them. I would have welcomed them with open arms.

The babe's body is black, bruised from head to toe, the flesh darkened by blood beneath the surface. I have closed his lids over the blood-filled eyes over and over, but they keep opening, the blood-red crescents somehow accusing.

"Kirin," Lia whispers. "You should come away, now. Let Livinia tend to the bod . . . to him."

"I killed him," I whisper. I feel Lia pull away.

"What? No, you certainly did not. You wouldn't . . . " she protests, but I hear the faint thread of distrust in her voice.

What wouldn't a woman like me do?

"I used the blood magic on the Mor," I say, my voice hoarse, as if my throat is full of graveyard dirt. "When I did, their power flowed into me, and I reveled in it. I kept taking more, and more. I never even thought about what it would do to him. I wasn't thinking about him at all . . ."

"Kirin, it was an accident. You didn't mean to . . . to hurt him."

"I've killed my son. Whether or not I meant to matters not. When the blood of the Mor went into me, it must have . . . it must have gone into . . . into . . . oh *gods!*"

I fall to the floor, my body torn with racking sobs. I fear that such grief surely cannot be endured. That it will kill me. A moment later, I fear it will not.

Lia pats my shoulders, the gesture somehow feeble and awkward, then kneels beside me. Blindly, desperately, I clutch her. She holds me, for hours maybe, I am past knowing, until exhaustion finally sucks me into its black undertow.

I WAKE TO SILENCE. The room is dark, lit by a single taper, burned low. Lia slumps in a chair beside the bed, her gentle, ladylike snores the loudest sound. She is still begrimed, her shift torn and stained. Traces of blood are on her face. A tremendous bruise swells her cheek, below the purpled circles that surround her closed eyes.

I rise from the bed, tentatively at first, expecting pain. I feel fine. Better than fine. There is no pain, although I suspect that there will be, later. I feel strong.

The blood of the Mor, my sister whispers, *is potent. You used it to heal yourself.*

I stop. It has been months since she last spoke to me, long enough that I feared that she had left forever. I feel tears begin, stinging and hot, at the thought that I am not alone.

I walk into the manor's main room. It is empty; those that huddled here have gone. The fire is low, little more than embers. My roving eyes encounter a small, swaddled shape, laying in a basket atop the table. I walk to the basket, and look at what is within for a long time.

I carry the basket to the bedroom, staring into his pitiful face. In the candlelight, he could be a statue, or a doll, carved from some dark wood.

I see movement, and realize that, while I have been staring at him, my secret eye has opened. I see his shade, ghostly and pale, crawling towards me across the floor.

Then, he is on the bed with me, his wizened face dominated by a pair of opal, staring eyes. He stares, wordlessly pleading for me to bring him back. The hunger he radiates is enormous, bottomless, enough to swallow an ocean of blood.

You mustn't, my sister breathes. *Do not even consider this thing. Whatever comes back will not be him.*

My words are a whispered plea. "But, he is my flesh. My blood. Mine and Jazen's. And maybe, this time, it will be different. The blood of the Mor may have . . . may have ennobled him with their strength. This time may be different. He might rise, intact and whole."

You know he will not. What will return will be an abomination, in every way. If you do this thing, you will be damned. From this, you will never return.

"But certainly he deserves the chance, at least? If he comes back as . . . if he is damaged . . . I can send him back."

As you did with Hollern?

The words are like icy water, thrown into my face, shocking me back to the reality of what I have almost done. What I still yearn to do. My son's shade sits beside his dead body, waiting for me to restore the life that has been stolen from him.

Wordlessly, I reach out. My hand passes through his spectral flesh. His sightless eyes beg.

"I'm sorry. So very sorry, but you cannot come back," I say, the words passing like razors, each one cutting me, so deep. "You're not supposed to be here. Go. Go beyond, where you belong. Your father is waiting for you. Give . . . give him my love." I can say no more.

Even before my words end, his soul begins swirling, like smoke, like petals in a breeze, up and out of sight. The ghost of a smile plays across his pale lips. Then he is gone.

My son, the true child I thought I could never have, is gone, forever.

I cradle his tiny, cold form, tears streaming down my cheeks. My heart labors, each beat so full of pain and regret that I fear it must break my chest.

I hear a gentle sigh, and look up from my son's sad face. I see Lia watching from her chair. My whispered words must have woken her. Lightning flickers in her eyes. If I had chosen poorly, she would have ended it.

A vast relief floods over me at the realization, a sensation of such pure satisfaction that, for a moment, even my grief is eclipsed. My love for her shines forth, pressing back the darkness that has choked me for so very long.

Even now, even after all I have done, I am not alone.

With a sigh, I lay back, and let sleep, true, healing sleep, claim me.

EPILOGUE

I close the diary, pushing away from the table with a sigh. I set aside the journal and my quill, capping the precious ink, then massage my hand. It is cramped and sore from so much unaccustomed exercise.

Writing everything down was Lia's idea; gods know that I would never have thought to do so on my own. It was her notion that purging my mind of such memories, of the details of my life, might help with the nightmares.

She was right. I think. Once I began to write, recalling those first terrified days following Gamth's Pass, the words spilling, faster and faster, from my pen, I found I could not stop. Many evenings I stayed up far into the small hours of the night, as Lia snored on her blanket, writing by firelight until my head pounded from the effort of recalling.

The more I wrote, the more the dreams faded, becoming less severe, less damaging. I still wake every other night, screaming, the vision of my . . . of my dead son, branded in my mind's eye alongside the visions all of the men I have killed, or resurrected.

Still, that is an improvement. At least now I can sleep for a few precious hours and, some nights, not see his small, sad face staring into mine.

I rise, wincing at the stiffness in my back and legs. The Mor's blood, whatever inhuman vitality that it contained, that wasn't also killing me as it killed (my son), did much to heal my body of the wounds that I suffered in childbirth. But, even days later, my flesh seems to recall, like an echo, the tremendous pain I have endured.

I move to the doors, my erstwhile guards following my movements. I do not mock them, or even embarrass them by deigning to notice their presence. We both know that they could do noting to stop me should I choose to free myself. They deserve better than that, and, even after all I have sacrificed for them, even after the way they now look at me, I find that I cannot blame them for their mistrust.

For, in the end, the Mor were finally defeated, brought low by the refugees' surprising courage (some might call it desperation, but I know better) and the power of Lia's elemental allies. Despite the toll in lives, despite the price paid by so many, in broken and burned bodies, in lost children and mothers, in sons and fathers, the people survived, even as I labored in the relative safety of the keep.

"You saved them. Saved us, I mean," Lia told me on the first day, after she and Livinia managed to get me to my feet. "If not for you thinning their numbers, they would have overrun us. If not for what you taught them, they would have given up." Livinia, walking with us, still my nursemaid then, nodded agreement, even as her eyes refused to meet mine.

Everywhere that we walked, that first day, whispers followed us. The tales of what I had done, of my blood magic, reaching out to tear the life from enemy after enemy, ran amongst the people. Tales of me, covered from head to toe in black blood, belly swollen and *moving* beneath the sodden fabric.

I could not refute, nor explain it; it was what it was. I was done with hiding. Done with asking for forgiveness, for I was beyond forgiving.

For Livinia it was worse. She had been there when it—when my son—was born. She had liked me, had stood beside me before witnessing the terrible price that I paid, that he paid, even if she knew nothing of the real struggle, of the moment when I almost faltered—

But did not. Thanks to Lia. Dearest, Lia. She who watched, and would have done the right thing had I succumbed to my son's terrible plea.

I wonder where the midwife is now. When it was clear that the wounds of childbirth were healed, faded to pale scars by morning, and when it was apparent that I would not die from sheer, overwhelming grief, she left, disappearing into the night.

As is my habit, I stroll out to the courtyard directly after the midday meal. Soon, Lia emerges from the mercy tent, where the last of the wounded are being tended. Burns mainly, almost all superficial, not life-threatening but painful. Those that were more deeply wounded, crushed, or torn, or burned, had all perished and been buried days before; even Brother Ato's goddess could not help them all.

As I stroll in the midday sun, my guards trail behind. *You are not their prisoner, certainly not, but you also are not free, never forget that,* my sister whispers inside. I nod, accepting the widsom of her words. Since that night, she has spoken to me, hesitantly at first, then with greater strength, as if she were recalling the sound of her own voice.

She seems calmer now, the madness and spite that always seemed to thread through her every word diminished, if not entirely gone. I wonder if it is as Lia says, that she is indeed no more than a voice of my own creation. I shrug. It does not matter, for she will be with me, always, I feel it, as certain as my own body, my own blood.

Ato follows Lia out. He spots me and glares at me with a lingering, resentful stare. I return it, like for like.

Even after his refusal to tend to me, to soothe the pain of my mending flesh with the power of his goddess, I still might have forgiven him. After all, I had made promises. Promises I had broken, or that I had so desperately *wanted* to break that there seemed little difference between the wanting and the doing. I had earned his wrath.

But, standing beside the tiny grave, so small amongst the rows of heaped soil, the final resting place for so many, and listening to his refusal to bless such a . . . such a *thing* with the final rites. Standing beside my son's grave, I felt my heart turn to stone as the gods once and for all turned their faces from me.

Good riddance and damn them. Damn them all if such is their mercy.

Lia walks to my side. She is still pale-faced, her bruises faded greenish-yellow, but she moves better, her gait free from the old lady's stiffness that seemed graven into her bones just days before.

Like me, her power has marked her, but unlike mine, those marks may fade in time. I pray it will be so.

"Are you up for a walk?" she says, grasping my hands. I nod. Together, we stroll through the open gates and down the road. The guards, as ever, trail behind, close enough to watch me but not close enough to intrude.

Down in the valley, where the water pools when the rains are heavy, the great cairn that the people have piled over the bodies of the Mor stands, the pale stones shining in sun, white like skulls.

"I still dream of them," she says, pausing beside the road. "Still see them coming through the gate."

I nod. I know all about dreams, hers and mine.

"I would have died, there before the gates, if not for Natalie," she says in a rush. I nod again. She has told this story often, as if this singular event has the power to haunt her, rising above all the horrors of the past few days.

Once again she speaks of Natalie, the most promising of my young archers, she who stood with me on the wall and who helped loose the rain of stones upon the Mor. She tells me of how Natalie saw the burning knife aimed at Lia's heart, and how she pushed her aside, taking the stroke in her own breast. I listen as Lia tells me of the way she held her as she died, just as I had held Jazen, telling her that she would be fine, that she would be going to a better place.

If we were not sisters before, we were then.

"Her sacrifice gave me the strength to call down the lightning once more. Again and again, until I was blind, was deaf, but still fighting," she says.

"And then, they were running, were *retreating*. Gods, what a sight. We had broken the Mor. We were safe."

I squeeze her trembling hand and lean my shoulder against hers, feeling the tiny tremors of unshed tears coursing inside her body. Soon, one day, those tears will come out, and on that day I pray I shall be there, as she was there for me in the dark whirlwind of the battle and of its aftermath. Pray she will let me be there for her.

We walk on, until the lake and the valley are spread out below us. I see smoke rising from chimneys, see the tiny, dark forms of the women in the fields, laboring to bring in the second harvest before the inexorable arrival of the cold.

"I wish to be gone from this place," I say. "These people . . . they are not mine. They never were. It was foolish for me to ever hope they would accept me, I know that now."

Lia nods. "Ato can never forgive you, and without his blessing, I fear they can never forgive you either," she says. "Where shall you go?"

The words send a spear of ice through my breast, one that I ignore. She will make her own decision, either way.

"If I leave soon, I should be able to beat the first of the late summer snows," I say, striving to sound matter-of-fact. "Rory knew these passes well, and if he was right, then they should be passable for another week or two."

"Can I . . . Can I come with you?" she breathes, so soft that I can barely hear her. I stare, open-mouthed.

"Can you? Oh, gods, I wished for nothing else," I say, turning her to face me. Her face blazes red in a deep blush, so very like my prim and proper Lia, so comically embarrassed I can scarcely stifle a laugh.

She flinches a little, then seeing that I truly mean it, she breaks into a smile more radiant than the zenith sun.

We embrace, settling together, bodies interlocking as if designed for exactly that purpose, arms encircling tight, half laughing, half crying with relief.

We turn and, together, head back to the manor. We have much to do, she and I, before we leave. I know that Brother Ato will be glad to see me go; I doubt Lia's leave-taking will be half so joyous for him.

I smile, trying to imagine the priest stopping her. The smile lasts all the way to the walls.

ABOUT THE AUTHOR

Matthew Cook graduated from the School of the Art Institute of Chicago in 1991 and wasted no time in beginning a family. As many Fine Arts graduates do, he took a normal, respectable job, one good for paying the bills but terrible at nourishing the soul. He spent several years trying to keep his illustration, digital graphics and photography skills sharp, even resorting to wedding photography when things were truly dire. More than ten years later, he was still no closer to making anything resembling a living in the visual arts, so he turned to his other great love: literature. In a bout of desperate optimism, he began on a mammoth undertaking: an urban fantasy trilogy set in his beloved Chicago. Four years later, while "taking a break" from editing that (still unfinished) project, he had this strange idea for a necromancer named Kirin . . .

Matt's second book about Kirin (*Nights of Sin*) will be published by Juno Books in 2008. He lives in Columbus, Ohio.